DAMAGED
FRUIT

Eunice Chapman

WARNER BOOKS

A *Warner* Book

First published in Great Britain in 1995 by Warner Books
This edition first published by Warner Books 1996

Copyright © Eunice Chapman 1995

A CIP catalogue record for this book
is available from the British Library.

ISBN 0 7515 1124 2

Typeset by M Rules
Printed in England by Clays Ltd, St Ives plc

Warner Books
A Division of
Little, Brown and Company (UK)
Brettenham House
Lancaster Place
London WC2E 7EN

To Lil Harrigan
and Harry Chapman

Acknowledgements

My thanks are due to my parents who both wrote accounts of their lives. These records and the stories I was told as a child provide the background for this book. The Island History Trust, the organisation which has compiled a history of the Isle of Dogs, gave me invaluable assistance in allowing me to draw from material in their archives.

Contents

Chapter 1

Street Games

The boy's mouth had gone dry in the excitement of the game. Fog drifting in from the Thames as it looped the Isle of Dogs, blurred the street lights and obscured the figures flitting back and forth across the road. A mournful music of low bleats and wails from craft passing on the river heightened a delicious sense of danger. The boy kept his back pressed against the wall, the better to avoid being seized from behind, and waited his chance.

On the other side of the narrow street, the girls' pinafores made swooping patterns in the dusk as they spiralled round the lamppost on a rope slung over the crossbar. Light and noise spilled from The Three Feathers on the corner, the volume increasing in sharp bursts every time someone pushed open the door to the saloon bar, mostly to go in. It was early yet, few were coming out. A handful of little kids on the pavement watched hopefully for signs of their mothers' return, but their waiting was not over. It was East London, 1910, and the only nursery was the street.

The agility and speed of the one chosen to be the hunter added to the thrill of the game. He rushed past the boy's hiding place without seeing him, intent on taking more prisoners. The boy shrank back into the shadows, scanning the street. From the entry to the flats where he lived, he saw the naked figure of a tiny child come at a wobbly run. Scattering the playing girls, she hooked a fat little arm round the lamppost, did three rapid circuits then, followed by their shouts and laughter, streaked back the way she had come. Friday night: it was his sister Daisy. Mum was bathing the little ones.

In the gloom he could see a skinny figure by the railings that marked one boundary of the imaginary compound, hopping up and down in his impatience to be liberated. The hunter's attention was held trying to corner someone in a doorway. The boy darted out and touched the 'prisoner' on the shoulder.

'Release!' he yelled at the top of his voice.

Farther up the street, a door opened and another voice was raised. 'Jimmy,' it screamed. 'Come and get your tea.'

The game was over. It was getting too dark to see anyway. From alleyways and porches where they had been in hiding, boys emerged and gathered on the cobbles, shouting, shoving and jostling to take their leave of each other.

Voices summoning them indoors were becoming a chorus. Kate Collins was flicking her rope trying to free it from the crossbar of the lamppost. She called to him. 'Get it down for us Danny.'

The boy went over, knowing that this was just a ruse to get near him. She could get it down herself all right, but he shinned up far enough to free it and handed her the end. 'What's the matter? Afraid of tearing your drawers?'

He sneered partly to save his face in front of the other boy, but partly to deny that he liked her.

They turned towards home. Flats in a grim row of four blocks that stood at the poorer end of the street. At the other end were classy little houses with bay windows; no gardens – nothing grew here.

They walked without speaking. Kate, untouched by his insult skipped along behind. Her brother Charlie caught up and fell in beside Danny.

'Come on Danny, we'd better hurry up,' said Charlie. 'My old man'll give us both a belting if we're not there in time.'

'Where you going Danny?' asked Kate.

'Mind your own business.' Her brother turned on her fiercely. 'Tell Mum I've got to wait for Dad. I don't know how long he'll be.'

They reached their porch. Within it were two front doors, one on either side of a wooden staircase. Behind the door on the left lived old mother Poulter, never known to come out, except when she brought offerings of baked potatoes for the kids in the street. The other door was open and at it stood the mountainous figure of Rose Collins. She frowned at the two boys. 'It's gone half past five. Get up there quick, or you'll cop it.'

'Where are they going Mum?' Kate persisted. Rose ignored the question and reaching out a long arm sped her daughter indoors, not so much by clouting her as scooping her over the threshold by a hand at the back of the neck.

'In' was all she said.

Not a hundred yards from them, Rose's husband had a hut tucked against the high wall that surrounded Millwall Dock. In it he kept a small stove burning winter and summer for the continuous brewing of tea and the

3

frequent frying of bacon, a shovel being improvised as a pan.

His duties as master of the dry dock demanded his skilled but intermittent attention. They included overseeing the positioning of vessels in the dry dock so that they were held securely on the stocks and in such a way that no damage befell them when it came to floating them out. He operated the sluice gates and raised and lowered the bridge that formed both the entrance to the dry dock and part of the roadway that intersected the great complex of basins.

It was his particular pleasure, at about five minutes to eight on some mornings, to raise the bridge just as the crowd of girls on their way to work at the sack factory were about to cross. To see them run to try to beat the bridge; the vigorous way they danced about and hurled foul and colourful abuse at him, filled him with glee and made him laugh till his belly quivered.

Dry Dock Tommy was well loved and had many callers at his hut. Earlier that day he had been discussing with two men – one a crane driver, the other a ship's painter – the cargo of a freighter that was lying alongside in the inner dock. She had arrived from the East Indies the day before and was presently receiving the attention of the stevedores as they swarmed about emptying the holds.

'I'll give you the wink, then,' the painter had said. 'As soon as I see him come in here, I'll go to the rail with me paint pot and wipe me forehead with me scarf. If I haven't got me paint pot and I light a pipe, you'll know it's off for tonight.'

'Yus, right.' The crane driver, not a talkative man, swigged from his mug.

'It'll be all right,' said Tommy, 'he'll be hungry by then and I've got a nice bit of gammon the Dutch bargee give me. He's tuppence short of a shillin' anyway.'

Their plans laid, they finished their tea and went back to work. The dock master picked up his palm and needle and resumed fashioning a rope mat. The painter made his way along the dockside and descended a gangplank to disappear into the bowels of the freighter. The crane driver scaled the ladder to his cabin.

Tommy worked until the light began to fade, then got up, pushed the shovel into the coals to heat and put the kettle on to boil. He strolled outside and did a stately circuit of the dry dock, checking that all was in order. Satisfied, he turned his steps to the main gate.

'Evenin', he greeted the constable on duty. 'It's getting nippy. Fancy a cuppa tea?'

The constable looked doubtfully up and down the sweep of cobbled road. Nothing was likely to come through now and it was half an hour before the dockies knocked off. 'Yeah, all right, thanks. Just a quick one.'

Back in the hut, Tommy handed him a mug of strong tea sweetened with a large spoonful of condensed milk and placed two thick gammon rashers on the shovel. The rich tantalising smell of frying bacon wafted round the hut. 'You hungry, mate?' he asked, looking up into eyes alight with hope. 'Fancy a sandwich? Go on,' he added, sensing hesitation. 'I'll keep a look out.'

The policeman sat on the wooden chair, his fist full of crusty bread that was quickly becoming saturated with the fat oozing from the bacon. Tommy stood at the door looking at the forest of cranes and the crowded berths that were his life. Beyond the bridge, on the far side of the inner pool, he could see the painter in position against the ship's rail. He raised his hand in salutation and saw him pick up a pot of paint with one hand and with the other, mop his brow on a red neck scarf.

The crane driver who had been manoeuvring crates out of the hold all the afternoon and dumping them on the quay to be removed to a warehouse, positioned the hook and waited for the signal that it was in place. Majestically, and deviating only slightly from the appointed course, the crate rose in the air, swung in a slow semicircle above the hut and over the wall to land gently on stony waste ground in Bermuda Street.

Danny and Charlie sprinted towards the stonefield, about half an acre of hard clay covered in stones that formed a boundary between the blocks and the prim terraced houses at the posh end of Bermuda Street. The dock wall, twice the height of a man, ran along the back, so that it was enclosed on three sides, making it an ideal meeting place for dogs, cats and kids. The boys arrived in time to see the crate looming above them in the twilight.

It settled with hardly a jolt and they freed the hook. In a moment it began to rise again. They watched till the sight of it swinging away was blotted out by the wall.

Charlie sank to the ground, leaning against the crate. 'Whew! Thank Christ,' he said.

Danny glanced round the shadowy field and shivered. 'I'll have to go. Mum'll be worried.'

'You're not going to leave me out here on me own are you?' protested Charlie.

'I'll have to. We don't want her to come looking for me do we?' He turned and soon disappeared round the corner.

'You rotten sod!' Charlie yelled after him. He was

not seriously troubled. His instructions were to wait by the crate until his father came. It could be an hour or more but he dare not desert his post. It was quite dark but he feared nothing, except that a copper might come by on the beat. That wasn't very likely. Policemen were a rare sight in these back streets on the Isle of Dogs. They always came in pairs and never after dark. Charlie settled down to a long wait for the master of the dry dock.

Danny went upstairs, covering the small round impressions left by Daisy's toes with the soles of his hobnail boots. At the top, two brass-furnished doors like those below faced each other across the landing. The immediate neighbours, the Carters, were on polite but distant terms with his family. They were Protestants. On the fourth side of the landing, a similar wooden stair descended to the back yard.

The door to the left yielded to his push and he made his way along the dark passage, guided by the clamour and the smell of mutton stew coming from the room at the back. It was crowded with furniture and children. There was a heavy mahogany sideboard, made by a shipwright, which itself had come into the family's possession over the dock wall. Two armchairs – one wooden, one padded – stood on either side of the range. A round table with a missing ball from a ball-and-claw foot of the central pedestal replaced by a lump of coal, filled the centre space so that there was little room for his brood of brothers and sisters to move. Danny found a place to sit at the table. His sister Sarah's mouth was open wide in a loud wail.

His mother bustled in from the scullery, carrying a

saucepanful of hot water to add to the tub that stood before the fire. She was a slight woman with a worn face, her luxuriant pile of dark hair the only indication that Charlotte Cavanagh was still young.

'What's the matter with you now?' she demanded of Sarah, a scrawny seven-year-old who stood undressed, waiting her turn to go in the tub.

'Daisy piddled in the water!'

Daisy was standing astride in the tub, little patches of foam sliding down her rosy body.

'I never,' she said.

'She did! I saw her.'

'Daisy!' admonished her mother, moving her one place along in the production line by wrapping her in a towel and setting her down on the matting to await the attention of Florrie. Florrie, at twelve her mother's indispensable right hand, knelt by the fire drying baby Paddy. Clean underwear hung warming over the fire-guard.

'I'm not getting in there,' shrilled Sarah.

'Get in!' Charlotte gripped her daughter by the arm and forced her over the edge into the bath. 'A little drop of maiden's water won't hurt you.'

Sarah was silenced before she could draw breath to scream again by Charlotte pouring water from an enamel jug over her head and beginning a vigorous application of Sunlight soap.

'Hold your noise or you'll get something to cry about.'

Florrie carried the two little ones to their bed in the orf room, so called because it opened off the scullery. A double bed pushed up to the wall occupied almost the entire space, so that she had to edge along the opposite wall to put Paddy in his place next to the brass rail at the

8

foot. She positioned him carefully, laying him across the width of the bed. Daisy was lifted in to the middle where she wriggled ecstatically, revelling in the sensuous pleasure of clean linen against clean skin.

'Don't kick him and don't make a noise,' Florrie ordered. She left a space at the head for Sarah. Until Paddy had grown too big to sleep in the bottom drawer of the chest in their mother's room, she had herself shared the bed, but now she slept on three chairs placed together under the window.

'Don't put the light out Florrie,' pleaded Daisy.

'I'll leave the door open a little bit so you can see the light in the scullery.'

Between them, she and Danny carried the tub into the scullery, emptied its scummy contents down the sink and returned it to its nail on the wall. The dirty washing was stuffed behind the soap box kept under the sink so that the girls in the family did not have to wait to grow tall before they could be useful.

When they returned to the now orderly kitchen, Sarah was clamped between her mother's knees, having her head scrutinised for lice. Once she had gone to bed, the rest of them could eat. Charlotte believed in sending the little ones to bed with full bellies. They had already been given bowlfuls of mashed potatoes moistened with the rich liquor from the pan simmering on the range. The older ones must wait until their father chose to return. An event to be both anticipated and dreaded.

The first heavy footfall in the passage, when it came, brought chatter to a stop. All eyes turned towards the door. They heard the hiss of a drop from the stewpan falling on the range as they listened with practiced ears for the second tread. Much could be learned from how soon it followed the first, whether it was firm or dragging. It came a second later, deliberate, accompanied by a swishing sound as the homecomer leant against the wall for support.

Sarah scuttled under the table and crouched peering out through the fringe on the red chenille cloth. The knob turned slowly. Charlotte got up and stood by the fireguard. Danny took up a position behind her right shoulder, Florence by the scullery door.

Dermot Cavanagh swayed slightly in the doorway, filling the frame, his round belly in advance of his whiskered face. He looked older than his thirty-five years. Hardly breathing, Charlotte watched her husband take off his coat and carefully hang it over the corner of the door. He took off his cap and slowly raised it to rest on top of his coat. It was a significant sign. Charlotte let out her breath. He was just far enough gone. If the next critical half hour could be negotiated, he would fall into a deep sleep.

'Hello, Dermot.' Charlotte bustled forward, pitching her voice with care so as not to provoke him. 'Your dinner's ready.' She took his arm and steered him to his seat. Easing him into the chair she nudged Sarah out from under the table with her foot. The child slunk out behind Florrie and fled to the refuge of her bed.

Dermot ate his generous portion from a four-pint pudding basin. The others spooned theirs rapidly into their mouths from an assortment of plates and bowls. No one spoke, the children having learned the wisdom of being seen and not heard and of eating while the going was good. Charlotte remained on the alert, placing the pepper-pot in his line of sight, the bread in reach of his groping hand.

He pushed away the basin, indicating that he was done. Had he wanted more, he would have signalled his wish to have the bowl refilled by rapping his spoon against the side. A thought had occurred to him and he turned a bleary look on his wife.

'When's he leaving school?' he asked, jerking his head towards Danny.

'When they break up for Christmas. In a fortnight's time.'

The look swam round and settled on Danny. 'You'll 'ave to shape up then, won't you?'

'Yes, Dad,' said Danny. His fourteenth birthday loomed in his mind: leaving school and starting in the docks with his father to learn the craft of ship's painter. He'd always known it would happen, but now it was on him.

'Dad, Charlie's dad's got him a job on the sailing barges. They go up and down to Gravesend every week. They leave on the first tide Monday and they're back on Friday.'

'Are they,' said Dermot. 'And that's what you'd like to do is it?'

'Yes, I would.'

'Well, you can forget that as quick as you like.'

'Why, Dad?'

'Because you're startin' where I can keep an eye on you.'

'But Dad—' He didn't finish the protest. Charlotte's warning look burned into him and he fell silent, his eyes on his plate.

'Think yourself lucky to be learnin' a trade from a

master craftsman. Do you hear me? Do you hear me?' he roared again when Danny made no answer.

Alarmed, Danny forced his answer through an aching throat. 'Yes, Dad.'

Danny got up to help his mother as Dermot moved to leave the table.

'Why don't you have a lie down?' she wheedled. 'You look tired.'

It was vital to get him to the bed before he passed out, but there must be no hint of ordering about.

'Come on, I'll get your boots off and you can have a little nap.'

With an arm across each back, Dermot suffered them to half lead, half drag him back along the passage to the adjoining room. The marital bed was high, the feather mattress being supported by two of horsehair; the whole topped by several blankets and a bulky eiderdown. They heaved and manhandled him in.

As he sank back on to the pillow, Dermot gripped Danny's arm.

'The stuff's all right is it?'

'I left Charlie keeping an eye on it.'

He grunted and released him. Waving Danny away, Charlotte took off his boots and neck scarf. By shoving and rolling him from side to side she got him out of his trousers and hung them on the bedrail. Covering him, she left him to sleep it off, which if God was merciful would not be until the morning.

Her limbs throbbed with fatigue. She sank into Dermot's big armchair, certain that he would not be claiming it that night. She glanced around her kitchen at the fat roses on the wallpaper, the kettle singing on the hob and knew a moment of contentment. The day's work nearly done. Florrie was in the scullery doing the washing-up. A good girl she was turning out to be. She called to her. 'Florrie, where's Danny gone?'

'He's gone down to see Charlie.'

Contentment evaporated. She liked to have her children safely under the roof at nightfall, but he was nearly a man; he'd be bringing in a wage soon.

Until she'd had Paddy eighteen months ago it had seemed that Danny would be her only surviving son. There had been others: another boy after Danny – Teddy – but she'd lost him at four to diphtheria. Florrie was twelve now. She'd lost two after Florrie. Both boys. Richard, stillborn and Thomas who lived only for a month. She didn't know why. 'Failure to thrive' was written on the black-edged memorial card that she kept in the drawer with all the others. It had pictures of cherubs on it that reminded her of Paddy. She shut out the thought and glancing at the crucifix over the sideboard crossed herself as a precaution against further divine punishment.

The three younger ones were robust and looked strong enough to survive the whooping cough and measles they were sure to get. After Sarah there had been a stillborn girl, Charlotte, but she was so small she could not have survived for long. She'd lost no more till last year when she had miscarried, so early she would hardly have known if the bleeding had not gone on for so long. Dermot had given her a good hiding over something.

Guilt at her idleness prodded; she reached for her workbasket and put in a few stitches to the neckband of the flannel petticoat she was making for Daisy, before weariness overcame her and her head drooped in sleep.

Florrie came in and took the kettle to refill the washing-up bowl for her own wash down. Looking at her mother swallowed in her father's chair, she was glad to find herself the only one awake in the household.

For a long time she had not had to stand on the box to reach the sink and Charlotte had banned her from bathing in front of the fire saying: 'You're a big girl now.' No other explanation was given and it had taken Florrie a while to realise that it was because she was growing breasts. It filled her with burning embarrassment.

She didn't risk stripping in the scullery, in case Danny came back, but balanced the bowl on a chair behind her bedroom door where some light was cast and she could watch through the crack for intruders. Beginning with her hair, she washed her body from top to bottom. The Mass tomorrow would cleanse her spirit. She put on fresh underwear. The chemise was tight across her chest, flattening and consoling her.

She arranged herself on her three chairs to sleep. In the morning, if she got the chance, she would look at herself in the mirror in her mother's room to see if the bumps showed through her clothes.

The coals in the range settled with a sigh. Charlotte started as Danny came in.

'Are you all right love?' she asked.

He came and sat on the wide fender beside her. She pushed her fingers through his thick brown hair and let her hand rest on his shoulder. So broad he was growing.

'It won't be so bad in the docks when you get used to it. You'll see.'

'I know, Mum.' The head sank against her. 'It's just that I'd like to go on the barges.'

Charlotte smiled. 'Charlie will only be gettin' eight

bob a week, and nothing but a coil of rope to sleep on. You'll get twenty-five shillings. You'll have to give me a pound for your keep, but you'll be able to get yourself a decent suit, go up The Queen's once a week.'

'Suits cost two pound ten, Mum.'

'You can give me a shilling a week and I'll pay it off for you.'

He sighed and looked glum. He had been taken once to The Queen's music hall in Poplar, where the performance by a soprano of limited talent, singing 'Velia' had poisoned his mind against classical music forever. The prospect she painted did nothing to lighten his spirits and she grew impatient. 'You'd best be getting to bed. I'm just going to bank up the fire, then I'm going myself.' She stooped to pick up the empty scuttle.

'I'll do that for you, Mum.'

'Thanks, love.'

She heard him go along the passage to the tiny room over the void of the stairs where the coal was kept. Dermot would not have it shot into the shed in the yard because there was no way to keep the other families in the block from stealing it. It would have been nice if Danny could have had a bed in there, but there was nothing she could do to alter things. She just scrubbed the lino round the edge of the coal heap once a week, to try to keep the place clean.

Danny wished her goodnight and went to lie on the sofa in the parlour. Charlotte changed into her nightgown in front of the fire, turned out the gaslight and crept to her bedroom door. A movement from inside kept her standing in the drafty passage listening. Dermot was peeing copiously into the chamber pot. She waited until she heard him grunt, the bed creaking as he clambered back in and for his deep breathing to resume. When she was certain that he slept again, she moved stealthily to her side of the bed, and making as little disturbance as possible, slipped beneath the covers.

Her feet were icy cold. She inched them towards the warmth encircling Dermot's body. It was a mistake. He rolled towards her and began fumbling with the fastening at the neck of her nightgown.

Chapter 2

Eight Shillings

Dermot swung along the road in expansive mood, anticipating, as he approached the corner to Bermuda Street, the pleasure of the little ones when he gave them the liquorice and the sweet, shiny locust beans that he was bearing home in his pockets.

He had enough tobacco from that last drop stowed under the chicken shed to keep him in smokes for months. It had netted a few quid too, enough to rig him out in a new satin-bound shirt and black jacket. Better still, he'd come up on the accumulator, on the strength of which he'd slipped out of the dock early. A few pints with some pals, then he'd been shopping. In a flash of paternal foresight, he had paid for two sewing machines, one each for Florrie and Sarah. A good standby for a girl. She could always make a few bob if she had one of those. Daisy's would come later. Plenty of time for her. He'd get her one when he had the next win, which he would surely have. He turned the corner with his shoulders squared and a swagger in his step. All things considered, he was a hell of a fellow.

Daisy was sitting on the kerb, enjoying the novel sensation of having a seat of convenient height. She ran towards him when he whistled and, feeling a surge of love for her, he swept her up on to his shoulder.

'Hello, Nin, wait till you see what I've got for you.'

'What you got, Daddy?'

'Wait and see.'

She laughed and clung to his head as he carried her up the stairs, deposited her with a bump into his armchair and filled her hands with the sweets from his pocket. Charlotte hurried to make tea, panicked by his unexpected arrival. 'You're home early, I haven't got the dinner ready yet.'

'I won't be wanting any dinner. I'm going out. I just come in to have a shave and change me gear. Don't worry about making tea, I won't be stoppin'.'

He picked up the simmering kettle and went through to the scullery. 'Put some socks and a shirt in the bag for me,' he called.

'When are you coming back?' Charlotte's voice was tremulous as she dared to ask the question. His expression hardened under the lather. 'When I'm ready,' he said.

He went through to the bedroom and emerged a few minutes later wearing the new shirt and jacket with a spotted silk tie.

'There's no doubt about it,' he announced to no one in particular, 'there's only two men in the world and the other one died on the way over.'

'Dermot,' said Charlotte, 'what about me money?'

He didn't answer but stretched his arms so that his cuffs showed to his satisfaction.

'Daisy,' said Charlotte sharply, 'save some of that for Paddy.' She turned again to Dermot. 'The landlord comes on Monday and I haven't got the money for the rent.'

'How much is the rent?'

18

'Eight shillings.' He fished in his pocket and put ten shillings on the table.

She stared at it for a moment. 'What about money for food, Dermot? I can't manage on that.'

'Can't you?' he said. 'Then don't manage on it.' He gathered up the coins and put them back in his pocket. Charlotte looked at him aghast, her colour draining. Unmoved, he picked up his bag and left, slamming the front door as he went.

For long minutes Charlotte sat dazed, while Daisy, chewing on her twig of liquorice, watched her wide-eyed from the other side of the fire.

'What shall I do, what shall I do?' she moaned, rocking back and forth, until the desperate urgency of her situation focused her mind.

'Daisy, you stay here a minute. I'm going downstairs to see Mrs Collins. Eat your sweets. Come and get me if Paddy wakes up. I'll only be a minute.'

She pushed open the door of the flat below and stepped into the passage. 'You there, Rose?'

'Yes, come in, I'll put the kettle on.'

'I can't stop, I've left the kids upstairs and the others'll be in from school in a minute.'

'What's the matter, love?' Rose asked gently. 'Has he gone off again? I heard the door slam.'

'I don't know where he's gone. I was wondering if you could let me have the lend of two bob till he gets back?'

'Course I can.' Rose took a jar from the dresser and produced four shillings. 'Sorry it's not more, but I tell you what, I know the missus at The Feathers wants someone to do a bit of washing for her. I could speak for you if you like.'

'Thanks, Rose. I've got tonight's tea, but after that I've

19

got nothing for the kids. I can't even borrow from the rent. He didn't leave it for me.'

'The landlord'll just have to take it out on the knocker,' said Rose. She had been looking closely at her neighbour. 'I'm going to make some tea. The kids'll be all right for a minute; I'll send Katie up to keep an eye when she comes in.'

They sat at the table in the little flat, a replica of Charlotte's own except that it was neater and there was an absence of wet washing. Rose poured, then said quietly, 'You've fallen for another one, haven't you?'

Charlotte nodded. Tears welled up in her eyes and coursed down her cheeks. 'How far gone are you?'

'Only just.' The signs of pregnancy were so familiar to her that she could tell almost in the first week. That morning she had felt so nauseous she had barely managed to carry the pail of slops down to the lavatory before vomiting.

Rose put a hand on her shoulder. 'Never mind, love, you know what they say: "They bring a loaf."'

'If it wasn't for the little ones, I'd chuck myself under the next horse and cart that came along.'

Rose let her weep freely. 'You could try jumping down the last six stairs a few times. That might shift it,' she said.

'Yes, and it might only half shift it; end up with a kid that's simple or got one leg longer than the other. Besides, I couldn't do it.'

'Annie got something from the chemist that worked. Mind you, she wasn't half bad. For Christ's sake, don't tell anyone. If her old man finds out he'll kill her. I don't know what it was. Only you'd have to do it soon. Can't leave it too long.'

The information about her nearest neighbour diverted Charlotte sufficiently to move her to dry her eyes. 'Annie Carter?' she said incredulously. 'What's she want to get rid of one for? She's only got three.'

'She had her own reasons.'

'Well it's all right for a Proddy, but it's against our religion. It's a mortal sin.'

'You'll just have to have it, then. Does Dermot know?'

'He'll know soon enough.' Charlotte dropped her head in her hands.

'Look, love,' said Rose, 'You'll get over this. I know. How many's this for you?'

Charlotte hesitated. 'Ten, counting the ones I lost.'

'I've had twelve. They're all gone now except Charlie and Kate. I nearly done meself in when I fell for her. I thought I'd finished. I was over forty and Charlie was four. Then all of a sudden here comes another one. But you get used to the idea and settle down to it. And it might not be so bad. Your Florrie's a big girl. Old enough to be a help. And Sarah's coming along.'

Charlotte turned on her a look of utter hopelessness. 'Do you mind if I don't drink this tea? The smell of it turns my stomach.'

When Danny got home from the docks, his dinner was placed before him by Florrie, which nettled him slightly. Finding that his father was expected to be absent for some time, he sat at the head of the table and would have liked to have his mother's ear, to tell her about his day at work. He was finding it difficult to adjust to the long working hours, but in truth it wasn't as hard as he had feared. Dermot had proved surprisingly considerate

21

and had set him to work sandpapering below decks out of the biting January wind.

Charlotte noticed his return only to ask if he had brought his wages. She was at the sink up to her elbows in suds, finding the smell of soap easier to tolerate than the smell of faggots and onions. A pile of unwashed sheets and clothing waited on the floor behind her, a basket piled high with loosely wrung linen stood on the draining board. The floor was awash.

The sight deepened Danny's depression. He hated Mondays because of wet washing draping the kitchen, robbing it of what little comfort it had to offer. This was Friday, the day he'd looked forward to all week.

'Danny, give me a hand down to the yard with this,' said Charlotte, taking hold of one handle of the basket.

'Can't Florrie do it?'

'Florrie's already got plenty to do. Now take hold of this.'

'But Mum, it's dark. Can't you do it in the morning?'

'The woman wants it back on Sunday. I've got to get it dry. Now get hold of this before I clout you, even if I have to stand on the box to do it.'

By the faint light from the flat below, they dragged the mangle away from the wall and placed the bath tub on the ground to receive the washing.

They worked together, Charlotte deftly folding sheets and feeding the heavy wooden rollers, Danny turning the handle until his arms grew tired. They changed places and the work slowed, he being not so expert. It was late in the evening when they started work on the last load of shirts and underwear while, upstairs, Florrie draped the finished sheets and pillowcases in every available place to dry.

Danny's legs ached, his resentment as bitter as the wind scouring the yard. At first he didn't realise that anything was amiss, his fingers and senses too numbed to feel to the full the crushing pressure of the rollers on the tip of his middle finger. He withdrew it sharply and stared at it in disbelief. The flesh, as white as the shirt hanging from the mangle, was split to the bone. It took a moment for feeling and blood to return. As the first ruby drops splashed on to the linen in the basket, he let out a scream of pain.

Charlotte snatched a sock from the basket and wrapped it round his hand, then drew him towards the window where she could see and judge the injury in better light. Cradling his head against her shoulder she looked and quickly rewrapped his hand.

'It's a bad cut, Danny. We'll have to go to the hospital to get some stitches in it.'

She felt him sag against her and he moaned softly. 'Come on, let's get you upstairs and tie this up properly, then I'll take you to Poplar Hospital.'

'What about the washing?'

'I'll worry about that later.'

In a few minutes, with his finger bound in strips of rag and heartened by a sip of his father's whisky, they started on the long walk to the hospital, three miles away.

They saw no one, passing rows of unlit parlour windows, life and brightness showing only in the pubs that stood on the corners of almost every little street. Charlotte supported Danny around the waist and with her shawl covering them both, they covered the ground quite quickly.

The cavernous hall that served the hospital as a reception area for those in need of emergency treatment was

23

cold and gloomy. They took their place on a bench about three rows from the front. They were in luck. This not being Saturday night there were few drunks and fight casualties waiting to be seen. Danny kept his head turned away from the sight and smell of the ulcerated leg stretched out next to them, unbandaged, ready for the doctor's inspection.

Charlotte shivered. Now that she had stopped moving, chill was striking through to her bones. She was anxious. The rag round Danny's finger had become saturated and blood was beginning to drip on to her skirt. The boy was white-faced, concentrating on not whimpering, breathing through his mouth.

They were taken into an anteroom at last, and the wound was cleaned and stitched, a procedure which left Danny feeling sick and shaken. The clock on the church in the high street was showing eleven as they started for home. As they reached the long perimeter road that looped round the island, it started to snow. A light fall, not settling, but stinging faces and hands, wakening numbed feet into painful life.

They held the shawl tightly round them but the wind found those places where wet clothing clung and pierced them to the flesh. They battled, heads down between the towering walls of the dock. Danny, steadying his mother when she stumbled, got his shoulder under her arm and pressed himself against her side, trying to match his stride to hers, as though in a three-legged race, so that they might make smoother progress.

'How far have we got to go?' she asked. He looked up. Difficult to tell. Gas lamps glimmered faintly into the distance and round the next bend, indistinguishable from the last. 'Nearly there now,' he said, not knowing if he lied. She didn't answer, but plodded on, one foot after the other, till she saw the lamp on the corner of Bermuda Street shining on the tiled façade of The Three Feathers, closed now and shuttered.

They dragged each other up the stairs. Florrie had banked up the range to speed the drying of the washing and the room was filled with dank steam. Charlotte cleared the armchair and sank into it.

'You sleep in my bed, son. I'll stay here by the fire.'

'It's all right, Mum, you go to bed.'

Charlotte lay back and closed her eyes. 'The parlour's too cold. You'll never get warm in there and you need a good night's sleep. Anyway, I don't think I've got the strength to move.'

With his good hand Danny ladled some of the remaining faggot stew into a basin. His mother was already asleep. Comforted by the food, he left her to crawl into his parents' bed.

Charlotte lay with her black hair tumbling over the side of the chair, steam rising from her wet clothes. She hadn't moved when Florrie came out in the morning, her head against the antimacassar, cheeks flushed from the warmth of the fire. But it was a false warmth. She had been dead for some hours.

Three days later, Dermot was halted half-way up the stairs, not so much by the sudden appearance on the landing of Rose Collins as by the cold contempt glittering in her eyes. Looking up at her stony face and majestic bosom, he was reminded of the ship's figurehead he had been recently painting.

'Hello, Rose. Is something the matter?'

'You'd better come indoors.'

She stepped inside ahead of him and he followed meekly, the sense of something amiss and his curiosity overcoming his amazement at her bloody cheek. It was usual for callers to scuttle away on his return. The unusual emptiness and neatness of the flat struck him at once.

'Where's Lottie and the kids?'

'The kids are in my place having some dinner. I'll tell you where Charlotte is. Sit down.'

Bluntly, she told him what had happened and for a moment was gratified to see his stunned look. Then she took pity and added, 'The kids are all right. Course, Paddy and Daisy don't understand what's going on. Bloody good job you've turned up. We'd have had to get the parish to bury the poor little cow if you'd been gone much longer.'

'I've been—' he began, but Rose cut him short.

'I don't want to know where you've been, but now you're back you've got to see about them kids.'

He couldn't take it all in. It was a thunderbolt. 'Where is she?'

'The undertakers laid her out. She's in the bedroom. You can still see her, but they'll have to screw the lid on her soon.'

She gave him tea in his huge pint-size cup, and waited while he lifted it with a trembling hand to take a sip. 'I hope you won't marry again, Dermot. You don't know how to treat a woman.'

'What am I going to do?'

'I dunno, mate. There's Barnardo's or the Salvation Army.'

'No,' he said vehemently. 'No. I'm not putting them away. We'll have to get by.'

'Well, me and Annie'll give an eye. Let's get the funeral over, then we'll sort things out.' She got up to leave, having stayed too long alone with the man.

'Rose?'

'What?'

'What did she die of?'

' 'Igh po-thermia. Whatever that is.'

Only one carriage followed the hearse, there being few mourners. Charlotte's only sister Edith and her husband had never visited and were strangers to the children. Beyond sending a card at Christmas, there had been no contact. Edith had preferred to keep away from this neighbourhood and from Dermot. She considered she had made a rather better marriage, living in relative comfort in a spacious house in Clapham as Albert Kemp made ponderous progress up the career ladder of Lloyd's Bank. They had not come to the hastily arranged wake and had no plans to return to the flat after the burial.

From their upstairs window the Carter family watched the spectacle provided by the two black horses, draped in purple velvet, shining necks arched from bearing reins, their heads adorned with black feathered head-dresses. Other neighbours lined the pavement, among them Dry Dock Tommy, standing beside Rose with Paddy in her arms, Sarah and Daisy holding on to her skirt.

Florrie and Danny rode with their father, maintaining their customary silence in his presence. Dermot made no attempt to lessen the tension between them and his in-laws.

On muffled hooves, the horses pulled them away from

the kerb. For a moment as their faces drew level, Danny found himself looking deep into the sorrowing eyes of Kate, as he set off to accompany his mother on her last journey, in more splendour than she had ever known in life.

Chapter 3

Easter

Spring showed itself even in Bermuda Street by a raising of the light level and a flowering of wives sitting on doorsteps to talk as they shelled peas or peeled the spuds.

On Easter Saturday afternoon the door to the public bar of The Three Feathers was propped open so that the waiting urchins clustered in the opening, craning their necks to catch a glimpse of their mothers. Sometimes, cheered by the sunshine a mother would take out lemonade and buy herself an extra ten minutes peace.

Outside the blocks, it made the kids laugh to see the women stretch a thirty-foot length of thick dock rope across the road and begin to skip. Daisy was thrilled to see Dermot, joined by some other men drifting out of the pub, take an end and turn the rope, making it strike the cobbles with a loud crack as the women, with skill remembered from childhood, ran in and out, timing their jumps to the beat. Sometimes they joined hands with a daughter and together executed their steps, the crowd chanting the skipping rhymes, breaking into laughter when a foot caught, whooping and cat-calling when a pair of drawers flashed in the sun.

On Sunday Dermot bought a pint each of cockles and

winkles from a barrow outside The Feathers, where trade was brisk. Later, sitting down to tea, he looked more relaxed than he had for some time; he was almost genial as he showed Daisy how to take the cap off a winkle and extricate the flesh with a pin. Things were a bit easier with Florrie home on holiday from school. Nearly three months after Charlotte's death, they were getting by.

For all his motherless brood, the loss had been hardest on Florrie. Rose and the other neighbours were good, but most of the housework now fell to her and she still had to attend school whenever she could. Dermot's application to the school board to allow her to leave early had been refused. The nuns were fairly understanding about her frequent days away, provided she put in regular appearances at mass. He did what he could. Every night he prepared a meal for the next, and he paid for the washing to be taken to the bagwash, a job which seemed to have devolved to Sarah. Twice a week she loaded it into the old pram and struggled round to the laundry in the next street. She became expert, adding blue to the whites and soda to the coloureds, then loading it, still damp, to trundle it home again, the weight almost lifting her off her feet.

Dermot watched Florrie get up to refill his cup, noticing her new shapeliness. Seeing her slender wrists tremble under the strain of lifting the big, blue enamel pot, he felt a pang. He pushed back his chair and reached for his jacket, hanging as usual over the corner of the door. 'Here,' he said handing her half-a-crown. 'Take the nippers to Blackheath tomorrow. Get some ice-cream.'

Astonished, they made their preparations. Every

bank-holiday there was a fair on Blackheath. Florrie persuaded Kate Collins to go with them. The old pram was cleared out and wiped over, dripping was applied to the back axle to deaden the squeak and it was ready.

Early next morning it carried Paddy and Daisy and a parcel of jam sandwiches wrapped in the *Daily Mirror*. Sarah clutched the handle and Danny – who decided at the last minute to join them – jolted it over the cobbles to the Island Gardens.

The little park at the island's southern tip housed a few trees, a patch of grass and the domed entrance to the Greenwich foot tunnel. It also afforded the most amazing of city views.

The Thames flowed by in a wide arc, the pale sun cutting its grey surface into flashing diamond shapes, forming a fitting foreground to the beauty of Wren's Naval Hospital on the other side of the river. Behind it a steep green hill was crowned by the low white buildings of the Queen's House and the Royal Observatory. Danny stood with his head against the railings, looking across the choppy water, mesmerised. The wash of a passing tug slapping against the wall carried to him the smell of ships and tar and the open sea.

'Look, Paddy,' said Florrie, pointing to the matching dome on the other side. 'That's where we're going.'

'How we gonna get there?' shrilled Sarah.

'We're going under the river, through the tunnel.'

'S'pose it breaks!'

'It won't break.' Florrie laughed and, putting her head down, set off at a run for the entrance to join the stream of pleasure-bound islanders.

Having the pram, Florrie was obliged to wait for the lift, but Danny seized Kate's hand and together they ran down the seemingly never-ending spiral of the stairs, shouting and yodelling, rejoicing at the echo bouncing off the white-tiled walls.

For half its length the path sloped gently downwards. At about the middle, when they all had to give a hand to get the pram up the incline, Sarah screamed as she felt a drop of water on her face.

'It's leakin'!'

'It's only condensation,' said Danny, but she wouldn't be pacified and started to bawl.

'Oh shut up, Sarah,' they shouted in unison, the tunnel taking the sound and tossing it behind and ahead of them, to mingle with the calls of other youths strung out along its length.

They emerged on the Greenwich side and toiled upwards through the ancient park. Gusts of steam organ music drew them on. Reaching the flatter land of Blackheath, Danny abandoned the demeaning job of pram-pushing and dropped behind to take Kate's hand again. When Florrie grew exasperated at continually having to look back to make sure they were following, he seized the chance to break away.

'If we get separated, we'll meet you on the seat in front of the Observatory at five o'clock,' he said, and deliberately slowed until the ragged little train melted into the crowd.

Together Kate and Danny wandered among the rides and round the sideshows till they were footsore and hungry, their last three ha'pence spent on viewing a fish-tailed woman, displayed in a tiny tent in very dim light. At five they turned their step towards the park again and reached the meeting place ahead of Florrie.

They sat on the bench at the top of Observatory Hill,

gazing at the Thames looping round the Isle of Dogs, craft on the river appearing like toys. They tried to pick out places they knew from the black density of the island's interior, but it was all too far below and too lost in haze.

'I can hear Florrie coming,' said Kate. 'The dripping must have worn off.'

The pram came round the corner, listing and squeaking, dragging a dirt-streaked Sarah. Paddy was asleep; Daisy, sitting at the handle end gripping the sides, looked contented, unlike Florrie, who was trying not to heed a blistered heel and looked exhausted. She drew alongside and flopped down to rest.

'I had one go on the swing boats and she,' she said, pointing at Sarah, 'had a go on the hoop-la and bawled because she didn't win the rag doll. We've had saveloys and ice-cream and now there's no money left.' She kicked off her shoes and rubbed her feet through the damp grass.

'My feet ache,' Sarah whined.

'You can have a little rest, then we'll have to get home. Dad'll be in in a minute.'

They hadn't gone far when they realised they couldn't hold the overladen pram. There was a danger of it running away down the steep hill, so they re-grouped. Danny and Kate took the handle, Florrie and Sarah braced their backs against the front. Slowly the scruffy procession descended through the ancient royal hunting ground.

By the gates at the bottom, Danny put Daisy on his shoulders and Sarah rode the rest of the way home in her place, her spindly legs dangling over the sides.

About eleven o'clock one morning soon after Easter, one of the two coppers patrolling the West Ferry Road parted from his companion, arranging to catch up with him a little farther ahead and turned down a deserted Bermuda Street. He trod steadily to the foot of the stairs in the block where the Cavanaghs lived and, without hesitating, went up and into the flat.

It was quiet, the door to the kitchen closed. The family had settled back into their newly established routine. The older children were at school, Dermot and Danny at work. Only Daisy and Paddy were at home.

Paddy was tied into his high chair with a piece of webbing criss-crossed across his chest. He had fallen asleep with his cheek resting in the bowl of mashed potatoes Dermot had left there to sustain him until Florrie returned in the afternoon. A similar bowl had been placed on a chair within Daisy's reach. There had been no need to lock them in. Daisy still couldn't reach the doorknob.

The policeman took a towel from the overhead airer, folded it and, gently, without waking the baby, put it under his head in place of the potatoes. Daisy clung to the tablecloth and watched him silently.

'Do you want a drink, love?' he asked her. She nodded and he fetched a cup of milk from the scullery. 'I'll put some here for the baby. You give it to him when he wakes up like a good girl. Florrie will be home soon.'

He left her then, calling at the Carters and the Collins on his way out, but no one was at home. It was not ideal, everyone knew that, but it was the best that could be managed and the arrangement worked. It was Sarah's fault that it came to an end.

Dermot had had a visit from the only school-board inspector brave enough to deliver a warning that if Florrie's absences continued, he would be prosecuted.

The inspector only just escaped with his hide intact and for days Dermot had raged that he wasn't going to be dictated to by anyone, but on the day of the month when his life insurance premium fell due, he decided to keep Sarah at home to pay the agent. Rose Collins often did such small favours for him, but he felt she already knew too much about his personal affairs.

After the first hour, time began to drag for Sarah. She wandered from kitchen to scullery carrying cups and plates to the sink. If Florrie came home and found the table not cleared, she would tell Dermot, then there would be trouble. It had taken her ages and it still didn't look any clearer. The clock's ticking was getting on her nerves. She never noticed it when everyone was indoors but it served to remind her that she had no one to talk to. She put the last cup on the pile in the sink and, with relief, rolled up the cloth to shake the crumbs over the fireguard.

Daisy gave a shriek of protest. She had been playing house under the table in the tent formed by the cloth. Its sudden disappearance enraged her and she came out fighting. She bit Sarah hard on the behind. Sarah then burst into tears and retaliated by delivering Daisy a stinging slap across the cheek. Paddy strained at his bonds and added his despairing wail to the general squalling.

'Now look what you've done,' sobbed Sarah. 'You've started him off.'

The din was awful. She had to shut him up. She snatched up her father's discarded paper and pushed the rolled-up end between the bars of the fire. It flared, and the crying stopped immediately as she waved the brand around her head.

'Hooray!' shouted Sarah and circled it faster so that she seemed to be ringed in beautiful orange flames. The children were entranced. When the paper burned down and Sarah threw it into the hearth, Paddy screwed up his face in preparation for another bellow. Hastily, Sarah lit another sheet and waved it with more vigour.

The tail of Dermot's shirt, hanging lower than the other garments on the airer, caught fire first. In an instant it had spread and bits of burning clothing began dropping on to the floor. Sarah cringed, fending off the showering fire. The shirt dropped and enveloped her right hand. She ran about the room in agony, trying to shake it free, saved from being totally engulfed by a damp towel descending on her head.

Downstairs, Rose detected the difference in the wails. From anger and misery, they turned to pain and terror. She made for the stairs and was lumbering to the rescue when she was passed by the copper taking them two at a time.

The fire had only just begun to take hold. The ropes suspending the airer had burned through at one end and its load had slid down the slats to the floor, temporarily dampening the flames. They hadn't reached Paddy or Daisy.

The policeman tore off his jacket and threw it over Sarah, dousing the fire. There was no time to give her more attention. The fire was recovering and licking its way up the slats of the airer towards the ceiling. Quickly he rolled the burning linen in the coconut matting and threw it from the window, down into the yard, then turned on the scullery tap and set about throwing water over the remaining pockets of fire until he was satisfied that it was truly quenched.

Rose led the hysterical children to safety, through the women crowding the stairs, into Annie Carter's flat. There were many arms ready to cradle and rock the two little ones while Annie and Rose attended Sarah.

They lay her on Annie's bed. She moaned and sobbed, summoning her spent energy to scream again as Annie tried to peel away fragments of shirt clinging to the injured hand. Below the elbow to the wrist, the skin was red and blistering. Below the wrist, the flesh had shrivelled and curled, leaving only the thumb and first finger recognisable. From the remaining bloody, blackened pulp, two little claws like sticks of charcoal emerged. The little finger appeared to have gone.

Annie sucked in her breath and got a warning poke from Rose, who said, in a matter-of-fact tone: 'We'd best get Dr Lambert to look at this.'

'Shall I put flour on it?' asked Annie.

'No. You go for the doctor. You'll be quicker than me. Tell him what it's like. I'll stay here and get her to drink something.'

Annie seemed to be gone an age. Some women were in tears, unable to bear the child's suffering. Rose tried to give her water but she would not take it. She sent runners off to fetch Dermot and Florrie. The policeman came in and was administered tea. Hot, to drink, and cold, applied to a blistered hand.

The women fell back respectfully as the doctor arrived. He had – to Annie's disbelief – stopped to have his pony harnessed to the trap and she had enjoyed the second drama of the day, driving down Bermuda Street beside him. She soon saw why he had delayed.

'Annie, can you get me something clean to wrap her arm in? I'll take her to the hospital myself.'

37

A pillow-case was produced. Dr Lambert eyed Annie doubtfully. He would have preferred Rose to accompany the child, but her bulk would slow the pony. Florrie's arrival ended the quandary. Sarah was carried to the trap and laid across the seat with her head in her sister's lap. As they drove away, Florrie, not for a moment considering defying the doctor's orders, reflected that there would be hell to pay when Dad got home, found her gone and that he had a doctor's bill to pay.

She returned from the hospital in the evening, alone and on foot. Dr Lambert had handed Sarah over to the nurses and left to get on with his other work. Florrie had waited in the great hall while Sarah's hand was dressed, the distant screams echoing dolefully down the tiled corridor, reminding her strongly of the recent day when she had dragged a tiresome but whole Sarah through the foot tunnel. She had been allowed to see Sarah before going home.

She lay in a high-sided iron cot in the children's ward: a large square room with a fire burning in the centre and a balcony outside. She was quiet at last. The sides of the cot were too high to lean over to touch her. Florrie crouched until their heads were level.

'I'll come and see you Sunday,' she whispered. 'I'll bring you some sweets. Be a good girl.' Sarah didn't speak. Her eyes followed Florrie to the door, staring out through the bars, her face as white as her pillow and the bandages that swathed her arm.

When Dermot reached the flat, it was to find an army of women scrubbing, cleaning and putting the place to rights. Someone had even found a piece of coconut matting to cover the charred floorboards in front of the range. The policeman was waiting for him and drew him aside.

'This is no good, mate. You can't carry on like this. You'll have to get someone to look after them kids, or you'll have to take 'em down the workhouse.'

Chapter 4

Dolores

The problem of how to keep his family together occupied Dermot's mind to the exclusion of everything else. A few days after the fire, he carried his drink through the noisy throng in the saloon of The Feathers and sat in brooding silence at the end of the bar, aware that he was the object of interested looks from a knot of women shucking peas in the booth near the door.

They discussed what they knew of his affairs in low tones, with much shaking and nodding of heads, their animated faces curiously white and mottled, the effect of the light shining through the reversed lettering on the frosted window. When Dry Dock Tommy came in and stood looking blankly about, missing Dermot from his usual central position, they motioned him to the corner, verbal directions rendered useless by the enthusiastic vamping of the pianist.

Tom ordered up two more pints and went to join Dermot. 'Hello, mate. How's the nipper?'

'Not too bad, thanks for asking, but it's going to be a long job.' Dermot stared sorrowfully into his stout, then spoke with difficulty. 'They're talking about grafting a bit of skin from her leg.'

'Poor little bugger. Have you seen her?'

'No, I couldn't, Tom. I couldn't stand seeing me kid in one of those places. Florrie went. Said she cried when she had to leave her. It would just choke me.'

'When's visiting?'

'Half hour on Wednesday night. Six to half past. Then an hour on Sunday afternoons.'

'I'll get our Kate to go with Florrie. Take her a bar of chocolate.'

'That's good of you. I wish Florrie was a bit older. Take a load off me, it would. I don't know what I'm going to do, Tom.'

'Well, I was wondering.'

'What?'

'Well, it's just an idea but it might be worth trying. I thought Bobster's old woman might come round and help you out for a while.'

'No, she wouldn't. Why should she?'

'She's a relation of yours, ain't she?'

'Yes, she's me cousin, but I can't see her taking on five kids. Anyway, what about Bobster?'

'I thought you knew. He's gone inside for six months.'

'Are you sure?'

'Yeah. I took him on casual, cleaning out the bilges on the Greek ship. That's how I know. Anyway, he didn't turn up one Monday, so I sent a boy round to find out what the matter was. Seemed he'd carried on signing on with the Relieving Officer while he was working. They found out and he's got six months' hard labour. Dolly might be glad of a place to go.'

'Ain't she cooking down the Anne Boleyn?'

'No. The missus got rid of her. The grub was going missing.'

41

'I still don't think she'd do it. She ain't used to kids. She's never had any.'

'She'd be a bloody sight better than what you've got now, and you won't know if she'll do it till you ask her.'

Dermot took a long swig. 'You're right, Tom.' He finished the pint in a long smooth swallow, then stood up, decisively wiping his whiskers. 'I'll see you tomorrow.'

Setting his cap well down on his head, he astonished the clientele by steering a direct course to the door, a good two hours before closing time.

Dermot got off the bus in Poplar High Street, mulling over how best to approach his cousin Dolores O'Lambert. He had seen her only once since he attended her wedding ten years before, and that had been when he'd bumped into her by chance when they were both browsing the stalls in the Chrisp Street market. He hadn't avoided her exactly, but he didn't like the way she dominated her huge, good-natured husband, and had never sought them out.

His mother and hers were sisters. Forty years before, on their way home from mass in Ireland, they had, on impulse, pooled their money and joined a ship bound for England, lured by stories of the easy money to be made. By the time their father had saved the fare to come and take them home, they were both pledged to young immigrant Irishmen.

Dermot walked along Chrisp Street looking for the mean little turning where the O'Lamberts rented the top half of a tiny terraced house, his feet kicking against lopped-off cabbage leaves and other garbage left from the day's trading. The long summer day had ended and it was dusk. He was not sure of the number and was peering up at the doors hoping some feature would stir his memory, when he found her. She was sitting on a doorstep, her knees under her chin, her long skirt trailing in the grime, at her feet a large bundle of belongings tied in a tablecloth.

He stopped in front of her, looking down at the plaited rope of hair coiled several times round her head. Her face, when she turned it up to him, looked worn. It gave him a start. The pronounced widow's peak, high cheekbones and glittering dark eyes reminded him strongly of his mother.

'Jesus, Dermot! What are you doing here?'

'Looking for you, Dolly. I want to talk to you. Can we go indoors?'

'We could have done half an hour ago, but the landlady's turned me out. God rot her!'

'What for?'

'I'm a wee bit behind with the rent. Then she heard about poor old Bobster and that did it. I'm out on me ear without a second chance. The stingy cow! May she melt like the froth on the river!'

'Where are you going to go?'

'I've enough to pay for a night's lodging. I'll go to the RO tomorrow and try to get some work. I'm not going to the workhouse. I'll sleep rough if I have to, till I find me feet.'

'Do you fancy some pie and mash?'

'Do I! God love you, I've had nothing all day and I'm famished.'

With uncharacteristic courtesy, Dermot helped her to her feet. He drew the line at carrying her bundle, but cupped his hand under her elbow while they walked to one of the many pie shops plying along the high street.

She ate while he talked, shifting mountainous quantities of mashed potatoes smothered in a liquor made bright green with parsley. By the end of the meal she had agreed to take charge of his household until Bobster came out of prison. Her last doubts were removed when Dermot pointed out that fate must have made her stop to rest on that doorstep just at that moment. Another few minutes and he would have missed her. It might have taken him months to find her again.

That night she took the sofa in the parlour. Danny shared his father's bed. In the morning they would make other arrangements. The first of many in the new regime.

Danny's loathing of Dolores deepened with every week that passed. He was big enough to be exempt from the clouts that she liberally dealt the other children, and her incessant nagging to fetch the coal or take out the slops bothered him very little, but within a week of her arrival she had taken his mother's place in his father's bed. For a couple of nights, Dermot had made a show of settling for the night in his chair by the fire while Danny reclaimed the sofa and Dolores went to his bedroom, but he soon gave up the pretence.

Danny never spoke of it, fear of his father keeping him silent on the subject. He avoided speaking to Dolores except to answer in monosyllables, but Dermot, watching his son closely, noted the way he flattened himself against the wall when Dolores passed, the eyes carefully kept expressionless, and was aware of the anger that consumed him. Dermot too said nothing and Danny waited, consoling himself that when her husband got out of prison they would be rid of her.

In the new order everyone worked, though Dolores reserved her own energies for cooking and organising the household, which under her direction became clean and orderly. Even little Paddy was given a blunt knife and potatoes to scrape, not for the help it gave, but to train him in what would later be expected of him. Daisy learned to scrub the lavatory seat, graduated to scrubbing the lavatory floor and then the long passage that led from the front door. The bulk of the work still fell to Florrie.

At first, Dolores had walked out once or twice a day, to the shop on the corner or the butcher's in the next street, but quite soon this stopped. Essential trips down the stairs to the yard left her breathless and Florrie took over running all the errands except those which Daisy could manage in her dinner hour. Dolores explained that she couldn't go herself because she was suffering 'a touch of the dropsy'. She did not explain or admit even to herself that she dreaded meeting Rose or Annie Carter on the stairs. They could only guess at her new status of fallen woman, but it was enough to keep her confined to the flat.

By the time Sarah came home from the hospital, Dolores' overpowering presence had been felt in the house for five months. It was a Monday when Florrie was sent to fetch her. As usual, Dolores lit the copper at midday and by four had 'a lovely lot of suds' ready for the wash. Florrie's evening was spent rubbing it against the ribbed glass of the washing board until her knuckles were raw. She then went down to the yard where Dolores dropped the items to her from the window, one at a time, to be pinned to the line. She was most particular that this was done correctly and leaned

45

over the sill shouting instructions about which way to hang the shirts and sheets to take best advantage of the wind.

Strangely, Dolores took to Sarah immediately. She made no pretence at affection or even liking for the others, but suffering had changed Sarah, left her quiet and uncomplaining, oddly unchildlike.

In their attempts to graft skin to the back of her hand, surgeons had removed what remained of the little finger. The operations had failed and she was left with a contracted claw covered with a layer of red, inflexible scar tissue which did not grow and in winter would split and bleed. She was excused all work.

Danny kept out as much as he could. Rose Collins became used to him dropping in after work in the evening. Sometimes he came down again after his meal and played a game of cards with Tom and Charlie, when he was home. Soon it was accepted that when he left, Kate saw him to the door and spent a few minutes talking to him in the porch.

One evening in August, he turned into the entry and found her waiting for him.

'Danny,' she hissed in excitement, 'your Uncle Bobster's home. I don't know what's been happening upstairs. There's been a terrible shindig going on all day. It's quiet now, but he's still up there.'

Danny went cautiously up the stairs. Sarah and Daisy, with Paddy between them, were sitting on the step.

'Where's Florrie?' he asked.

'She's indoors,' said Daisy.

'And Aunt Dolly?'

'She's asleep.'

'She's drunk,' said Sarah 'They're both drunk.'

Florrie was at the range. She spun round, a look of terror on her face when he went into the room.

'Oh Danny! Thank God. I've been praying you'd get home before Dad. There's going to be murder when he gets in. They've drunk all his whisky and Bobster threw the clock at her and smashed it. The fire's gone out and there's no dinner ready.'

The two were insensible, Bobster slumped in the armchair, his mouth slack and drooling, Dolores sprawled at the table with her head on her arms, snoring.

'What are we going to do?' Florrie pressed her hands to her cheeks. 'Can we get him out before Dad gets home?'

Danny looked at Bobster's huge bulk. 'I can't shift him,' he said. He thought for a moment. 'Look, you take the nippers next door to Mrs Carter. I'll go and find Dad. Don't worry. He'll know it's not your fault. Don't come out till I fetch you.'

Annie let them in without asking unnecessary questions. Danny saw them inside then went back to the living room. He picked up the clock, thought better of it, left it where it had landed after missing Dolores' head, and set off unhurriedly to where he knew he would find his father.

Outrage at Danny's sudden appearance in the bar of The Feathers deepened the red of Dermot's face to dangerous crimson. The cronies flanking him on either side stared in astonishment. He spluttered on his beer. 'What the bloody hell do you think you're doing coming in here?' he bellowed.

Something about the way the boy quietly stood his ground and the hint of mockery as he met his eyes made him change his tone.

'What do you want?'

'Uncle Bobster's back. I think you'd better come home.'

He knew better than to say more in public. He waited for the moment it took Dermot to absorb the information and to finish his pint, then followed him outside. Almost every customer in the bar fell in behind them, anxious not to miss what promised to be the most spectacular fight the street had seen for years.

By the time he reached the landing, Dermot's blood was up. It was deflating for him to discover, when he burst into the room, that his adversary was already unconscious. He glowered down at Bobster, then bunching the front of his shirt in one fist, he raised him out of the chair as far as the strength of his left arm would allow. He drew his other fist behind him and landed a punch on the jaw with all the force he could muster.

Bobster cried out and dazedly got to his feet, shaking his head. He took a few tottering steps towards Dermot, who stood back, waiting for him to come round enough to stiffen his knees and stand upright. He threw another punch at the face which loomed a good six inches above his own. Bobster retaliated with a blow to Dermot's eye, connecting by chance rather than judgement. He was too drunk to defend himself properly.

From the doorway, Danny judged that it would soon be over. He turned to rouse Dolores, anxious that when Bobster's ejection came, she would be alert enough to be sent packing with him. He shook her hard and hissed in her ear, 'Aunt Dolly!'

'She grunted and stirred but would have sunk back

into stupor had Dermot not crashed against the table, reeling from the impact of a chair brought down on his head. The familiar sound of splintering wood jerked Dolores awake. Hazily she took in what was happening. For the moment, Dermot seemed to be getting the worst of it.

Danny made no move to stop her as she staggered to the range and picked up the poker. He expected to see her lay about Dermot, but instead she amazed him by bringing it down with cracking force on her husband's skull. It was too much. Bobster turned and made for the door. He stumbled down the stairs, his shirt torn, his nose bloody. The crowd in the entry fell back to let him pass. Someone shouted after him, 'Never mind, Bobster, you're well shot of her.'

Upstairs, Dermot slumped in his chair, too tired to give Dolores the thrashing he had in mind for her. He looked across to where she sat gasping in the opposite chair. A parting swipe from Bobster had split her lower lip and she was half-heartedly stemming the trickle of blood with the back of her hand. She had partly redeemed herself.

He wanted a drink. The fire was out, no chance of tea. He groped for the mug of cold tea that always stood on the fender and realised that Danny was still in the room.

'Danny. Run down The Jug and Bottle and get me a quart of stout. Put it on me slate.'

Danny clenched his fists, the nails digging into his palms. Rage rose in his throat, threatening to choke him, but he stepped over the wrecked chair to get the jug from the scullery.

'While you're out there,' said Dermot, 'fetch her a cold flannel to put on that.'

'I'm not touching her.' Danny rounded on him with venom. 'I'm not going anywhere near her.'

Dermot started to haul himself out of the chair, but sank back, unable to make the effort.

'She could be a mother to you, if you'd let her, you lippy little bleeder!'

'She's a whore!' spat Danny. 'A religious whore. And don't you talk about my mother!'

He had dared too much. He had to escape. Not break down in front of his father. At the door he turned and said in a strangled voice, 'You can fetch your own fucking stout.' On the landing he hesitated, not sure of the best way to run in case Dermot should come after him, then he turned and went softly down the back stairs into the cool and blessed darkness of the yard. In the safety of the space between the back wall and the chicken shed, he cried until he could cry no more, then sat for a long time, thinking. When he got up, he knew what he must do.

He washed his face under the outside tap then went back upstairs. He pushed open the door to listen. Deep snores reverberated down the passage. It was safe to get Florrie.

They decided to leave Paddy where he was. Annie had tucked him up beside Johnnie, her own two-year-old. Florrie could collect him in the morning. Sarah and Daisy, white-faced with tiredness, obeyed absolutely when Danny warned them not to make a sound. Florrie went ahead and silently pushed open the living-room door. Only Dolores remained sitting beside the range, fast asleep, her head lolling at a painful angle. Dermot had left her and gone to bed.

As they crept past Florrie said, 'We ought to find something to put under her head.'

'I hope it drops off,' said Danny, but Sarah took a towel from the fireguard and they wedged it between Dolores' neck and the rails of the chair back. Her snoring quietened.

They had not eaten. Florrie gave her sisters bread spread thickly with dripping to eat in bed, then spread more for herself and Danny. They stood together in the scullery, whispering as they ate.

'I've got to get away from here,' Danny told her. 'She's here for good now. I can't stick it.'

'She does look after Paddy while I'm at school,' said Florrie.

'I don't care. I hate her. I wish Mum was here.'

'Not much good wishing that. It won't bring her back.' Florrie began to weep quietly. 'I don't like her either.'

'Well I've made up me mind. I'm going to see if I can get a job on a Thames coasting barge. Charlie told me there's one tied up in the Victoria Dock. The skipper might be looking for a boy. I'm going to try me luck.'

'When are you going?'

'Tonight. Dad's gonna kill me if he finds me here in the morning. You needn't worry,' he added, seeing her stricken look, 'you can pretend you didn't know anything about it. Pretend you don't know where I've gone.'

'Where are you going to sleep?'

'If I get tired I'll kip in a doorway. If I start walking now, I'll get there at daylight. Be first in line.'

'When will we see you?'

He considered this. 'I'll most likely be back in about a week, if I get the job. I'll wait for you at the school gate one dinner time.'

Florrie had to be content with that. She helped him collect his clothing into a bundle and saw him off at the door. At the foot of the stairs, he turned and looked back.

'Tell Kate where I've gone,' he said. 'Tell her I'll get a message to her.'

Chapter 5

Barges

Danny found the coaster berthed alongside the Millenium Flour Mills. There was barely enough pre-dawn light to identify her and he paced along her length until he could make out the name: *Scot*. Nothing stirred on board. Uncertain what to do next, he sat on a bollard and waited.

Visions of his father waking and finding him gone pushed into his brain. It would not be long, he knew, before Dermot found out where he had gone. News would travel along the waterfront and reach Dry Dock Tommy, who would pass it on before the day was out, perhaps before the *Scot* was safely in mid-river. Perhaps Dermot would come looking for him to take him home, if only for the wages he could earn. He was not a man to feed a boy till fourteen only to watch his investment walk away.

He rehearsed how he was going to ask to be taken on as a hand. He didn't consider what he would do if he didn't get the job. He had to get it. The fate that had forced him to leave home and brought him to this cold dockside would allow no other course.

For an hour he sat, as the sky slowly brightened, cold from his unyielding seat striking up through his trousers till his backside was as numb as his spirit. At about six, there was movement on the barge and a head emerged from the cabin top. 'Have you come to join us?' it shouted.

Danny jumped up. 'Yes!' he yelled, and passed his bundle up to the little bow-legged man who appeared on deck. He had barely clambered aboard and got beyond giving his name to the mate when, amid the quickening scene on the waterfront, a dinghy appeared, being sculled alongside by a huge red-haired man with a florid face.

'Here, Tod,' he shouted to the mate, 'Get the boy to cook that.' He picked up a brown parcel and lobbed it on to the deck.

'He can't cook yet, Mac,' Tod shouted back. 'He's only a kid.'

'He'll bloody soon learn aboard here. What he buggers up, he goes without.'

The parcel contained about three pounds of rump steak and the same quantity of bacon sliced into thick rashers. Tod led the way down the steep fo'c's'le ladder to show Danny where it was to be cooked and to outline his duties.

Four large racks occupied the cramped space below, two on either side, holding ropes, blocks and canvas. The after-rack, where the thick tow rope was coiled, with the staysail tucked between, was pointed out as Danny's bunk. The cast-iron stove, a simple contraption with a few bars in the front, glowed malevolently in the centre.

Tod showed him where the frying pan was kept, gave the briefest explanation of how the skipper liked his eggs and fried bread and left a quaking Danny with instructions to bring it to the cabin when it was ready.

After about three-quarters of an hour and having broken the yolks of several eggs which he put aside for himself to eat later, he managed to cover two plates with food. Black speckled and greasy, but definitely eatable. He had been acutely conscious of the minutes passing, imagining the skipper clutching knife and fork, waiting for his breakfast. Panic seized him when he realised he was going to have to climb the ladder carrying the plates. He decided one at a time would be wisest.

At the top, he immediately attracted the attention of scavenging seagulls and had to come down the ladder again to get a second plate to cover the first. By the time he reached the top for the second time, he was feeling fatalistic. They could only chuck him off the ship.

The after cabin was luxurious in comparison with the fo'c's'le. Oak pannelled lockers on all sides, cushioned seats, two bunks – one port, one starboard – each with a curtain hanging on rings from a brass rail. Overhead, a skylight let in the morning sun which twinkled on the brass clock/barometer.

The skipper regarded him stonily and didn't speak. Tod helped to lay the table, then he and the skipper fell on the food without comment. They didn't tell him what he was supposed to do next and Danny stood awkwardly eyeing the stove in the centre of the cabin. Superior to the one he'd been battling with – it had an oven that shone with black lead and a brightly polished copper flue disappearing out through the deckhead. The whole thing was mounted on a whitened slab. It was obviously an object of pride. He could guess who would be responsible for keeping it in this gleaming condition.

Tod stopped chewing. 'What's the matter? Something you want to know?'

'Yes,' said Danny, 'What happened to your last boy?'

A slow grin spread across Captain MacFarlane's face. 'You go for'ard,' he said, 'get some grub, then come back and we'll have a talk.'

Danny obeyed, joy surging through him and sending him sliding down the fo'c's'le ladder. He was in. He knew it!

Once the dishes were clear and the cabin restored to splendour, Danny stood before the skipper while he set out his terms of employment.

'You'll get eight shillings a week and your grub, if you don't bugger any up. All crockery you break while we're in the London river, you pay for, also any scrubbing brushes you sling overboard by mistake. There are no set hours of work aboard here. While we're underway, so are you.'

That was it. The rest Danny gleaned from experience and the things his two sailing companions told him, a gradual process since they seldom spoke to him beyond giving orders. The skipper and the mate received from the owners a small sum per ton of goods delivered. His wage was paid from that, so he learned quickly that time was money and not to be wasted.

His first voyage was to the Isle of Wight, carrying oil cake, a kind of cattle feed. The skipper had laid in supplies, that is, he had taken a large kit bag to the Home and Colonial stores and bought a huge hock of smoked bacon, a lump of salt beef, tins of coffee, potatoes and onions. Any unfilled corners of the bag were stuffed with bread. Stowing these provisions in the cabin locker, Danny wondered how long they would be away, but thought it prudent not to ask.

On the way down river, they anchored for the night at

Grays. The skipper had on board line and mackerel spinners to tow astern when they were underway and he wanted some mussels for bait. He pointed out to Danny the sunken wreck of an ammunition ship, which had become a rich breeding ground and sent him off in the dinghy with a bucket.

Danny had had a little experience of skulling in the flat waters of the dock and, setting out from the *Scot* on an ebbing tide, he found progress to the wreck smooth and easy. In half an hour he had the bucket filled and turned to skull the short distance back.

After several minutes of strenuous effort, he realised he was making no headway against the running tide. He made for the shore, hoping to come up against the *Scot* at an angle. Keeping his eyes on his target, he put his back behind the figure-of-eight motion he was making with the oar to keep the dinghy on a straight course, his dexterity increasing with every stroke. It began to grow dark. Pausing briefly to get his breath and reckon the distance that still lay between him and the ship, he felt himself bump against the wreck again.

A despairing sob broke from him but he checked himself. He couldn't get back tear-streaked and get back he must. The skipper was waiting for the mussels. For several hours he tacked back and forth arriving alongside as the tide began to slacken, with barely enough strength left to climb aboard. Captain MacFarlane stretched out a hand to help him. Looking up, Danny saw him smirk and knew he had been given one of the skipper's unique lessons in seamanship.

By the time they entered the English Channel, Danny was beginning to get his sea legs. The weather had been fair and he had been allowed to take the wheel on some stretches, with instructions to keep an eye on the sails and the flag at the mast in relation to the course he was steering. Loaded, there was only about a foot of free-board amidships, so he became used to being constantly wet and to snatching sleep at odd moments. Sometimes he nodded off while standing up. When he could be spared from deck, he contrived hot meals from whatever was left in the locker.

At Newport, they unloaded and began their slow return round the coast, stopping at several ports of call, some of them tiny villages. In one, Danny was overjoyed to see the *Norman*, their sister ship, and the one on which Charlie Collins worked, riding at anchor. He was mustering the nerve to ask permission to skull across to see him, when the voice of the *Norman*'s skipper boomed across the water. 'Mac, you coming ashore?'

Danny could see Charlie lowering a boat. He waited in hope for the Skipper's answering holler: 'You get 'em in. I'll see you inside.'

Danny was impatient to get going. 'That's my mate, Charlie,' he told them, but he was made to light the riding lights and leave everything shipshape before he was allowed to haul for the shore. On the stone slipway in front of the pub, he and Charlie greeted each other like brothers.

The boys were not invited to join their masters, but were given twopence to go to the pictures. As they trudged up the road, Charlie remarked: 'Blimey, you ain't half skinny.'

Danny grinned. 'I'm doing the cooking.'

They discussed the various character traits of their shipmates. 'My old man's a bastard,' said Charlie, 'but I know how to handle him. I put a drop of whisky in his tea in the mornings. Don't let him sober up too quick. What's yours like? Can't be worse than your dad.'

'Was there a row when he found out I'd gone?'

'I dunno. He never said nothing to me. Well, he wouldn't, would he? But I was down in the yard that Saturday, feeding the chickens, when the meat and two veg and all the plates come flyin' out the window of your house. Florrie said he just come in and tipped the table up. So I don't think he was none too pleased.'

They joined the audience in the village hall, most of them noisy lads who appeared to be related or who certainly knew each other very well. The film was about India in the monsoon. As the images flickered and jerked across the screen Charlie and Danny struggled to follow the action, craning their necks and leaning from side to side as the boy in front repeatedly jumped to his feet to pour rice on to a tin tray to provide the sound effect of rain teeming down on tin roofs. His efforts were almost drowned out by a chorus of voices reading the subtitles aloud and Charlie yelling at him to make it rain harder.

Back on the slipway, the boys waited under the stars for the pub to turn out. 'Charlie,' said Danny, 'tell Florrie you've seen me; and Kate.'

'I will if I get home first. We're going up to Malden when we leave here. Look out, here comes the old man.'

The three mariners emerged, Captain MacFarlane holding himself stiffly upright with Tod tottering from side to side, as though treading the deck in a force eight gale, supporting Charlie's skipper whose knees buckled with every step. Danny helped to get him in their dinghy and pushed it into deep water. 'How you going to get him on board?' he whispered as Charlie took the oars.

'If he can't climb up, we'll leave the old bugger in the boat all night.'

Danny had no trouble with his charges. They sat in the stern without speaking and boarded with the agility of monkeys. In the morning, when he came on deck, the *Norman* had already gone.

Outside Dover, where they were to pick up a load of coal for Southend Gasworks, they hit rough weather and had to run for shelter. For ten days they stayed at anchor waiting for the wind to change. Danny was kept busy, polishing and scrubbing. He was in the cabin one day rubbing the copper flue and all the bright work with an emery cloth when he found *Brown's Nautical Almanac*. Ted and the skipper were ashore. Fascinated, he picked it up and lay back against the cushions to read.

He leapt up and straightened the cushions when he heard footsteps on deck and felt the boat rock slightly under the weight of the skipper's step. When Captain MacFarlane put his head in, Danny was diligently rubbing the clock. He braced himself, waiting for the bellow, but it didn't come. He looked innocently at his employer who picked up the almanac from where it still lay on the bunk. The bushy red eyebrows came together in a frown.

'What you doing with this?'

'Just looking at it.'

'You got the dinner on?'

'I done that first. Then I come in here to clean up.'

'What we havin'?'

'Currant pudden.'

'Well, we'll have some of these as well.' He thrust the kit-bag containing potatoes and cabbage towards him. 'I tell you what,' he said, stooping to look him menacingly in the eye, 'if you've let that pudden boil dry, and it's been burnin' while you're in here lookin' at books, I'll make you eat the bleedin' lot.'

Danny beat it for'ard. He'd become good at performing culinary miracles in one pot. He suspended the potatoes and cabbage in nets above the pudding, then served it all together as one course.

That night, the wind veered and lessened to a fresh breeze and they set sail again, arriving at the mouth of the Thames as night fell. They dropped anchor and waited for the tide to turn. In the fo'c's'le, with only the glow from the stove for light, Danny curled up on the staysail, glad of the chance to sleep.

Tod shook him awake. 'The skipper wants you.'

'What for?'

'Ask him yourself.' Tod disappeared and Danny, befuddled and apprehensive, climbed to the mist-shrouded deck, muttering some newly acquired cuss words as he went.

The skipper was at the table, *Brown's Almanac* in front of him. 'Can you read?' he asked.

'Yes.'

A calloused finger tapped the almanac. 'Can you tell from that which lighthouse is flashing?'

Danny swallowed. 'Yeah, course I can.'

'Right, come on, then.' The captain led the way on deck with the hurricane lamp and held it while Danny found the place. Away to his right, a light showed intermittently, penetrating the pitch blackness. Presently, he began to discern other lights as his eyes adjusted, but he could not judge their distance or direction. The one point he was certain of was down, as the deck rose and fell beneath his feet. The next gust of wind brought billows of fine rain, soaking them and splattering loudly against the glass of the skylight. The skipper was impatient. 'What's that one, then?'

'Wait a minute. I've got to count the flashes.' He read aloud from the almanac, studied the sequence of flashes, then announced, 'That must be the Chapman Light.'

'That's what I thought.' The skipper grunted and went inside. 'Can you write and all?'

'You can't really do one without the other.'

'Is that right? Well, smartarse, you can write a letter for me.'

He took paper and pen from the locker at the head of his bunk and dictated a letter to the owners in Fenchurch Street, concerning payment and delay in delivery because of the recent bad weather. There were many 'respectfullys' and 'begging to reminds'. He closed with 'I have the honour to remain, sir, your obedient servant'. Danny wasn't too sure of the spelling of all these words but since, by now, it was obvious that neither the skipper nor Tod could read or write and were therefore unable to check his work, he finished with a confident flourish.

'Is that all?' he asked. He was soaked and his teeth were beginning to chatter.

'No. I've got another letter.'

'Can I just go and fill up the stove? We don't want it to go out.'

'Tod'll do it.' The skipper motioned to the mate who went without protest.

The next letter was to Mrs MacFarlane, the skipper's wife, in Gravesend. It contained nothing of an intimate nature, only details about being stormbound in Dover and hopes for her good health, but Danny was hard put not to grin. 'Hoping this finds you in the pink as it leaves me at present,' he penned, then looked up expectantly, waiting for the closing line. The skipper was looking at him through narrowed eyes.

'What have you put in it?' he demanded.

'Only what you told me to put,' said Danny.

'You lyin' little bleeder.' It was said without rancour and he took the paper and laboriously signed his name himself.

'Can I go now? I'm perished,' pleaded Danny.

'Go on. Hoppit.'

The fo'c's'le was snug. Danny took off his clothes and spread them round the stove to dry, a facility the cabin didn't have, but which its occupants didn't seem to miss. He was happy as he lay down in his bunk; he hadn't been spoken to with such warmth and affection since his mother died.

He had risen so far in the captain's esteem that on the long reach past Barking Creek, while Tod took the helm, Danny was allowed to cut his hair. Preparation, Danny thought, for a few days ashore when they tied up in Victoria Dock again.

At Rotherhithe they lowered all the gear to the deck – topmast, main and all the sails – and continued under tow, shooting under the bridges to Battersea, where they offloaded and, to Danny's bewilderment, picked up fresh cargo. When the skipper came back from his usual foraging expedition, he felt bold enough to question him about it.

'Ain't we going into Victoria Dock then?'

'We got to make up the time we lost in Dover. Here,' he added, 'this'll cheer you up.' He passed over the kit-bag which Danny almost dropped on the deck, it was so unexpectedly heavy.

'What is it?' He looked inside and found, among the

potatoes, a cobbler's last and several thick sheets of leather.

'It's a hobbing foot,' said the skipper. 'I'm going to learn you to mend me boots. Give you something to do of an evening.'

That was all. On the way down river, they passed the causeway where had spent so many hours as a school-boy. He could have walked to Bermuda Street in a couple of minutes, but the *Scot* being still under tow, the street rapidly disappeared astern. It surprised him to find his eyes smarting with tears and he went below so that Tod and the skipper wouldn't see.

At Rotherhithe once more, the gear was checked to see that it was in good running order, the mast was winched up and they set sail again, for Southend. It was to be three years before Danny saw home again.

Chapter 6

Talleymen

Dolores' housekeeping skills, or her powers of delegation, kept the flat shining and ensured that Dermot always came home to a hot meal even on those days when the children had to go hungry; but her skills did not extend to budgeting. She received thirty shillings a week. Eight should have been set aside for rent, though seldom was, leaving twenty-two shillings to meet all the other demands including providing only the best quality food for Dermot.

She could not get more out of him, though in the early days of their living together she tried, showing tremendous daring by tackling him on the subject every pay night, after he had been to the pub and filled his belly with beer. It led to fights. Every Friday without fail she would be cuffed about the head, to which she responded with the courage of a bull terrier and hit him back with any implement that came to hand.

Florrie and Sarah advised her not to keep on answering back; it would be over much quicker if only she would shut up. But she couldn't bring herself to let him have the last word. She would back-chat him till her dying breath, if need be. Once or twice he did knock her senseless but usually the fight was suspended with him

65

storming down the stairs, to be continued on Saturday and, very often, Sunday too.

Dolores scorned to resort to the wiles other women were driven to. She would not wheedle or cajole – in any case she lacked the subtlety to be convincing – but cunning did come to her aid. She quickly realised that Dermot was easily taken in by stories of hardship. He was quite unmoved by his own sons' lack of underwear, but stories of children without shoes or bread reduced him to tears.

She had been in residence only a few weeks when, after a particularly violent row, she was banished from Dermot's bed. Had it not been for the children's need of her, he would have thrown her out of the house. She was just too unlike his meek and slender Charlotte. There was no other place for her to sleep but on the sofa vacated by Danny. It was not to her liking and she made one of her rare expeditions to Chrisp Street and arranged for delivery of an armchair which opened out into a single bed, to be paid for in weekly instalments.

How to get it into the flat without arousing Dermot's wrath occupied her mind all the way home on the bus; the rest of the scheme was already in place. By the time she arrived, it was complete. She waited until mid-week, when there was a lull in the fighting, to put the first stage into action.

'Dermot,' she said, as he pushed back his plate, 'you know the McGuires? Well,' she went on as he grunted an affirmative, 'you know they're packing up and going to Australia? The poor man's been out of work these six months and one of the little ones has got consumption. Well, they're just a few quid short of the money to emigrate and they're selling some of their bits and pieces to scrape it together.' She rushed on see-ing that she had his interest. 'I was wondering if we couldn't help them out a bit. There's this chair-bed they have. It would come in handy for us, with Florrie get-ting bigger and all.'

'How much?' asked Dermot, and the thing was as good as accomplished. She had the chair for the price of a down-payment and a useful lump sum besides.

Dermot inspected it in its new position in the parlour. He opened it out and lay on it, bouncing up and down on the modern springing. He looked about at his sur-roundings; the aspidistra on its jardinière in the bay window, the pair of pictures of camels in the desert above the piano, and decided that such a setting was too good for the likes of Dolores. He had his own belongings moved in and Dolores went back to the back bedroom where, to ease the crowding in the off room, Sarah took to sharing the bed with her.

Windfalls accrued by cunning did Dolores no good. Had she been able to use this gift for strategy to think beyond the immediate crisis, she and the family might have prospered, but her wit was constantly employed in devising means to extricate herself from difficulty. As Dermot was the one wage winner since Danny's depar-ture, it meant constantly looking for fresh ways to outwit him.

She ordered a new suit to be made for Dermot, taking the measurements from an old one he kept folded in a box under the double bed. When it arrived, she sent Florrie to pawn it for a third of its value, then waited for the right opportunity.

After dinner, in his chair by the range, buried behind the *Racing World*, Dermot's concentration was spoiled by a faint sniffling. Dolores was sewing and, from time to time, dabbing at her eyes.

'What's the matter with you?'

'I'm just thinkin' of poor Aggie Hennessey in Kingston Street.'

'What's the matter with her?'

'Her husband, a fine big man like you, died all of a sudden last week. They've been having hard times and he'd pawned his best suit. Only just had it made and he's died before he had the chance to wear it.' A tear splashed on to her work. 'It's never been on his back. Now, if Aggie can't sell the ticket, she can't pay the rent.'

The outcome was exactly as she planned. Dermot bought the pawn ticket; Dolores had some ready cash, from the pledge in the first place and the sale of the ticket. As a bonus, Dermot redeemed the suit, found it ill-fitting and refused to wear it, leaving it available to be re-pawned when needed. She did not include in her calculations the weekly visit from the tailor's tallyman to collect payment on the suit.

Tallymen were her downfall. Salesmen, selling on credit all kinds of goods, from essential pots, pans and brushes, to the almost obligatory parlour piano, toured the neighbourhood constantly. Dolores couldn't resist them. She seldom committed herself to more than a few pence a week, but her purchases became so numerous that she soon had two tea pots hidden in the sideboard, one stuffed with dockets from tallymen, the other with pawn tickets.

It took ingenuity to keep Dermot in ignorance. On Saturday mornings a child had to be posted on the stairs to head off any tallymen who might be coming to call when he was still at home. The tallymen themselves grew sly and realised that their best hope of actually collecting any money was before he got home, or after they had seen him leave. It worked fairly well but, inevitably, sometimes Dermot would meet a debt collector on the stairs.

That was not the way the first fight that Daisy could clearly remember started. She couldn't understand the reason for it, or why it always seemed to happen just as the dinner she had been waiting for was placed in front of her, but she felt the sickening apprehension shared by them all as Dermot's dragging step was heard in the passage. He wasn't staggering drunk, only moderately so.

He hung his jacket over the door, raised his cap a foot or so, then paused to let his baleful glance fall on each wary face in turn, before putting it in its customary place. It was the worst possible sign. Sarah started the scramble to escape, but before she could get down from the table, the first bowl of food had hurtled across the room and smashed against the range, its contents hissing and congealing against the bars. The tablecloth was torn off, sending china and cutlery crashing to the floor. Florrie grabbed Paddy as he started to scream and the children made for the door. Dermot didn't try to stop them as they fled for sanctuary in Annie Carter's flat; his sights were set firmly on Dolores.

The children huddled together in silence. Annie did her best, but nothing could distract them from the crashes, shouts and screams that came to them through the walls. Jack Carter was home from his baker's round, but he sat grimly behind his paper, not speaking, obeying the law more rigidly observed in those parts than the ten commandments: do not interfere in domestic disputes.

After a while, they heard their front door slam. Annie went to look out of her parlour window and came back to report that she had seen Dolores going up the street towards The Feathers.

'She'll be going to the laundry doorway,' said Florrie. It was where Dolores usually settled on the nights she was banished from home. It had a deep porch where some warmth from the steam pipes lingered.

'Can we go home?' implored Daisy.

'In a minute,' Florrie promised. 'Let's wait for a little while and see what happens.'

When quiet had reigned for half an hour or so, they decided to send Daisy ahead, knowing that Dermot would not hurt her, to see if it was safe to return. She didn't want to go by herself, so Sarah agreed to go in behind her. It was most likely that Dermot had gone to bed to sleep it off. He hadn't. He was in his chair, surrounded by the wreckage. Unafraid, Daisy walked up to his chair and regarded him reproachfully through round blue eyes.

'Hello Nin,' he said. Daisy didn't answer. She was looking at the lovely meat and potatoes spewed across the hearth. Guilt smote Dermot.

'Come on, love, tell the others to get their coats. I'll take you all down the pie shop.'

'No.' Sarah piped up vehemently. 'It's all right Dad, we ain't hungry.'

'You must be.'

'No. We don't want to go.'

Dermot, seeing the fear in her eyes, didn't argue. 'Well, I'm going. Here. Here's some money for fish and chips.' He put coins on the table, took his cap and jacket and left.

As soon as he reached the door, Daisy started to protest. 'Why can't we go to the pie shop with Daddy?' Sarah gave her arm a vicious twist. 'Shut up. Do you want him to kill her? You know our coats are in pawn.'

Between them they cleaned up the mess, then Florrie set off to get the food and find Dolores. She was where Florrie expected her to be, sitting on the ground, her back in the angle of the laundry porch.

'Aunt Dolly?' The face that peered out of the gloom was swollen and misshapen, the right eye almost closed.

'Florrie? Has he gone to bed?'

'No, he's gone out. I don't think you'd better come back tonight. I've brought you a blanket and some fish and chips. Oh, your poor face!' Florrie added, as Dolores shuffled into the light of the street lamp and she got a better view of the damage.

'I'll put that cowson in hospital when them kids are older, you wait and see. You got any cribbings?'

'Yes, it's not much.' Florrie handed over the change from the fish and chips. 'Cribbings' was Dolores' word for any small profit made by overcharging Dermot for groceries, which she could then pocket.

'It's not enough for a cup of tea,' she grumbled.

'I know, but I'll come back in the morning. I might be able to get you back indoors. I'll try and bring you some more.'

Dolores had to be satisfied. She listened to Florrie's footsteps returning towards Bermuda Street, then sank back into the porch. She made a pillow with the blanket, rested her throbbing face and tried to sleep.

*

Monday was a good day for the Rag and Bone man. He toured the streets with his horse and cart every day, exchanging plates, cups and bowls for bones and rags, but Monday was always particularly fruitful. Crockery was used as a convenient missile on Saturday nights in many households, not just the Cavanaghs'.

Florrie heard his call carrying across the streets while she was still in bed and she got up quickly, to rummage through the washing to find anything she might exchange for a few plates. Last night's fight had left them with nothing. They were going to have to eat out of pot lids. She tried not to make a noise, but as she passed the parlour door, it opened and Dermot stood in his longjohns, glowering and ashen-faced.

'Where do you think you're going?'

'The Rag and Bone man's coming.' As if to bear her out, the cart turned the corner into the street and the cry of 'old rags for china' came to them as musical and as penetrating as the mewing of seagulls.

'We ain't got no plates left, Dad. You got anything I can give him?'

'Wait a minute.' He went back into his room and came out with a couple of frayed shirts. 'That's all I can find,' he said handing them to her. Florrie got six thick white soup bowls in exchange for her rags. She put them on the table, quite pleased with herself. Dermot picked one up and turned it over. 'I'll get us some more plates,' he said.

'Better get some tin ones,' said Florrie sadly.

Dermot groaned and sunk his head in his hands. 'I know. I shouldn't lose me temper. I'm going to sign the pledge.'

She'd heard it before, but she asked, 'Do you want me to talk to the priest for you?'

'No, don't you worry. I'll see about it. Are you going to school today?'

'I can't, can I?'

'Will you get into trouble?'

'No. I went to mass yesterday, so I'll be all right. I'll tell Sarah to say that Aunt Dolly's not well and I've got to stay at home. Can I go and get Aunt Dolly, Dad?'

'No.' He banged his fist on the table. 'I'm not letting that scheming cow back in here.'

Florrie had no love for Dolores, her own life being barely more tolerable with her than without her, but she couldn't leave her to starve in the street. Plainly Dermot could. His response was sharp and angry when she persisted: 'How we going to manage? Who's going to mind Paddy?'

'Shut your row! I ain't havin' a bit of a kid dictating to me. I said we'll manage!' He didn't say how, but it was no use arguing any more. Later, when he was a bit more mellow, she would try again.

Dermot left for the docks and Florrie went back to the laundry, dragging Daisy and a whining Paddy along with her. Dolores was waiting in the street. She had had to quit the doorway when the workers started to arrive. Florrie gave her the bread she had brought.

'He won't let you come home. I asked him this morning.'

Dolores chewed thoughtfully on the good side of her jaw. 'Did he leave you any money?'

'Two bob. I can't give you much of that. I've got to get his tea tonight.'

'Go down the butchers and get some bullock's cheek and then get a pennorth of specks and make a stew. You can spare me a couple of coppers then. I'll tell you what else to do.' She outlined the plan that had rapidly taken shape in her mind.

On the way home from buying the specks – damaged fruit and vegetables that greengrocers were glad to sell for a few pence – Florrie tried to explain the plan to Daisy, since she was a vital part of it, but it was not easy.

'But I do want my dinner,' she protested.

'Just pretend you don't want it. I'll save some for you and you can have it later on.'

'But I'm hungry now.'

'You're always hungry,' snapped Florrie. 'All right, I tell you what, I'll give you your dinner before Dad comes in. You mustn't tell him you've already had your dinner. I'll give you another one when he comes in and you sit there and don't eat it. Say you're not hungry.'

Daisy didn't understand but she was eager to please. Florrie rehearsed her and Sarah again in the evening and made sure Daisy had her fill of the stew before the family sat down to dinner. She served Dermot first, then the others, placing a full bowl before Daisy.

Dermot was sober. He had called that afternoon at the Salvation Army Mission and signed the pledge. He was deep in thought and it was some minutes before he noticed that Daisy had not touched her food.

'Come on, eat your dinner,' he told her.

'I don't want it,' said Daisy, with a glance at Florrie.

'Come on,' said Dermot, picking up her spoon. 'You won't grow up a big girl like Florrie.' Daisy turned her head away. 'I don't want it.'

'What's the matter with her?' frowned Dermot. 'Ain't she well?'

'She's fretting, Dad,' said Florrie.

'Fretting?'

'She wants Aunt Dolly,' said Sarah.

Dermot scanned his youngest daughter's chubby face. Perhaps she was a bit pale. Daisy returned his gaze unflinching. 'All right,' said Dermot after a pause, 'you'd better go and get her.'

Chapter 7

Hop-picking

Dermot's sobriety after he signed the pledge, a roughly biannual event, usually lasted about two weeks, during which he was quiet and amenable. Every evening he passed the pub, eyes resolutely facing front, to go home for his meal which he ate without voicing criticism.

His presence for so much of the time was disconcerting for the family, but particularly for Dolores. After dinner, during one such lull in the fighting, when the little ones had gone to bed and Florrie sat at the table with her sewing, she could not be at ease. She settled in the chair opposite Dermot, breaking the uneasy quiet by crunching sugared almonds and trying to read *Pam's Paper*. She kept glancing up, afraid that she would find his eyes on her which, often, they were. She could not fathom what was behind his brooding look but it made her uncomfortable, so when he threw down the *Racing World* and announced that he was off out 'to find old Tom', she felt a sense of relief. He would surely come back staggering drunk but at least she would be in a familiar hostile territory.

Dolores was glad she had extracted from him, in this brief period of passivity, the money for train fares to take the children hop-picking. With the end of abstinence Dermot would make up for lost time and go on a series of blinders that could be threatening to her hair, eyes and teeth, if not to her life.

She had another reason for being keen to go: high summer brought an opportunity for her to bring her finances into balance. Until she came to live with the Cavanaghs she had been hopping every year. Not a holiday, but an annual change of scene, and she missed it. She calculated that with the children's labour, she could earn enough to clear her debts and be left with a hefty sum to pay into the Christmas loan club run by Levene's, the grocer. Paddy, at four-and-a-half, could only be expected to work for short intervals; Sarah's burnt hand was a drawback, but she still had a useful thumb and forefinger. Their combined contribution would not be insignificant. Under her eye, the others could put in a good day's work.

Before dawn on a mid-September morning Dolores loaded the children and the huge two-handled basket she had been packing for weeks on to the greengrocer's donkey cart and they were hauled, lurching and rattling, over the cobbles to Stepney station, where they caught the connection to London Bridge.

The concourse was buzzing with families arriving to board the hop-picker's special to Faversham, in Kent. Each woman carried a bundle and shepherded several children. A good many had babes-in-arms. A queue was lengthening in front of the ticket barrier, violets denoting grandmotherhood bobbing among the daisies and fruits on the hats of the younger women.

Some of the money Dermot handed over had had to be used to get necessary clothing out of pawn but Dolores had her contingency plans. She took Daisy aside. She favoured Daisy least of the children, finding her too saucy and defiant, but she was the sharpest of the bunch. She could be relied on to twig the meaning of the eye signals and body language she frequently had to fall back on when Dermot was around. It had to be admitted, Daisy was now quick on the uptake. She stooped to get good eye contact.

'Listen, when we get to the ticket man, you hold Paddy's hand and walk in front. Whatever happens, don't turn round. Keep on walking and wait for me on the platform.'

Daisy's eyes widened in alarm but she knew better than to ask questions. She noted her instructions and nodded. They joined the queue and shuffled towards the barrier. Daisy could see the crowd fanning out as it passed through and the shiny leather belt round the ticket inspector's waist coming into view. She took firm hold of Paddy's hand.

They had advanced a yard or so when she felt Florrie and Sarah cannon into her from behind, propelled by a mighty shove from Dolores. Daisy tottered against the child in front but managed to keep her feet and her grip on Paddy as the wave-effect travelled to the head of the queue and a dozen kids surged through the barrier at once, some of them landing in a heap.

Ignoring the shouts and curses that broke out behind, Daisy steered Paddy round her fallen fellow-travellers and marched him towards a gap in the crowd. Half-way along the platform she looked back. Florrie and Sarah were through the barrier. Dolores was helping children to their feet and solicitously dusting them down. This done, she showed her ticket and walked down the platform, puffed but unhurried to meet them.

There were more briefings once they were on board the train, but the first hour of the journey was uneventful, the children excitedly looking out of the windows. They were sharing a carriage with a family from Stepney, Dolores and the mother occupying one seat while the children squeezed on to the other. Dolores opened her basket and handed round slabs of cold, spicy bread-pudding.

Ten minutes out of Faversham the two women were deep in conversation when Dolores cocked her ear. She signalled to Daisy, who at once ducked under Dolores' seat, dragging Paddy with her. There they crouched, her hand on his mouth.

Dolores spread her skirts and her companion, taking her cue, did likewise, barely interrupting their conversational flow as the ticket inspector did his rounds.

A smoother ride in a cart driven by a dark-haired man wearing a red neck-scarf brought them to the pickers' huts standing on a rise at the edge of a wood. Theirs was at the end of a row of seven, specifically requested by Dolores in her correspondence with the farmer because it was closest to the standpipe and farthest from the earth-closet.

All had been made ready for them. The walls had been whitewashed, fresh straw piled on to the wide shelf that ran along one side to serve as a communal bed and an old pram, even more decrepit than the one at home, stood at the door.

The dark-haired man, who seemed to know Dolores, helped her to get the big basket inside. As he left, he ruffled Daisy's hair. 'Hello, Fairy,' he said.

'Is that the farmer?' asked Daisy.

'No. That's Ruben. He works for Mr Whiteley.'

Dolores was untying the cloth that covered the basket.

'Is Mr Whiteley the farmer?'

'Yes.'

'Has he got any chickens?'

'Yes. Now hold your noise and get stuffing these.' She hauled bundles of striped mattress ticking out of the basket.

While the children stuffed the mattresses with straw, Dolores unpacked a huge, three-legged, iron pot from where, along with ladles, mugs, plates and spoons, it was embedded among blankets and clothing. When she had finished, she turned the basket upside down in a corner where it served them as cupboard and table-top for the duration of their stay.

Drugged by the sweet smell of the straw, Daisy went to sleep before the light had gone, to be woken by the customary slap on the bottom before it had returned. A quick sluice of the face in cold water, a mouthful of milk and she was stumbling, holding on to the pram bearing a groggy Paddy and food and water for the day, across a rutted field.

They were first to reach the hop garden. Daisy could sense rather than see that she was in a long tunnel, could smell and hear the vines rustling overhead. It was cold. Dew from the grass seeped through to her stockingless feet. She and Paddy huddled together shivering.

'Come on, get busy,' shouted Dolores, 'that'll warm you up.' She had taken a large umbrella from the pram, opened it and stuck its spike into the ground. 'Here,' she said to Paddy, lifting him and sitting him down beside it, 'this is how you do it.' She took one of the lower runners and dexterously picked off the hops, dropping them into the upturned umbrella. 'When you've got it nearly full, tell me and I'll put 'em in me basket.'

Daisy could see now that a line of empty baskets, each with a white line painted inside below the brim, waited for the pickers. Dolores and Florrie began at once to fill one of them. Daisy was assigned to help Paddy fill the umbrella while Sarah was allowed to wander between the two.

Dolores stripped each branch by drawing it through her closed fist. She then rapidly removed the leaves and twigs that fell with the hops into the basket and reached for the next branch. She worked to a steady rhythm, her speed increasing, and with the arrival of full daylight and the first of the other families, her basket was half full.

The sun climbed as they worked. Dolores tolerated Paddy's lapses in concentration, tempting him back from his wanderings among the pickers with bits of barley sugar, but Daisy, considered at seven to be out of infancy, was kept hard at it. Once, when her attention wandered to a game of tag being played in a neighbouring row, a clod of earth landing below her ear brought it rudely back to the job in hand. 'Get on with your work,' shouted Dolores. 'This ain't a bleedin' excursion.'

Dolores herself worked without pause. As the contents of each bushel basket neared the painted line she plunged her arms in and lifted the hops, letting them fall slowly so that they rested lightly against each other and reached their target sooner.

At mid-morning, a cart driven by Ruben and carrying half-a-dozen other swarthy men appeared and began moving down the aisles between the arches of hop poles, collecting the full baskets and handing over tokens in exchange. Dolores took the chance to break off and pass round water in a tin mug with wedges of bread and marge.

'Don't anyone knock against them baskets,' Dolores warned.

Daisy bit into her lunch and screwed up her face in disgust. The smell and taste of hops from her engrimed hands had tainted the bread. Sarah threw hers on the ground. 'This tastes 'orrible. I can't eat it,' she said

'Go without then,' said Dolores, stuffing her own mouth.

Ruben reached them. He kicked the first basket, and with a sidelong look at Dolores, he topped it up from the children's crop in the umbrella before loading it on to the cart.

'Still getting up early in the mornin's I see, Dolly,' he said.

'Yes,' said Dolores tartly, 'but I ain't catchin' many bleedin' worms.'

Ruben clicked his tongue, the horse took another plodding step and the cart moved on. Ruben looked back over his shoulder, grinning. 'Do you want a couple of rabbits?' he asked.

'Yes. Gawd bless yer.'

The afternoon wore on. Men with hooked sticks came to pull down the high vines to be stripped before the pickers moved on, leaving destruction in their wake as though a swarm of locusts was passing through. Daisy, hot and weary, looked back and mourned the loss of the lovely leafy tunnel.

'Right,' said Dolores at last. 'Pack it in for today.'

She sent Florrie flitting ahead to fetch water and start the fire while she laboured up across the fields with the smaller girls helping to push the laden pram. It was dusk by the time they neared the huts at the top of the rise. In the next valley a fire was already burning. Daisy could see caravans grouped together and brown and white horses grazing.

'Look,' she said to Dolores.

'Yes. That's the gypsies.'

'Is that where Ruben lives?' asked Daisy, remembering his hand ruffling her hair.

Dolores, saving her energy for the last few yards, did not answer. Back at the hut, she did not permit herself to rest for long, but summoned the breath to blow on the smouldering twigs Florrie had gathered. A little deft rearrangement, a few faggots added to the pile and she soon had a blaze crackling round the iron pot and licking up to heat the water in the billy suspended above.

They supped on the two rabbits they found inside the door. Later in the evening the cart came round with supplies of food and milk, for which the women could pay with the tokens they had earned in the field.

The meal was cleared away. Daisy sat with her back against the door post, her belly tight, enjoying the few minutes before she would be sent unwashed to bed. Dolores took up the singing someone farther down the row had begun. 'On Mother Kelly's doorstep, down Paradise Row . . .' This, thought Daisy, breathing in the scent of wood smoke, this is Paradise Row. It was a moment she would try throughout her life to recapture.

On Thursday of the first week, Florrie complained of feeling unwell. Dolores assured her that she would soon work it off in the fresh air but on Friday, after Florrie fainted at her work and had to be carried into the shade, she conceded that perhaps something should be done. She gave her a dose of Syrup of Figs.

'What you need is a good clear-out,' she told her.

This was achieved, but on Sunday morning, before Dermot was due to arrive on his weekend visit, Florrie awoke with a distinctly yellow tinge. Dolores was annoyed, but consoled herself with the thought that the children probably wouldn't have earned much that day anyway. It was traditional for fathers to take their off-spring on an afternoon walk before heading back to London on the early evening train. Sarah and Daisy were looking forward to it, but as soon as Dermot arrived, he declared the walk out of the question.

'She's got yeller jaundice,' he pronounced as soon as he saw the drooping Florrie. 'She'll have to come home with me.'

'No. She'll be all right tomorrow.'

'She won't be right for a fortnight. I had it once. I'll take 'er home and get Dr Lambert.'

'So long as you've got the five bob to pay him.'

'I ain't got no money. You must 'ave got some by now.'

Dolores surprised him by putting up no further oppo-sition. It had suddenly occurred to her that if Florrie had something catching it would be better to get her out of the way before the farmer found out. She could see her-self facing an angry mob if it swept through the hoppers and brought picking to an end.

'I've only got a few tokens up here. I'll have to ask Mr Whiteley to let me sub on what's owing.' She thought fast. 'Sarah, you'll have to go down to the farmhouse.' Sarah let out a wail.

'I can't. I'm scared of the cows.'

'Don't be so bleedin' daft. Daisy will go with you. Now, listen. Don't let on that Florrie's not well. Just say that she's going home with her dad because he can't manage on his own. Ask for a sub on me wages. Enough for her fare and a bit over.'

The two girls set off, Daisy by no means certain of her own feelings about cows but, she reasoned, they were not as big as the milkman's horse, and she often played games running underneath his belly and he'd never hurt her.

'Go to the back door. Mind you say please, and don't eat any berries,' Dolores called after them.

Much more terrifying than cows were the geese they encountered in the yard. Their clamour brought a woman out of the house.

'What do you want?' she asked, flapping her apron and seeing off the geese who had them cornered. They explained the errand and were led inside, through the kitchen to a wide flagstoned hall, where they were told to wait on a wooden settle.

The woman went down a passage in search of Mr Whiteley. Daisy had never been in such a big house; she could not have imagined that such a splendid house existed. Opposite, a large panelled door stood ajar. She slipped off her seat and peeked into the room.

A huge rug spread its many colours before a stone fireplace, empty now except for a jar of chrysanthemums. Two soft sofas stood one on either side of the fireplace, a low table between, but what made her stretch her eyes were the curtains: Rose pink brocade looped up in swags across the top of the wide window and falling in a rich cascade to the floor. Each curtain was held elegantly to one side by golden cord. Daisy scampered back to her seat as she heard footsteps returning.

She was relieved to see the farmer appear carrying a large cash box and a notebook. He was apparently not going to argue the toss about handing over the advance. 'You put that in the pocket of your pinny,' he told Sarah, counting coins into her good hand, 'and tell Aunt Dolly, even though she's subbed on her money, you kids and her have still got more to take home than anyone else.'

'Don't tell her what he said in front of Dad,' said Sarah, when they were clear of the gate. The woman in the apron had escorted them that far, either tò make certain they were off the premises or to give them safe passage through the ranks of the geese. They couldn't tell from her manner which.

'If he knows how much she's got, he'll get it off her.'

'She's promised to buy me a white frock and shoes for my first Communion,' said Daisy.

'Well, you've got to have a white frock for that, but you might have to wear the one I had.'

Daisy would have protested, but the path had led them past the front of the farmhouse, where a girl of about her own age was swinging on the gate. She was leaning back so that her long, shining ringlets, caught at the back of her head by a pink satin bow, hung clear of the crisp pinafore. Behind her, on a smooth lawn, a swing still moved gently to and fro.

She straightened as they approached and stared at them. Daisy dropped behind Sarah, so that they passed in single file. Scrubbed and clean as she was in her Sunday best, Daisy knew, without being told, that she was not good enough to speak to the girl on the gate.

Chapter 8

Incest

Florrie embarrassed her father by vomiting twice on the way home, once on the train and again on the walk from the bus. She was sagging by the time they reached the landing. A smell of sweaty socks and stale cigar smoke hit them as Dermot opened the door. It woke no response in Florrie. There was nothing she could do about it. She wanted only the sanctuary of her bed. Dermot brought her tea but she could not drink it.

He decided against calling the doctor, believing in the local axiom that ailments got better in seven days with medical attention but would take a week without. On Monday morning he left her with a glass of water and asked Rose Collins to call on her while he was at work.

It was Kate's face at the end of the bed when she opened her eyes.

'Blimey,' said Kate, 'you look just like that old Chinawoman down Chrisp Street. You know, the one with the funny feet.'

'Thanks,' said Florrie, 'it ain't my feet that's giving me bother.'

'Mum sent you a drop of soup. See if you can drink it.' Kate waited while Florrie took a tentative sip, then said, 'Danny's downstairs.'

'Danny? How long's he been here?'

'Since Friday. He'd like to see you but he don't want to bump into the old man.'

'What time is it?' asked Florrie.

'About half-past six. I just got home from work.'

'He'd better not come up here. Dad's not usually home till about nine, but there's just a chance he might come home early because I'm laid up. I'll come down.'

'No. It's all right. I'll keep a look out. If I see him coming round the corner I'll shout up the stairs, "Are you all right, Flo?" and he can nip down the back stairs.'

Danny had changed; he was wiry and weatherbeaten, with a hint of tremendous strength in the arms that went round her in a hug.

'Better not kiss me,' she laughed. 'You might turn yeller.'

'You've altered such a lot, Florrie,' he said, sitting on the bed, 'but nothing else round here has.'

'I ain't always this colour.'

'I don't mean that.'

'I know what you mean. You've been gone a long time. I put my hair up two years ago. Why didn't you come home before now?'

'I've been close. I wanted to come, but I didn't know how Dad would take it. I've seen Charlie and I've written to Kate and sent you messages.'

'Yes. She told me. Are you two courting?'

'Sort of, I s'pose. Mrs Collins let me stay the night in Charlie's bed.'

'When are you going back?'

'I'm not going back. I left the ship at Gravesend.'

'Why? I thought you liked it on the barges.'

'I did. I loved it with Tod and Captain MacFarlane. He

was training me up to be a skipper, but about a year ago the company transferred me to another boat. Their boy left and I didn't like it so much.' His face clouded at the memory. 'I hated it,' he added.

'Did the skipper treat you bad?'

Danny flushed. 'He was a depraved old bugger.'

'What you going to do now?'

'I've been trying to get another boat, but there's nothing going. I'll have to get a job. Could you speak for me where you work?'

'I ain't got a job.'

'Kate told me you was working in the sack factory.'

'I was, but I got me cards.'

'What for? What did you do?'

'I had a birthday. They always get rid of girls once they turn sixteen. They have to pay 'em more money if they keep 'em on. They can get another one who's fourteen for less. They chucked me out last month. That's how I could go hopping. I'm going down the jam factory once I shake this off, but they ain't been taking anyone on lately. I wish I could get shop work.'

'Don't look too hopeful for me, then. I s'pose I can get work in the dock. Scalin' boilers or something.'

'Dad'll find out about it.'

'I ain't worried about him any more. I just don't want to start any trouble for you and the littl'uns.'

'Do you want me to get him to let you come home?'

'No. I wouldn't come back here. I'll get lodgings. I looked in the newsagent's window. There's a few places around.'

'Have you got any money?'

'Some. I'll be all right.'

'Wait a minute. Dad give me some money.' Florrie got

out of bed and was crossing to the door on spongy legs when Kate's voice rang out below.

'Florrie, are you all right?'

'Oh God! Dad's coming!' She fumbled in the pocket of her coat hanging on the back of the door. 'Here, take this.' She held out ten shillings.

'I can't take that.'

'It's my money. It's some of what I earned down hopping. Take it.'

She looked as if she was about to pass out. Danny took the note.

'Thanks. I'll pay you back.'

'Oh, hurry up! Nip down the back stairs. He'll be here in a minute.'

Danny seemed to deliberately try to put the wind up her by sauntering along the passage. She heard his steps start down the back stairs as Dermot's climbed the front. She released her grip on the edge of the door and got back into bed, looking up at him through feverishly brilliant eyes when he put his head in a moment later.

'You all right, girl?'

'Yes, Dad.'

He crossed to her. 'You're in a muck sweat.'

'I'm 'ot.'

'Keep the blankets round you. Sweat it out.' He drew the coarse blanket up to her shoulders and laid his hand across her forehead. 'Yes, you've still got a temperature.' The hand moved up to smooth back the dark hair and lingered to finger a tress that lay on the pillow. 'You've got hair just like your mother's. You've grown into a lovely girl. Lovely face and figure. You couldn't wish for better.'

Florrie squirmed under the covers. Kind words from

her father, rare compliments, but she didn't want to hear them and didn't know how to stop them without rousing his anger. His hand moved down to her shoulder and on down over her nightgown until it cupped her breast.

'You could fit into one of your mother's frocks now,' he said in a soothing voice. 'There's a nice one in the drawer. I couldn't throw it away, but I wouldn't mind seeing you in it. Try it on when you're better. Or if you like, I'll buy you a new one.'

She dared not push his hand away but she had to rid herself of its violating pressure, its loathsome warmth. In a convulsive movement she turned on her side, her back towards him, hunching her shoulder to shield herself from him.

Dermot didn't try to hold her. She shut her eyes tightly when he tucked the blanket into her neck and rested his hand briefly on her back, but presently she felt the bed relieved of his weight as he stood up.

'You have a kip. I'm going out for a pint. If I see a nice little crab on the stall, I'll bring it back for you.'

She lay still while he moved about first in the scullery, washing and shaving, then in the parlour, drawers opening and closing. Then, at last, there was the click of the front door behind him.

Florrie was on fire; her skin itched and prickled under the weight of the blanket. She tried to bear it, to sweat it out; it might be better in the morning. But she could stand it no longer and kicked the covers off. In the scullery she let the tap run over her wrists and, taking the flannel, she sponged the back of her neck and under her arms, heedless of the soaking her nightgown was getting. She pulled the front of it away from her and let water trickle freely down her body as the memory of Dermot's hand surfaced in her mind. Perhaps he hadn't realised she was not a little girl any more.

She took a long drink, went back to her room and opened the window. She lay letting the soft breeze play on her wet nightgown, cooling her so that at last she was able to fall into the first deep sleep she had had since she fell ill.

Dreams swarmed through her brain, dreams of gypsy men with hooked poles of hops balancing one on another. A giant presser foot on a sewing machine raced along to the pounding rhythm of train wheels on a track. Her head threshed from side to side, trying to escape the smell, but it grew stronger till she caught her breath and gasped. Beer. The smell of beer, then the touch of damp whiskers on her cheek. Her eyes opened. Dermot was kneeling beside the bed.

'I only want a cuddle. I ain't had a cuddle for a long while.'

Florrie struggled to sit up, but the dead weight of his arm was across her waist. 'No!' She gripped the coarse tweed of his sleeve, perceiving that he was very drunk indeed. It gave her hope. She threw off the arm and rolled over towards the wall, scrambling to her knees and then her feet. She stood on the bed, her hands pressed against the wall behind her, her heart thumping, looking down at him, watching him for his next move.

'Florrie. Don't be silly, girl. I ain't going to hurt you.'

He partly raised himself, making a grab across the bed for her, but he was incapable of such co-ordinated effort and collapsed face down on the mattress. It was easy to side-step him. She gripped the low brass rail at the bed-foot, swung her leg over, groping with her toes for the bottom rail. She lifted the other leg clear, taking a fraction of time to ensure the nightgown didn't snare her on the little brass knobs, and ran into the scullery and on, out on to the landing. Not down to the yard – he could corner her there. Down the front stairs, padding along the street in the dark, to hide, panting, crouched behind the low wall surrounding a neighbour's area.

She knew he wouldn't follow her, that sleep would engulf him, but she stayed in hiding, keeping her head low, until she could breathe easily. What time was it? The street lamp had gone out. There was no way of knowing. Florrie sat leaning against the wall. She couldn't stay here. It might start to get light soon; people would be coming out of their houses, would discover her in the street in her nightdress. She would have to go back to get dressed.

Noiselessly she moved along the passage, avoiding the boards that creaked, knowing nothing would rouse Dermot except the need to pee. In the doorway of the off room she hesitated. He hadn't moved. The jerry under the bed was still empty. She would have to be quick.

Her skirt hung on the back of the door. Underwear she could gather from the airer. Boots lay under the bed. She stooped to pick them up and was hit by the stench of urine. Dermot had wet the bed. Quietly she backed out of the room and carried her clothing down to the yard, to dress in safety behind the bolted lavatory door.

No clear idea of what to do next had yet come to her but she felt steadier once her body was decently covered. Stealthily she drew back the bolt and came out into the yard. It seemed colder now she was dressed. She noticed the sharp nip of the September morning, and remembered how ill she felt. She hadn't stopped to collect a comb. She washed under the yard tap, drying her face and hands on the discarded nightdress, twisting her dampened hair into a knot at the back of her neck. The gush of water woke the bantam cock. He fluttered to the roof of the chicken shed and crowed. Florrie decided. She would go to early communion.

It was still too early. She sat on the bottom step of the front stairs to rest, leaning her forehead against the rough cold wall, opening her eyes to stare apathetically at Dry Dock Tommy and Danny when they came out into the porch.

'Gawd 'elp us, Florrie! What you doing there?' demanded Tommy.

'I'm going to mass.'

'You're frozen stiff. Come indoors and have a cup of tea.'

'No, I can't. I'm going to communion.'

'You ain't up to going to mass yet, Flo,' said Danny. 'Give it another couple of days.'

'No. I want to go.' She got unsteadily to her feet. Tommy put a supporting arm round her.

'You ain't going nowhere till you've had something to eat. Come on. The old woman will give you a bit of toast or something. You can go to church later.'

They led her back into the kitchen of the downstairs flat and handed her into the care of Rose and Kate, who were still sitting at the table in the dim light. Rose sat her in an armchair, covered her with a shawl and gave her tea. Tommy and Danny left for the dock. Florrie dozed. When she woke, the kitchen was brighter and Kate, too, had left for work.

'Sorry, Mrs Collins. I didn't mean to fall asleep.'

'Don't be daft. Come and get something to eat.' Rose

rested a loaf on her abdomen and sliced it towards herself. 'Afterwards, I want you to go down the doctor's and get yourself a tonic.'

'I'm all right. I feel a bit better now. I ain't got the money, anyway.'

'I'll give it to you and get it back from your father later.'

Florrie slowly spread jam on a piece of bread. 'Mrs Collins, how do people get jobs in service?'

'Well, sometimes they've got someone who'll speak for them. Someone who already works there, like, or you could try at the labour exchange. But it's mostly factory work round here. Why?'

'I was just wondering. I've got to get another job. I'd like to get something where I could go to work washed and dressed all nice, but I don't s'pose I can.' She had a vision of herself in a white blouse with a boned collar, working in a hat shop, but that was no good. She couldn't talk posh.

'Well, you can sew. You might be able to get taken on as an alteration hand down Chrisp Street, but all your money will go in bus fares. I can't see your Aunt Dolly wearing that.'

'I was thinking of a live-in, all found job.'

'Well, Gawd knows you ain't got much to keep you here, but your father won't like it. What does he say about it?'

Florrie steadily met her eye. The course of action that was beginning to take shape in her mind did not include seeking Dermot's blessing.

'I haven't told him yet. Thought I'd find something first. Perhaps I could go as a kitchen maid in a big house.'

'You might have to go up the West End for that. You'll need a testimonial.'

'Where do I get that?'

'Ask the priest. He'll probably give you one. Wait a minute, have a look in the paper. We got yesterday's here somewhere. Danny got it to look for a room. It's under the cushion on that chair.' Florrie got up and retrieved the paper from where she had been sitting on it.

'Did he find anything?' Florrie asked, turning to the back pages and Situations Vacant.

'He's going to see one in West Ferry Road tonight. I've told him, he can bunk in with us, but he's right, it would only start another rumpus.'

'There's lots of service jobs in here,' said Florrie. 'Here's one place, Queen Anne's Mansions, wants corridor maids. They want more than one.' Florrie pushed back her chair. 'If you could lend me half-a-crown, I could go up there after mass and find out about it.'

'I'll lend you the money, but be careful, love. You still ain't well and there's some funny people about.'

Florrie smiled. 'I know. Thanks, Mrs Collins. I'll pay you back.' A worry surfaced. 'P'raps I ought to take some clothes with me, in case I get taken on straight away.' She thought about going back into the flat. 'If Dad finds me, he won't let me go.'

'Your Dad's gone to work. I heard him go out while you were asleep. But you ought to leave him a note. Save him worrying.'

So Florrie went back into the off room and, keeping her back to the rumpled bed with its sour, yellow-stained sheets, she collected the best of her clothes into a small bundle. In the kitchen, she found pencil and paper.

Dear Dad, she wrote, *I've gone. I'm going to get a job in service. Will drop you a line to let you know where I am. Florrie.*

No love; no crosses on the bottom. She left it on the table and went out, feeling a serenity and a strange lightness as she closed the door.

When Dermot got home later that night, he screwed up the note when he'd read it and tossed it into the empty range, then he took a match and set fire to it, watching while it burned away.

Chapter 9

Bawley Boats

Dry Dock Tommy spoke on Danny's behalf to the man who ran a scaling company. They engaged men to stand on wooden rafts as the water was pumped out of the dry dock to scrub fungus and weeds from ships' sides with hard brooms, preparatory, in the case of steel ships, to chipping off the barnacles and rust ready for painting. This, the most congenial of the tasks that fell within the scope of the company, was already fully manned and cleaning out bilges and ballast tanks at four shillings a week was all that was on offer.

Danny and a group of other youths were each issued with a bucket, a small shovel, a bundle of cotton waste, a dozen green candles and a length of wire. This could be coiled round the base of a candle and formed into a hook so that it could hang from any convenient crevice or hole to provide illumination.

They were rowed out to a Greek ship where they were split into two parties. Danny was detailed to clean bilges: steel box sections that ran the length of the ship below the waterline. He was placed in the middle of the chain, between two experienced boys. One behind the other, they crawled into the ship's bowel and, kneeling in the slime, filled the bucket with sludge and muck, passed it to the boy in the next section who handed it back to the next, until it finally reached the manhole. After wiping dry with cotton waste, they all moved along to repeat the action in the adjoining run of filthy boxes.

All day they laboured, coming out into the air for a half-hour break at noon. At five they were released and, wet and stinking, Danny presented himself at Tommy's hut. Bilge fumes seemed to have entered his blood and filled his stomach. He could not eat the toast and dripping that came hot from the shovel and could swallow only a mouthful of tea.

The wages were not enough to cover the rent of a room, so he went back with Tommy to the blocks, too flattened in spirit to care much whether he met his father or not, but as it happened he did not run into him. Rose provided hot water and a meal, but all the evening Danny sat wooden-faced and hardly speaking. Kate could not divert him and he sat in the kitchen long after the others had gone to bed, trying to fend off the morning when he must go back to spend another day grovelling in the reeking dark.

Saturday afternoon marked the end of the working week. With a sense of relief Danny set out with Tommy to cross Daysfield, the broad piece of wasteland outside the dock gates. A small crowd had gathered in the corner.

'What's going on over there?' Danny asked, though he knew the probability.

'A couple of girls from the factory 'avin' a sort-out, I reckon,' Tommy replied. They took a detour to find out what the attraction was.

As Tommy supposed, a fight was taking place between two girls from the canning factory. It was their practice to save grievances till the end of the week and settle them once and for all with fists and nails. No one in the circle of watchers interfered or made a move to stop them as they flew at each other screeching like mating alley-cats, wrenching out handfuls of hair, scratching and biting. A murmur of satisfaction ran through the onlookers when a shredded blouse was finally torn from one protagonist's back. It seemed to mark the end of the contest.

The crowd was beginning to disperse, grinning and chattering, when Danny's eye was held by a figure on the other side of the ring: a stocky man in a flat cap, with little to distinguish him from the crowd except his extremely bowed legs and, as he turned to walk away, a stiffly rolling gait.

'Tod!' Danny yelled, and again, 'Tod!' as the man, not hearing him, continued to move away. Telling Tommy to wait for him, Danny sprinted after the man and caught him by the shoulder.

'Tod. What are you doing here?'

Tod's startled look gave way to one of his rare smiles. 'Looking for Bermuda Street.'

'You looking for me?'

'I come from Gravesend to find you.' Danny's heart leapt.

'You want me back on the *Scot*?'

'No, not so fast. I'm working on me own now. Mac's gone ashore for good. His old woman's ill. The company took on a new crew. I could have stayed on with a new skipper, but me and Mac been together so long, I didn't fancy it. Me and me brother Dick have got a couple of Bawley boats to go shrimping. He's going to skipper one and I'm going to work the other one. I heard you'd chucked your hand in with the other lot and, well, I want you to come as me boy.'

Tod came to the end of this lengthy speech and watched Danny hopefully. 'That's if you're not working already,' he added when a stunned Danny didn't answer immediately.

'No, Tod, I'm not workin'. I've been cleaning bilges and I don't mind jackin' that in. When do you want me to start?'

'Can you come back to Gravesend with me tonight? I'll pay your fare.'

'Just let me get me gear and tell Tommy and Mrs Collins what's happening and I'll be ready.'

Tod sipped tea while Danny got ready. He wouldn't stop for dinner, being anxious to get to the station in Burdett Road in time to catch the train to Tilbury. Tom and Rose rejoiced with Danny but Kate was put out, until he explained that he could be home every Saturday afternoon and could stay until Monday morning.

'Will it be all right if I come here, Mrs Collins?'

'You can come here, love. You can have Charlie's room. If Charlie's home at the same time you'll just have to bunk in together.'

Tod didn't say much on the journey except to explain that his father had taken over the pub on the waterfront, The Albion Shades. It had a slipway running down into deep water and this present enterprise was seen as an extension to the family business. The long silences didn't trouble Danny; he leant back with his eyes closed, savouring his happiness as the train clanked through the Essex countryside.

From the ferry they walked to The Albion Shades.

Tod's sister was in the kitchen at the back preparing a meal. She nodded politely to Danny when they were introduced, but he thought her manner frosty, and when she called the family to come to the table she remarked that she 'couldn't see how anyone could sit down to a meal with those filthy hands'.

Danny could not hide his mortification. He had scrubbed himself all over before leaving Rose's flat, but it would take more than one soaping to remove the oily grime ingrained from the Greek ship's bilges. He kept his head up, screwing up his toes inside his boots, conscious of his ragged trousers and the heat flooding his face. He tried to think of something to say. Tod came to his aid.

'Don't be silly. He can't borrow no one else's hands.' Danny sat down, his liking for Tod deepening into affection in that moment.

Next morning they loaded stores for the week aboard the boat, one of a small fleet of Bawley boats riding at anchor in the deep water. The most important commodity seemed to be the hundredweight sack of Russian salt, to be used in boiling the shrimps, the activity from which the boats derived their name – Bawley being a corruption of 'boiler'. That done, they took the dinghy and dug some blue clay out of the river bank. Danny asked what this was for, but Tod replied, 'I'll show you when we get underway.'

Tod's boat was modern. It had a petrol engine, though he had retained the foresail and used it frequently. They headed out to their fishing ground, shallow water along the shoreline where shrimps abounded, Danny steering with the tiller between his legs, a cleansing wind driving the drizzling rain into his face. He breathed deeply, filling his lungs with fresh, salt air on every exhilarating lift of the bow.

For an hour at a time they trawled, then hauled the nets and shot them away again. The trawl was cast over the side. Thirty feet of net, twenty feet wide. At the end of the morning's fishing it was Danny's task to winch it back, fifty fathoms of wet rope, which he accomplished with a small hand capstan and without a pause, a feat that impressed Tod and confirmed that he had done well to choose Danny.

A copper had been brought to the boil, the blue clay plastered along the seams to seal them where they gaped. Tod ladled in salt until the water was sufficiently dense to keep the shrimps afloat, then the first netful from the catch was lowered in. When the water came back to boiling point they were lifted out, tipped into sieves and left around the gunwale to cool.

By three in the afternoon they were back in Gravesend and Tod went ashore, leaving Danny to clear away. He busied himself, happily stacking the cooked shrimps in round bushel baskets, stowing them on the foredeck. For company, he had two swans, who appeared to be more familiar with the nightly routine than he was himself, falling on the small shrimps that had fallen through the sieves as Danny swept them up and threw them over the side. At five he went ashore himself to collect his dinner from the pub, part of his wages, which, Tod's sister made clear to him, he was expected to take back to the boat to eat.

The arrangement pleased him well enough. In the ensuing weeks he grew to love his new home. He slept alone on board in one of the two bunks in the cabin. It was bliss. He could lean out and make toast on the tiny

Kitchener stove without leaving his bed. His table was formed by a few boards cut out to fit round the mast that ran through the centre and were held in place by crossed ropes attached to the deckhead.

A whistle from the causeway at about four in the morning started the daily round. Danny was alert immediately and rowed over to fetch Tod, who brought bacon and sausages for him to cook as they ploughed up-river. Other seamen came to know that he would respond to a whistle late at night and would 'step them aboard' after an evening in the pub. Tips were left without a word on the thwart. Only later did Danny realise that it was against watermen's rules to offer or accept payment of fares. The perks swelled his fifteen-shillings-a-week and meant he had a little to spend when he got back to the island on Saturday night.

He looked forward to going once a week to The Dock House, a large pub with a small building in the yard, just big enough to hold a boxing ring and a couple of rows of chairs. All the boys from the working lads' club fought there under the direction of a retired professional, who, since taking a hammering from a lusty young docker, now shouted encouragement and instructions from the side. It was always crowded. One evening when Wag Bennet, the local star, was fighting, Danny was too late to get a seat inside and joined a bunch of his contemporaries on the roof where they hung over the edge of the skylight to watch the bout.

He was hoarse and happy as he made his way home to Bermuda Street, his companions dropping off one by one to go to their homes. The Three Feathers had turned out and a knot of men and women lingered, unwilling to leave each other until they finished their passionate rendition of 'Nelly Dean'. Among the figures weaving unsteadily along the road were Dry Dock Tommy and his father. Tommy had his arm around Dermot and was helping him to steer a more or less straight course.

All went well until they reached the entry to the flats, when Danny saw his father slump and slide down the wall. Tommy was making manful attempts to get him to his feet but Dermot, quite unable to assist, had slid even further towards the horizontal when Danny came up. He stooped and, tucking his head under his father's arm, he lifted him over his shoulder and carried him effortlessly up the stairs and into the parlour where he dumped him on the bed.

He was looking down at him, reluctant to touch him, when the door opened quietly. Daisy came in, barefoot and swamped by an old shirt of Dermot's. She looked at Danny without recognition and began to unlace Dermot's boots.

'Thanks for bringing him home,' she said.

'Daisy, don't you know me?' asked Danny. The blue eyes turned on him to study him with care, but no light dawned. 'I'm your brother Danny.'

'The one that bunked off without so much as a kiss my arse?'

'Well, no. I went away to get a job on a boat. Who told you I done that?'

'Aunt Dolly. She's always sayin' it.'

'How old are you now?'

'Seven.'

'You shouldn't say "arse". It's not nice for little girls to swear.' Daisy went on struggling with the laces, untouched by the rebuke. Danny watched, then helped her by tackling the other boot. He stood close to her working rapidly with his strong stubby fingers until the foot was free, then dropped the boot with a loud thud.

'Shh! You'll wake Aunt Dolly up,' said Daisy.

'Oh, blimey! We don't want that!'

'Now you're swearing.'

Danny laughed and took off the other boot and placed it carefully under the bed. 'Come on,' he said. 'I'll give you a carry back to bed.'

He picked her up and carried her to the off room. She clung round his neck breathing the faint but pleasing smell of tar given off by his crisp dark curls. She liked him.

'I'm in a procession tomorrow. Will you come and see me?' she asked as he put her down beside the sleeping Paddy.

'When is it?'

'We're leaving the church at two o'clock. We're going all down Poplar High Street carryin' the statue of Our Lady. I've got a new white frock and shoes.'

'Is Paddy in it?'

'No. He's still too little.'

'Well, I might bring him to see you. If you shut your eyes and go to sleep. Here.' He delved into his pocket but could find only a sixpence, a larger sum than he had intended to bestow, but gave it to her anyway. 'Buy some sweets for you and Paddy.'

Daisy turned over, clutching the coin in her hand and screwed up her eyes. Danny crept out.

He thought it probable that his father was too drunk to have any recollection of him carrying him up the stairs. He didn't see him the next day, but discovered that it no longer mattered to him whether he confronted Dermot or Dolores. He didn't frame the thought into words, but his new and developing strength gave him mastery. He knew that and carried the knowledge with a quiet assurance. He always paid for his weekend lodging with Rose and Tom in fish and shrimps. Next week, he would bring some for his family.

Fishing didn't start until Tuesday morning, Monday being spent in scrubbing the sacks used to transport the shrimps and making general repairs and preparation for the following week. Danny always took one of the weekend newspapers back with him to read to Tod at quiet moments. News scarcely touched them, but Tod liked the sports pages and cartoons. Hard news on the front pages was kept until all other reading matter had been exhausted, so they were vaguely aware of concern in government circles about the increasing might of the German navy.

No German warship ever intruded into their sphere, though it teemed with craft from all over the globe making their way up river to the docks. On one bright autumn afternoon, bracing themselves against the wash of a passing freighter, Danny asked, 'Tod, where's the Balkans?'

'Don't ask me. Must be up Lowestoft way.'

Towards the end of the year catches and markets began to fall off. The ordered routine had to be varied in an attempt to keep in profit. On a Sunday just before Christmas 1913 they cast the net at four in the morning and trawled all day. In the late afternoon they caught the tide and sailed straight up to Billingsgate Market with a good catch.

There were no takers. They didn't sell any and there was nothing for it but to turn tail back to Gravesend to dump them. To make matters worse, on the way in, they had reached Tower Bridge at the highest point of the tide and couldn't clear the bascules, the lever mechanism which lifted the roadway. The cost in time and money of opening the bridge had somehow to be met.

A silent Tod and a grieving Danny beat their way down river on a slackening tide. They both knew what must be done. The boat would have to be laid up. The operation simply wasn't worth continuing.

Chapter 10

War

Daisy stood on a footstool sliding a comb through Dolores' glossy hair. Dolores was growing steadily fatter and the effort of washing her hair had left her exhausted. She couldn't hold her arms up for long enough to plait it herself and it had been a long time since she was able to bend to lace her own shoes. Daisy now did these things for her. Sarah couldn't, because of her bad hand.

Dolores was keeping up a continuous diatribe, to which Daisy had closed her ears and her mind. Dolores' complaining, usually on the theme of the ingratitude of the young, went on almost without ceasing. She paused now in her invective against Florrie only to pop another sugared almond into her mouth.

'Soon as they start to find their feet, they're done with you.' Daisy could recite the next bit. 'You slog your guts out for 'em and what do you get? Shit for thanks.' The voice droned on as the braid grew longer. When I'm bigger, thought Daisy, I'm going to wrap this round her neck and pull it tight, but she said nothing and wound the first thick rope of hair over the head.

'Wait a minute. I'll just trim the end.' Silently, Daisy passed the end to Dolores over her shoulder. She took the scissors and cut off the final half-inch, as she did once a month. Her hair was her only pride. She passed it back and Daisy skewered it into place with hairpins, resisting the temptation to drive one into the skull.

'Run downstairs and ask Rose for the lend of half-a-crown till Friday,' said Dolores.

'Oh! Can't Sarah go?' protested Daisy. 'I've got to do the fireplace and I'll be late for school.'

Dolores considered her options and conceded. 'Yes, Sarah, you go. Tell Rose I'll let her have it back as soon as I get me money. And, Oh!' She remembered a rider as Sarah got up from the table and went to the door. 'Ask her how's her bronchitis.'

Paddy, who was sitting at the table finishing his bread, now received her attention. 'Come on, Paddy. Get your boots on and your face washed.' Her voice cracked like a whiplash, brooking no disobedience. He slid down from his chair and went to the scullery with Daisy following. 'You leave him alone,' said Dolores. 'He's big enough to put his own boots on.'

Sarah burst in breathless, having leapt up the stairs two at a time. 'Mrs Collins said her bronchitis is no better, thank you for asking, and she can't let you have the half-a-crown this week because Charlie's coming home and she needs it to get his dinner.'

Consternation seized Dolores. 'Jesus, Mary and Joseph!' she said. 'What am I going to do now?' She routinely borrowed money from Rose Collins on a Wednesday, to tide her over until pay-day. The talley-man who called on Tuesday nights to collect payment for lace tablecloths or bundles of sheets and pillow cases, all presently wrapped in brown paper and lying on the pawnbroker's shelf, swallowed the last of her house-keeping allowance. A good percentage of it disappeared on Saturday mornings when the weekly round of calls began and the landlord called. An oppressive silence descended while she pondered her next move.

'I know.' She tapped Daisy, kneeling before the grate, on the back. 'Nip home at dinner-time and take your father's best suit to pawn. He only wears it high days and holidays. Then take the money and get half a pig's head and some specks. Bring it back here. I'll have the suit wrapped up ready.'

There was no sense in arguing, even though it was plainly an appalling idea. Daisy and Sarah dragged Paddy, whose inclination was to dawdle, along the road to school, which lay on the other side of Millwall Inner Dock from Bermuda Street. Their route took them across a sliding hydraulic bridge which, at high tide, was opened to allow ships to enter and leave. It was their luck on that morning to arrive on the scene as the whole section of roadway spanning the dock entrance was lifted and rolled back on four great sets of double rollers, exposing the two huge pronged teeth which held the structure in place when closed.

A groan went up. They were not the only ones to be caught that morning. A group of eight or nine boys and girls hopped about in an agony of anxiety, waiting for the sedate passage of a freighter. The penalty for being late for school was six strokes of the cane across the palm of the hand.

'Oh, blimey. We're gonna cop it now!' wailed Daisy.

'We might not,' said Sarah. 'Not if Sister Mary Magdalen catches the bridger too.'

Sometimes they were fortunate. If one of the nuns who taught them was herself delayed, their excuses would be accepted. However, it was not to be. The ship passed into the outer dock and the attendant hauled on the lever that would send the bridge gliding across the gap. When all went smoothly the section of road settled with a shudder into its place, standing about four inches proud of the surface on either side. On this morning the pronged teeth failed to align with the slots on the other side and the whole mechanism had to be reversed for a second attempt. This too failed.

'All round the dock!' the cry went up, and the children set out to trudge round the perimeter of the Inner Dock, a distance of about a mile, to travel the twenty yards they needed to gain the other side of the bridge. Paddy began to snivel.

'Come on,' said Sarah. 'If we run we might get there in time.' She and Daisy took one of his hands each and rushed him along. 'Don't worry,' Daisy told him. 'You won't get the cane. If they've all gone in, we won't go to school. We'll go and play down the causeway.'

The end of the column of marching children was just disappearing when they arrived at the gate with the legend 'Mixed Infants' set in stone on the arch above.

'Go on! Run!' said Sarah giving Paddy a shove.

'I want you to come in with me.'

'Don't be daft! We've got to run.' His sisters left him to cross the grey, hostile expanse of playground alone. With a few other stragglers, they raced across their section of playground, divided by a high wall from the boys' and arrived panting in the cloakroom.

Sister Mary Magdalen was waiting for them, cane in hand. She stood tapping it against her shrouded leg, waiting for them to come to stand before her, which they did without being bidden. She began with one of their classmates.

'Why are you late?'

'I caught a bridger, Sister.'

'Were you at mass on Sunday?'

'Yes, Sister.'

'Very well. You may go.' The performance was repeated until she came to Daisy and Sarah whom she left until last, knowing, since she had not seen them there, that they had not attended church on the Sunday before. The question came as they knew it must.

'Did you go to mass on Sunday?'

'No, Sister.' Sarah first, then Daisy in a whisper, 'No, Sister.'

'Why not?' She waited, but both girls remained mute, staring at the floor. It could not be explained that they had spent most of Saturday night standing in the street with coats on over their vests and knickers while a fight raged above them in the flat. They had stood shivering and terrified until Annie Carter had given them refuge in her kitchen and Rose had taken Paddy in to let him sleep in the armchair.

'Aunt Dolly's not well,' Sarah lied. 'We had to stay home to do the work.' The truth was too shameful and would only lower them further in the sister's esteem, nor would it save them from the punishment to come.

'I see.' said Sister Mary Magdalen. She advanced upon Daisy and, with a long bony finger, poked her in the shoulder, every prod emphasising a word and arousing in Daisy feelings of the most intense hatred.

'No time for school. No time for God! Hold out your hands.'

Sarah held out her right hand with a defiant look, but it was flicked aside with the end of the stick and the other hand indicated. The nun's scruples would not

113

allow her to lay the cane across that scarred claw.

She was meticulous in this, as in all things, taking careful aim, arcing the cane through the air to bring it down with a loud swish to inflict its agony accurately across the fingers. Six strokes each. Sarah tried not to cry, but despite her best effort, tears rolled down her face. Daisy managed to hold them back, but her legs were trembling as she was dismissed and she turned to walk to her classroom.

Throughout the morning, whenever she could, she laid down her chalk and wrapped her hand round the iron leg of her desk, trying to cool the stinging. She heard not a word of the lesson.

At lunch-time she set off at a fast run for home to collect the parcelled suit. No point in telling Aunt Dolly about the caning. Low tide. No fear of another 'bridger'. With the suit under her arm she sped off again for the shops in West Ferry Road.

The pawnbroker was a kindly man. He always had a soft word and smiled down at her from behind his high counter. Today, he seemed not to be quite himself. The transaction was taking an age. Daisy was in a froth of impatience. She had to get back to school before the bell rang and there were still visits to be made, to the butcher's and the greengrocer's. She stood on tiptoe to see what he was doing and was surprised to see that the hand making out the ticket was trembling.

'What's the matter, Mr Goldberg, don't you feel well?'

'I'm all right my dear. I've just heard some bad news. Bad news for everyone.'

'What?'

'Oh, it's nothing you need to be frightened about. Ask your father to tell you about it.'

'Tell me about what, Mr Goldberg?' Daisy's curiosity was aroused but he was hustling her to the door.

'Here. Take your money.' He ushered her out and closed the door behind her. Looking back a moment later, she saw him come out again and start to put up his shutters. In the middle of the day! No time to ponder on these wonders. She did her errands at the shops and then was off again at top speed to deliver the goods back to Dolores.

Daisy reached the school gates with minutes to spare and stopped to lean against the railings to get her breath. She was hot; her head and her hands were throbbing. Before Sister Mary Magdalen came on to the steps to ring the bell she had made up her mind not to go back for afternoon school. From behind the gate pillar she watched the orderly columns file inside, then wandered off along the road without a clear idea what she would do next.

At the main perimeter road she crossed over and found her way to a narrow slipway running down to the river between two high buildings. There she whiled away the afternoon, dangling her feet in the murky Thames and watching a handful of truant urchins diving off a barge. It restored her a little. She stayed until she felt more at peace, and hunger told her it was time to go.

Questions about Mr Goldberg's strange behaviour burned to be asked, but when she got home Rose Collins was sitting at their table and, even more extraordinary, she had been crying. Mention of the visit to the pawnbroker's should wait until the family were alone, but on the other hand, if it was left too long her father would be home. Then she would have to keep her mouth firmly shut and her curiosity remain unsatisfied until the morning.

'Aunt Dolly? When I was coming along West Ferry Road, I saw Mr Goldberg putting up his shutters. It was only dinner-time.'

'Poor sod,' said Dolores with feeling. Rose nodded and wiped her nose.

'Why was he shuttin' in the middle of the day?'

'He's a German,' Rose explained. 'He's frightened he'll get a brick through his window.' Daisy looked blank. She couldn't imagine why anyone would do that to nice Mr Goldberg. Sarah enlightened her.

'There's a war started. It's in all the papers.' Considering her ordeal of that morning, Sarah seemed elated. 'Charlie's going to join the navy and go and fight!'

'Where?' asked Daisy, visualising one of the usual Saturday night battles outside The Feathers, with the opposing parties dressed as sailors.

'In France,' Rose told her.

'What are they fighting about?' But she had been the centre of attention for too long. Dolores frowned. 'Shut your row and get on with your dinner,' she commanded.

The war disrupted island life very little. Work became generally more plentiful and Kate Collins was taken on at the canning factory, which won a government contract to supply the troops with bully beef. In the Cavanagh household the differences were subtle.

The children were never told stories, as such, but they had grown up hearing about the persecution of the Irish by the English, usually in the course of one of Dolores' bitter monologues of complaint. Songs sung with heart-wrenching emotion at wakes and at St Patrick's Day knees-ups were Irish: 'The Rose of Tralee', 'Kevin Barry' and 'The Wearing o' the Green'.

Daisy had once asked to have a line in a song explained to her: 'They are hanging men and women for the wearing of the green.' Dolores was hazy about historical detail, but she was clear about the events that had passed into the folklore of her forebears. Young men had been persecuted and shot for fighting to free their country of the aliens who were robbing it of its wealth. Men, women and children had been hanged for wearing the colours of dear old Ireland. For centuries, the English had been cruel and tyrannical oppressors of the Irish people. It was puzzling, then, that there should now be such wholehearted support for them in their struggle to overcome the Germans.

It was an upsurge of patriotic feeling that led to Dermot's discovery that his best suit was not in its place – folded in a box under his bed – waiting for one of the rare occasions on which he might wear it. He had been drinking in The Feathers with Dry Dock Tommy since knocking-off time on a Saturday a few weeks into the war. They had been discussing the day's news when Tommy commented that Rose was pining because they hadn't had a letter from Charlie since he went away.

'Ah! Women don't understand,' said Dermot. 'You can't expect 'em to.'

'I told her. He can't post letters while he's out at sea. All of a sudden, we might get three at once.' Tommy spoke with stout certainty. He hadn't much experience of getting letters and, if they did come, they would have to be read by Kate.

'Yes. Don't worry. It's a marvellous chance for 'im.

It'll set 'im up; make a man of 'im. I tell you what, Tom,' Dermot gazed into the rich brown depths of his pint, 'if I was a younger man, I'd be out there with 'im.'

They agreed that fate had been unkind in its timing of the war.

It was on the way home that Dermot suddenly saw a way that he could serve King and country. The idea struck him with such force that he had to put a hand on Tommy's shoulder to steady himself and with the other hold on to the lamppost.

'I can't join up meself, but I can give 'em my son.'

'What, Danny?'

'Well, I can't give 'em Paddy! Danny's old enough. And a fine strapping lad! They'll be glad of a boy like Danny.'

'What if Danny don't want to go?'

'He may not be sleepin' under my roof, but he's still my son. He'll do as I tell 'im.'

Enthusiasm carried him up the stairs without stopping. He shouted to Dolores to dish up his dinner and went straight to his room. The noble act he had in mind could not be performed in his working clothes. He dragged the cardboard box out from under the bed and took off the lid.

Dermot always had his suits made for him by a Jewish tailor in Whitechapel, partly because of his awkward shape and size and partly from vanity. He always chose the same shot-satin lining, so at first, he noticed nothing amiss. The jacket lay folded inside-out, the rich material shading from inky blue to purple as he shook it out. It was only when he noticed the paint spots and the frayed cuffs that he realised it was the best suit before the last that he held in his hand.

He knew at once what had taken place. Dolores had folded it with the lining showing, so that on a quick inspection, he would never have known the difference. His best suit had gone to pawn. No doubt about it. Rage took possession of him and he broke from the room bellowing like a mad bull. 'You, Dolly!'

In the kitchen Dolores had known she was in for trouble the minute she heard him go into his room. There was no time for her to bring out excuse or explanation. No time for Daisy or Paddy to slip out of the way down the back stairs. Dermot crossed the room in a second and struck her a blow in the face that sent her reeling across the room. She might have kept her balance had she not stumbled against a chair which gave way under her weight. It fractured into several pieces, bringing Dolores to the floor. She struggled to get up but Dermot was on her again. He landed a kick in her ribs and, seizing a leg from the broken chair, began laying about her head.

Daisy rushed forward and tried to get between them, clinging to her father's legs. 'No, Dad. No! Please! Leave her alone!' But Dermot thrust her aside as if she were a fly and continued to rain blows and kicks wherever they would land. Daisy tried a second time and he took her roughly by the arm and shoved her into the scullery. Then he took hold of Paddy, pushed him after her and closed the door between them. He took a moment to wedge a chair under the handle so that they could not interrupt him and turned his attention again to his task.

Daisy hammered on the door, shouting, 'Don't hit her any more Daddy. Please, Daddy, stop,' but her shouting and hammering were lost in the din of Dolores screaming and Dermot roaring. She gave up and wrapped her arms around Paddy, who was crouching in the corner with his eyes closed and his hands over his ears. They sat on the floor, rocking to and fro together as though the motion would ease their distress.

Presently, Dolores' cries lessened and then stopped. Through the door the children heard their father grunting as he laboured and the steady thud of the chair leg striking home. Each blow was followed by a deep groan as though air were being forced from Dolores' body. After a while he seemed to tire. They heard him throw down his stick and leave the kitchen.

They waited. There were long minutes in which nothing broke the silence, then Daisy got up and pushed again on the door. It yielded an inch and after a little careful jiggling she managed to get it open far enough to get her arm through and push away the chair.

The wreckage was confined to one half of the room, that side under the window where Dolores had fallen. The figures of Jesus, Mary and Joseph on the sideboard were undisturbed, Our Lord looking down benignly, his palms outstretched. At first Daisy was afraid to touch Dolores, thinking she might be dead, but she crept closer and could see that she still breathed, though the rise and fall of her chest was almost imperceptible.

'Aunt Dolly?' There was no response and, not knowing what else to do, Daisy went to the scullery and fetched a cup of water and the face flannel. She mopped her forehead and dabbed gingerly at the cuts round the swollen mouth and eyes.

Sarah ventured in from outside and stood looking down at her aunt with a shocked expression. She had seen her after beatings before, but always she had got to her feet, bruised but defiant.

'Oh, Jesus! Look what he's done to her,' she whispered.

'I can't wake her up,' said Daisy. 'You'd better go and get Mrs Collins.'

Sarah fled. In the time it took Rose to get up the stairs, Dolores recovered enough to open her eyes. She lay looking blankly at Daisy, then raised her head to take a sip from the proffered cup of water.

Her injuries were worse on her right side, the left having been protected by being in contact with the wall. With Rose's help, they got her to her feet, then into the armchair where it was easier to wipe her wounds.

Rose tut-tutted as she put a cold flannel on the eye.

'Bleedin' hell, Dolly! Why don't you prosecute him? You're not his wife.'

Dolores' vacant gaze travelled round the room and came to rest on the figure of Christ. Her voice, cracking in the effort of breathing with a broken rib, was low and distorted.

'One day,' she mumbled, 'I'm going to put him in 'orspital.'

Chapter 11

Zeppelins

It was two years before Danny enlisted. He did whatever work came to hand in the dock, where Dermot's observation of his remarkable physique may have influenced him in changing his mind about going to the recruiting office to 'volunteer' his son. Possibly, the effort of thrashing Dolores half to death may have driven it from his mind.

Dolores recovered slowly over the weeks that followed, though she did not pander to her injuries and resumed the cooking almost at once. She had the use of her left hand only at first, the other having taken the brunt of the beating.

She seldom spoke when Dermot was in the house, saving her railing until she was alone with the children. Otherwise the battering did not change her in any way. Sarah was the only one not to come in for her carping criticism, perhaps because Sarah was the only one to show her any affection. The very sight of Paddy irritated her and he was repeatedly cuffed, slapped and told that he was 'not worth a light'.

Daisy hardened herself against the hidings and nagging that came her way, telling herself that Dolores was not her mother. Her mother would have been nice to her. This spiteful old cow couldn't really touch her as long as she remembered that her mother would have loved her. On Saturday mornings, when she washed the figures on the sideboard, she handled the Madonna with special care. That's what a mother must be like. Her mother must have held her once as Mary held Jesus. She tried to remember what it had been like, but to no avail.

There were no pictures of Charlotte in the house. Dermot had a lock of curling, dark brown hair wrapped in tissue paper, which he kept inside a vase in the parlour. Unwrapping it was always slightly terrifying, in case any of the hair blew away, but Daisy took it out and looked at it in secret from time to time, running it through her hand and letting it spring round her fingers. Whenever she judged that Dermot was in the right frame of mind she asked him about her.

It was no use asking when he was helpless drunk, which was how she loved him best; when she could steer him towards his bed and give him a little push to make him collapse on to it, then remove his boots and laugh, saying; 'You're too drunk to fight pussy.' She had to wait for one of those moments when he had had a win and just enough drink to remove any tiny doubt he might have that he really was Jack-the-Lad.

'What was she like, Dad?'

'Little. There wasn't two penn'orth of her.'

'What sort of things did she do?'

'Do? Well, she liked singing. She used to sing a lot.'

'What did she sing?'

' "Danny Boy" was her favourite. She used to sing that.'

'Do I look like her?'

'No. Your hair's fair.' This was a disappointment.

'Florrie's more like her, then?' But Dermot had had enough. At the first frown, Daisy had enough sense to desist. Next time the moment was ripe, she would glean a little more.

She compiled and carried with her an image of her mother. It sustained her in a barely tolerable way of life that, with her child's sense of time, seemed to her to stretch into the future without end. She did what she could to keep out of trouble and, because her mother would have wanted it, took the best care she could of Paddy.

Since she had stepped into Florrie's shoes, her days seemed to be spent working or running. Running for errands, running to get back to school before the bell and running with her father's betting slips.

Dermot studied form carefully, no random picking with a pin for him. His deliberations went on until the last possible moment, the children not daring to speak, then he'd say: 'Here, Nin, nip up the top with this,' and she was off again, to get his bet on before the start of a race or sprinting between the dock walls up to Pennyfields to place his stake with the Chinaman who ran the Pukka Poo.

Daisy, tearing out of the blocks and up the road, provided the kids in the street with regular entertainment. They looked forward to it, just as they had looked forward to her bath night dashes when she was a baby. A cheer would go up. 'Go it, Daisy!'

As she grew in strength and experience, she was better able to cope. By the time she passed her tenth birthday Daisy could manage a house as well as any woman, though Dolores maintained her own peculiar grip on the finances. Trips to the pawnbroker remained part of Daisy's weekly round, to put things in hock or to redeem essential belongings. Dermot's best waistcoat went in and out in a monthly cycle. Out in time for him to wear it to a meeting of the Grand Order of Buffalo and in again immediately after.

The pawn shop continued to flourish even though the name Goldberg remained above the door, its survival permitted no doubt because the local economy depended on it. Daisy did not see Mr Goldberg again; another, younger man took his place behind the high counter. The windows had remained intact through the violent anti-German demonstrations of the early days of the war, though several others in the neighbourhood had suffered. His had been saved by the heavy shutters. Rioters had had to content themselves with daubing the premises with red paint.

Such incidents brought to Daisy what little awareness she had of the war. She had no inclination to read the newspapers, which was just as well, because Dolores would not have tolerated it. Talk in the house had lately been concerned with the Easter Uprising in Dublin. Daisy was as hazy about the whereabouts of Dublin as she was of France. Fighting was going on in both places, she knew that, and she knew from Dolores' passionate outpourings against them that in Dublin it was the English who were the bloody villains.

None of these things were on her mind when she was hurrying home one evening after a trip to Pennyfields. She was crossing the bridge across the inner dock when she saw in the sky and reflected in the water a sight to bring the war sharply home to her. A Zeppelin in flames was drifting out of control above the island. She broke into a run and found an excited crowd gathered in Bermuda Street. Everyone, even Dolores, was making for the stonefield where they could get a more unobstructed view.

She saw Dermot and pushed her way to his side. He hoisted her on to his shoulder. The airship was blowing first one way then the other, flames stripping the fabric from its frame until the ribs glowed red-hot and naked. The wind gusted and momentarily cleared the smoke to reveal a tiny figure clinging to a strut.

'Oh! The poor man!' Daisy cried out in anguish.

'He's come here to try to kill you, love,' said Dermot, but his voice swelled the gasp from the crowd as the doomed man lost his grip and plummeted downwards. Bits broke off and fell earthward until in a few minutes the whole structure seemed to capsize and was gone.

'Where's it going to land?' Daisy sobbed as Dermot lowered her to the ground.

'Let's hope it drops in the river,' said a quiet voice beside her.

'Oh, Danny! Did you see that man fall? That poor man! Will he be killed?'

'Yes, I expect so.' Danny stroked her head. 'It will be all over very quick. He won't know much about it.'

'One bastard less to drop bombs on us,' said Dermot. 'Still,' he added sourly, 'he was fighting for his country, I suppose.'

It was the first time for six years that he had spoken even indirectly to Danny, who chose not to reply to the barbed remark and walked away.

*

Danny had found cheap lodgings in Limehouse. He had stayed with the Collins until it became clear that there was an 'understanding' between him and Kate, when Tommy had gently pointed out the unsuitability of their living under the same roof. Danny had moved out and Rose had allocated a bottom drawer in which Kate began to collect linen and small household objects in readiness for setting up her own home at some distant date.

On one of the long walks back to Bermuda Street to see Kate and eat with the Collins, which he did on most evenings, he tried to think about being married to Kate, but it was too far in the future. Ahead of him the King's Bridge jolted into motion and he put on a spurt to try to get across before it swung sideways and opened a chasm in the road, but he was too late. For once it didn't matter. Rose wouldn't make a fuss about him being late for his tea. He watched the ship slide out of the dock into Limehouse Reach, studying its lines with avid interest.

Waiting for the bridge to swing back into position, a picture of the burning Zeppelin and the man falling came into his inner eye. He could not rid himself of the image or Dermot's voice saying, 'He came here to kill you.' The question of whether or not to enlist had tortured him since the incident. Until then his conscience had been satisfied by the work he was doing in the dock. Essential work. He wanted no part in the killing and he was sodded if he would join up just to please the old man.

After supper, he played a game of draughts with Tom while Kate and her mother sat by the fire sewing. Kate was pleased about a length of cambric she had picked up in Chrisp Street for a shilling to make pillow slips. She showed him but he could not even feign interest and she went back to the work, her feelings ruffled.

To make it up to her he asked, as later they cuddled in the dark porch, what she would like to do that coming weekend. Usually they spent Sunday walking about the West End or in Greenwich Park. They were saving hard to get married and walking was the only pleasure open to them except when Kate permitted a treat.

'Oh, I don't mind,' she said, soothed by his kiss. 'What do you want to do?'

'How about going round the Naval Museum?' She laughed.

'Not again! No. Let's do something nice. Let's go up The Queen's Saturday night.'

Danny groaned. He was still scarred by the memory of the woman in the white dress screeching 'Velia'.

'Oh, come on. There's some good turns on, and we can get some pie and mash after,' said Kate.

'All right, then. Meet me half past six outside the Queen's.'

'Make it half past five. We can look in the shops.'

Grudgingly, Danny agreed.

Kate was a bit late, unusually for her. Danny stared into the drizzle gusting along Poplar High Street, watching for her. Her face appeared, bobbing like a bright lantern among the throng of late shoppers, her eyes shining with excitement when she reached him.

'You're soaked,' he said. 'You should have got the bus.'

'Not if you want something to eat as well. Listen! Charlie's home!'

'Is he?' Danny received the news with joy. 'Well, let's

scrub round going to The Queen's and get back to see him!'

'No. He's having a sleep. He got home at dinner-time, worn out. We can see him after.'

Elation lent appreciation of the evening's performance. Danny enthusiastically joined the booing and barracking of a comic desperately trying to render a monologue; whistled and cat-called the plump dancer billed as a 'dainty soubrette'. At the end of the evening they decided to give the pie and mash a miss and joined the stampede for the bus back to the island.

Charlie was in the best armchair, gazing into the fire when they got indoors. Kate stood back beaming as the two boys pumped their hands and slapped each other on the back.

'Charlie, mate! Am I glad to see you! How long are you home for?'

'I got ten days' leave. We're in Portsmouth for repairs.'

The smile lighting Charlie's eyes was as warm as ever, but it faded like a spark in damp kindling. He seemed desperately tired, thinner and older.

'We're hungry Mum,' said Kate. 'Can I make some sandwiches?' Rose cleared a corner of the table and fetched bread, pickles and brawn. The family pulled up chairs, eager to hear Charlie's news, but his answers were less than full.

'What repairs have got to be done?' asked Danny.

'We're holed above the water line,' Charlie said softly, with a glance at his mother. 'They might put me on another ship. I dunno yet. Depends how long it takes.'

'Where you been, son?' asked Tommy.

'Oh, all over. Up in the North, mainly. Bloody cold, I

129

can tell you, except when you're down below shovelling coal, and that's most of the time.'

'Is that what you have to do? Shovel coal all the time?' Kate was incredulous.

'Yeah. Well, I'm a stoker, ain't I? It's not so bad when you're steaming half-speed. It's when the old man wants full steam ahead it gets a bit hard.'

'What's the old man like?' Danny wanted to know. Question and answer went back and forth until Rose rubbed her eyes and announced that she was going to bed, or she'd never get up in the morning.

'You don't want to walk round the walls tonight, Danny,' she said. 'Why don't you kip in the chair? It's Sunday tomorrow.' Rose and Tom went to bed. Kate stood up.

'Goodnight, Kate,' said Danny. He couldn't kiss her in front of Charlie. 'I'll see you in the morning.'

The boys took the chairs on either side of the range, to finish the celebration stout Tommy had brought in.

'You don't mind if I bank the fire up a bit do you?' said Danny. 'Unless you'd like the pleasure?' Charlie grinned and lay back with his eyes closed. Danny heaped two scoops of coal into the range and opened the damper until there was a roar and a rewarding burst of flame. He adjusted the coals with the poker then settled happily back in his chair. Contentment vanished when he glanced across at Charlie.

His expression was wooden, head back and his eyes still closed. Tears were squeezing under his lids and running down his face. Danny didn't know quite what to do or say. Awkwardly, he put down his glass on the fender.

'What's the matter, mate?'

Charlie took a long sighing breath. 'I'm sorry. It's just

being home here, I s'pose. In the kitchen with Mum and Kate. Just sittin' in a chair. I dunno.' He struggled to express himself. 'Just being home.'

'Has it been bad?'

'No worse for me than anyone else.'

'How did you get the hole in the side?'

'We run into some rough stuff up North. Weather and all.'

'Where?'

'Jutland.'

Danny's breath was taken away. He'd heard about that. Reports of the battle had been in all the papers.

'I read about that,' he said lamely.

'It ain't so much being in the fighting,' Charlie began to tell him. 'I'm not sayin' I wasn't scared. I was. But when the guns are banging away, an' you're ploughing through the water and the old man shouts down to pile on the steam, you ain't got much time to worry about being scared. All you think about is shovelling the coal as fast as you can. Keeping in time with the other blokes. Faster and faster. And it's so bleedin' hot you think you're gonna fry.' He leant forward and looked earnestly into Danny's face.

'The thing I can't forget; the thing that sticks in my gullet is what they done to the midshipman.'

'What did they do?'

'Well, it must have been gettin' pretty hot up on deck. We didn't know what was going on down below. All we knows is that we're rollin' our guts out and the old man keeps bawling for more steam. More steam. We're giving it all we got, when this little snotty comes up at the top of the companionway with a gun in his 'and.'

'A gun? What for?'

'Well, the skipper knows we must be slogging our guts out already, but he's got to keep a full head of steam. To get in and fight and get out. And we was lyin' sideways on to a beam sea. He couldn't head into it because of where the Germans was. Anyway, he must have got it into his head that the stokers might start flaggin'. So he gets the idea that he'll keep 'em up to the mark.

'In the middle of all the bangin' an bawlin' and hollerin', we hear the snotty shoutin' that he's got orders to shoot anyone who slackens off or tries to leave his post. Well, that done it. There he is, this kid, with a revolver wobblin' about in 'is hand. He's shakin' so much he can't keep it still, sayin' he's gonna shoot us.'

More tears welled and Charlie wiped them away.

'Honest, Danny, he couldn't have been more than twelve or thirteen. We was already working till you thought your 'eart and lungs was gonna burst. We had no thought of chuckin' it in, then the skipper sends a kid to shoot us. The men couldn't stand it. They start peltin' this kid with lumps of coal.'

'What 'appened?'

'The kid stands 'is ground as long as he can, then he sort of crumples at the knees and starts cryin' for 'is mother. All the blokes was jeerin' at 'im.' Charlie shook his head and took a gulp of stout.

'I felt sorry for the poor little bugger.'

'What'll happen to him?'

'I dunno. Disgraced. He'll be dismissed out of the service, I expect. Some of the men are still under punishment. I got fourteen days in jankers, but I wasn't one of the ringleaders. I didn't chuck coal at an officer.'

'Are you dreading going back?'

'Well, I ain't lookin' forward to it. But I ain't gonna think about it yet.' He got up and smiled wanly at Danny. 'I'm going to give my bed a towsin' while I've got the chance.' He went to bed, leaving Danny staring thoughtfully into the fire.

Chapter 12

Shoplifting

Down the stairs, two at a time, Daisy made her dash for two hours of freedom. After supper on most nights, when there was no washing or ironing to be done, Dolores let her out to play with the other kids.

Games were in full swing, and as often happened, it was difficult to break into a group. Sides had already been picked and there was a reluctance to change the numbers half-way through. She tried to join Paddy in a game of High Jimmy Knacker, but they wouldn't let a girl play, so she tagged on to a gang off to play Knock Down Ginger in the neighbouring streets.

Sarah saw her trailing after them towards the corner and shouted after her. 'Where are you going?'

One of the boys answered for her, 'We're going round the Alpha Road.'

'Aunt Dolly'll murder you, Daisy, if she finds out!' Sarah warned.

'Who's gonna tell her? You?' the boy shouted back.

It was the boy Daisy passed every day crossing the bridge in the opposite direction on his way to the Church of England school. She didn't know his name, but he always yelled after her when they were safely separated by the bridge, 'Old dirty-drawers!' These encounters left her hot and indignant but she was grateful to him for putting Sarah down.

There were some other, older girls among them but she caught him up and asked, 'What you doing, playing round our street?'

'Me mate's got a football. We was gonna have a game, but his Dad won't let him come out tonight.'

He looked at her from the side of his eye. 'Ain't you that girl I see in the mornings?' he asked.

'You know I am. And you call me rotten names! Bleedin' cheek!'

'What's your real name?'

'Daisy Cavanagh. What's yours?'

'John Fletcher. Cavanagh? That's Irish, innit?'

'Cavanagh,' said Daisy, putting the emphasis on the second syllable. 'Yes, it is. So what?'

'Nothin'.'

They crossed to the other side of the dock, by which time Daisy had discovered that his father was a shipwright, and continued walking along the little side streets.

'I thought we was gonna play Knock Down Ginger,' said Daisy.

'We are, afterwards,' said her new friend.

'After what?'

'We're going round to see the Band of Hope. We always go and watch 'em practisin'. Here, you can have one of my lemons.' He took a shrivelled lemon from his pocket and gave it to her. 'Specks,' he said.

'What's this for?'

'I'll show you in a minute.'

The pub on the corner of the next street was famous in this district of ever-open public houses. It could be relied on to provide spectacular street fights every Saturday night and on most nights in the week. A small crowd already waited on the pavement outside as they arrived. Soon bandsmen in uniform began to turn up with their instruments until there were about a dozen, when the leader called them to order and they started to tune up. The cacophony was dreadful.

'Blimey!' said Daisy. 'Can't they play better than that?'

'Oh, they'll get together in a minute, don't worry,' said John. He pulled Daisy with him to a position in front of the trombonist and peeled his lemon, nudging her to do the same.

The bandleader raised his arms in preparation for the downbeat that would start the performance of uplifting hymns, when his glance fell on John. A look of horrified recognition was immediately replaced by the expression of one in an agonising dilemma. He could hardly shout, 'Piss off you little bleeder,' which his every instinct urged him to do, when he was here on a mission to save souls from perdition. John returned the glare with an understanding smile and the music began.

Daisy had never enjoyed herself so much. The music was rousing, the crowd in great good humour, The harder the bandsmen blew, the louder the kids sucked on the lemons. The trombonist tried valiantly to fix his eyes above their heads and ignore them but, in such circumstances, the will has no power over salivation. Soon he was swallowing hard and opening the tap on the side of the trombone to let out trickles of fluid.

'Why couldn't we bring oranges?' asked Daisy, screwing up her face and shuddering.

'No,' said John. 'Oranges don't make 'em dribble like lemons do.' 'Stand Up, Stand up for Jesus' ended in a long wet raspberry and the crowd collapsed into laughter. The band gave up. There were plenty more sinners in the next street. They collected their belongings and moved off.

'You comin' to play Knock Down Ginger?' asked John, as they walked back towards the bridge. Daisy shook her head. She was growing uneasy at having been absent from Bermuda Street for so long. If Aunt Dolly found out there would be hell to pay.

'No. I got some errands to run before I go to school tomorrow, I've got to be up early.'

'Which school do you go to?'

'St Edmund's.'

'Are you a Catholic?' The question was asked in a tone of mild astonishment.

'Yes. Are you a Protestant?' She pronounced it 'proddy-stent'.

'Yes.' The reply stopped her in her tracks. She knew he must be one, or he would have gone to the same school as her, but she'd never been this close to one before. She stared at it, fascinated that it walked and talked just the same as her.

John was regarding her with similar speculation. 'You don't say prayers to God, do you.' It was a statement, not a question.

'Course we do!' Daisy was outraged.

'You say prayers to the Virgin Mary.'

'Yeah, and you . . . you!' She choked, unable to think of one of the thousand accusations she could have fired at him. Aunt Dolly was always listing them. 'You have married parsons!' she finished, but it didn't have quite the sting she was aiming at, and she flounced off with a toss of her head.

Most of the kids had been summoned indoors when

she got back to Bermuda Street. Sarah hadn't waited for her. The rotten cow! It meant she would have to explain why they hadn't returned together and where she had been. She steeled herself for the row to come. Punishment preceded explanation. As soon as she got inside the kitchen door, Dolores landed a clout on the side of her head that made her ears sing.

'Where the 'ell have you been?'

'I've been playin' down the Alpha Road.'

'What for?' This accompanied by heavy slaps across the face and head.

'I was only playin'.' Daisy cowered behind her upraised arm, getting what cover she could.

'Yeah? What's wrong with playin' in your own bleedin' street? You think you're out of sight out of mind, don't you? Startin' to feel your feet, ain't you? Gettin' up to no bleedin' good with the boys, ain't you?'

At this, determination not to cry broke down. Humiliation and the injustice of the accusation reducing Daisy to wracking sobs. No worse insult could come from Dolores. To her, though the actual word never passed her lips, sex was the unforgivable sin. She had been drumming this into the children since earliest childhood. Daisy edged along the wall to put the table between her and the flailing fists.

'You little mare!' Dolores' face was distorted with hate.

'Here! Here! Go easy!' In the ruckus no one had heard Dermot come in. 'What's she done?'

'She's been playin' out till late, round Alpha Street,' said Sarah.

'She'll bring trouble home to this 'ouse, you mark my words,' said Dolores, backing off. She wouldn't hit her again in Dermot's presence.

'No, she won't,' he said.

Daisy felt a burst of gratitude for this support, but it was all she got. Dermot's loathing of Dolores was not strong enough to make him break an absolute rule. One partner did not undermine the other when it came to disciplining the children.

On the way to school the next morning, Daisy met John as usual as they crossed the bridge. They passed without speaking but as soon as he was a dozen yards behind her he turned and yelled: 'Old dirty-drawers!' Daisy gritted her teeth and refused to look round, but she resolved, if he said that to her once more, she was going to risk getting contaminated and give him a fourpenny one!

In 1916, as usual, preparations for Christmas began in early November. There was some rivalry among the women in the blocks over who would be first to make their puddings. Rose lacked some of her usual enthusiasm. There would only be the three of them for dinner. Her, Tom and a po-faced Kate. Danny had joined the Navy and wouldn't be coming and Charlie wouldn't be home. Dolores headed the field with a pudding that filled the copper and took the whole day to cook, filling the air with the smell of fruit and spice.

It started the excitement and the build up to the great day. Houses and flats were cleaned from top to bottom, bed valances washed and starched, fresh curtains at all the windows. Those who kept chickens began adding extra corn to the feed.

When the children were very young, they had hung up stockings and got from Father Christmas an apple, an orange stuffed down into the toe, a few nuts and a small gift such as a colouring book or a penny whistle. Once they turned five this stopped. There was no giving or receiving of presents but the tradition of feasting was kept well alive.

Most of the food shops ran savings clubs where the women of the street put away small sums to pay for the hocks of bacon and legs of pork. Sometime in early August, Dermot began paying into a loan club run by a neighbour. It would pay out at Christmas and buy new dresses and shoes for the girls. Paddy would get new boots. Everyone got a 'Christmas rig-out'.

About the end of the first week in December, Dolores began to wear a worried frown. She had been 'subbing' on Dermot's savings and when she went to collect the remainder to buy the new clothes, she got a rude shock. All the money had gone and she owed thirteen pounds to the club. She confided these problems to Daisy and Sarah.

'Bloody hell!' said Sarah. 'Looks like being a lively Christmas.'

'Your father's gonna want to know what we bought with your money,' said Dolores.

'Can't we just tell him we ain't spent it yet?' Daisy's idea did not appeal.

'He ain't gonna believe that. Listen, I've been thinking.' Sarah looked at Daisy, who looked at the ceiling. Their Aunt Dolly's thinking was always the forerunner to trouble.

'We'll go up Chrisp Street; I'll come with you. Pick out the frocks you want in the window and we'll all go in the shop together. Don't speak to me. Make out you don't know me. Choose a frock each, then when they're in the bag ask to see something else. I'll keep the other assistants busy. You walk out. Don't run, but keep on crossing the road. Don't wait for me. Come straight home.'

It was no use to protest. Dolores' life probably depended on their having new dresses to show Dermot, but they had no stomach for it. Daisy's heart was pounding as they elbowed their way through the throng of shoppers and a look at Sarah's set face confirmed that she was feeling no braver.

Dolores had picked a time when the market was at its busiest to make the getaway easier. They chose a shop which had velvet dresses on display.

'Might as well get hung for something we fancy,' said Sarah.

They stepped inside and into a tremendous fuss. The saleswoman was wringing her hands and twittering behind the counter.

'What's the matter?' asked Dolores, close on their heels.

'You'll never believe it!' said the saleswoman. 'Somebody has stolen a baby's set from off that stand! We've been so busy. I just looked round and it was gone!'

'No!' said Dolores. 'Did you ever? Some people got the cheek of Old Nick.'

'A decent-looking woman she was,' the distressed woman went on. 'Asked me if we'd got it in another colour. I went to look and when I came back she was gone, and the set with her.'

'Oh dear, what a shame!' said Dolores. She waited sympathetically while the woman composed herself then asked if she could try on some hats. She planted herself in front of a mirror and didn't once look towards

141

Daisy and Sarah, who were receiving attention from a young girl.

They were well enough trained in the art of deception to put on a good performance, not making their choice so hastily as to arouse suspicion. Daisy tried on a green velvet with a cream lace collar. Sarah tried the same in red. There was some argument between them about who looked best in the green which they both preferred, but in the end they announced that they would settle for the ones they had first tried. The dresses were taken away and wrapped. The girl came back with the bags.

'Could we just see some of those petticoats with the lace trimming, like the ones you've got in the window?' Daisy asked.

The assistant trotted off to the stock-room. Together they made for the door, expecting the weight of the saleswoman's hand on their shoulders, or to hear her shriek, 'Just a minute!' But she was still engaged with Dolores and just at that moment the door opened and another customer came in. Not too fast, taking care not to glance in Dolores' direction, they made for the opening. The girl coming in politely stood aside, holding the door for them and they were out in the street!

Across the road, down a few yards past two or three shops then back to the other side again, zig-zagging their way back towards the High Street, fly enough not to go straight to the bus stop. They stopped in a shop doorway ostensibly to gaze in the window, but taking the chance to look back to see if they were pursued.

Once Daisy and Sarah left the shop Dolores took off the hat with the ostrich feather, which she would have dearly loved to own, and said to the woman, 'No. I think I'll leave it today, thank you.' She left before the girl returned from the stockroom and the second robbery of the day was discovered.

On top of the bus, Daisy pressed her head against the cool glass.

'Cor! Talk about jelly-belly,' she whispered to Sarah.

'Shh!' Sarah hissed. 'Sit up straight and act natural.' They kept up a flow of innocent chatter as the bus rumbled over the cobbles and they were deposited at the end of Bermuda Street. Euphoric with relief, they strolled home and up the stairs.

Dermot was home getting ready to go out again. He smiled at their glowing faces.

'What you got there, then?'

Eagerly they showed him the dresses. He said how nice they were, then suddenly noticed that Dolores wasn't with them.

'Where have you left old Dolly?'

'We lost her in the crowd,' said Daisy.

'We waited around for her, but then we thought we'd better come home. We thought she'd be here by now.' Sarah backed her up.

'You haven't left her to carry all them bags by herself! Go back and help her.'

'But Dad!' It was no use. Dermot bundled them out on to the landing and they were in the street again. They walked back to the bus stop and waited for her. She appeared an hour later, having taken the opportunity to dine out on pie and mash.

Chapter 13

Asylum

There was a fourth person at Rose's Christmas dinner-table. Florrie called after mass and was pressed to stay. She was thin but with maturity had acquired a quiet dignity and grace. The Collinses were delighted to see her. Rose exclaimed over her appearance and her blue wool dress. It was of excellent cut and quality, though it hung rather loosely on the hips. She put her hands on Florrie's shoulders and held her at arms' length, smiling into her eyes.

'Look at you, quite the young lady now. And what a lovely frock.'

'The missus give it to me,' said Florrie. 'She often gives me things when she don't want them any more.'

'Good of her to give you Christmas Day off,' said Rose. 'They're not usually that generous.' Florrie looked away.

'I've left that job. The family are going abroad and they can't take me with them.'

'Have you got another place lined up?'

'No. I thought I'd wait till after Christmas, then start looking round. I'm all right for money,' she added hastily. 'For a little while, anyway.' Rose didn't press her further. She bustled the family to the table, but she had caught a glimpse of despair and her suspicions were aroused.

'I thought you was a corridor maid in a big block of flats,' said Kate.

'I was, but I didn't like it there. Then the housekeeper heard that one of the ladies that lived there wanted a general maid in her house in Kent, and she spoke for me.'

'Why didn't you like it? Didn't you get enough to eat?'

'Not much, but that wasn't it. In some ways I liked it, you had your own room and everything. Nice after being three to a bed, but some of the people made sure you had a hard time.'

'Oh. I used to think I'd like to go into service, but not now me and Danny's gettin' married.'

'Are you? Oh, that's lovely. When?'

'I dunno. It'll be nineteen-twenty, the way we're going. But a service job wouldn't be no good. I'd see less of him than I do now.'

'No. They don't let you have followers.'

'Anyway, it don't suit everybody,' said Rose. 'It's all right if you get a good place, but sometimes the other servants can make your life a misery.'

'I'll bet,' said Rose sympathetically. 'Tell us how you come to change your job.'

Florrie glanced at her warily, but the warmth of the fire and the food had relaxed her.

'Well, I used to have to get up at five o'clock to get my section finished before breakfast at eight. Usually there's no one about and you can get on with it. If one of the nobs did come out while you were cleaning the stairs, you were supposed to carry your brushes and your mop and bucket all the way to the bottom, then wait round

145

the corner till they'd gone. They mustn't pass you on the stairs in case they should accidentally brush against you. And you're supposed to keep out of sight. They must think the place stays clean by magic. Well, one morning, I was near the top of these hundreds of stairs – and honest, they was about as wide as Bermuda Street – when a Nanny come out with a little boy, takin' 'im somewhere. She just stood there lookin' at me like I was dirt, waitin' for me to go down so she could pass. Well, she was only a servant, same as me, and he was only a little kid, so I said to her, 'Can't you come past me? There's plenty of room. I'll stand against the wall. You don't have to touch me.' Anyway, she wouldn't. She just stuck her nose in the air and went back to where she'd come from. She reported me to the housekeeper. I would have got the sack and no reference if it hadn't been for the housekeeper. She told the nanny that I'd be dismissed at once, just to satisfy her, then she spoke up for me to the missus. I was lucky.'

'Well,' said Tommy, 'you was lucky. If you've got a good job, you want to look after it.'

Rose had followed the account with close interest. It didn't quite add up. There was still something that she hadn't got to the bottom of. She would bide her time. After the meal, she and Tom settled by the fire to doze while the two girls tackled the mountain of washing-up.

'Are you gonna go upstairs to see everyone?' Kate asked.

'Yes. I do want to see them all. It's just . . . I'm scared they'll notice something. Your Mum has.'

'Noticed what?'

Florrie turned away from the sink and with soapy

hands pulled the fabric of her dress tight across her abdomen. It took a moment for the meaning of the gesture to get home to Kate.

'You don't mean? Oh, Florrie, no!'

'Yes. I'm in the pudden club. Isn't that what they call it?' she said bitterly.

'What are you going to do?'

'I was hoping your Mum might be able to help me. I haven't had the chance to ask her. I couldn't say anything in front of your Dad. I don't think I've got the nerve to ask her now. Will you ask her for me, Kate? Please.'

Kate went back to the kitchen and quietly roused her mother. Motioning her not to wake Tommy, she beckoned her into the scullery. She came straight to the point. 'Florrie's expectin',' she told a bleary-eyed Rose. 'We don't know what to do.'

'I guessed as much. How far gone are you?'

'About four months, I think. Maybe five.'

Rose pursed her lips and shook her head.

'You've left it too late. You'll be quickening soon. What about the father? Will he stand by you?'

'He might have done. But he was killed in France last month. He didn't even know about it.' Florrie began weeping quietly.

'He belonged to the family you been workin' for?' She nodded. 'And they've found out and chucked you out?'

'Yes. Don't tell Aunt Dolly, or Dad, please.'

'You bloody little fool! No, don't worry. I won't tell 'em. There may be something we can try. If that don't work, there's nothing else for it. After Christmas I'll come with you to see the mother superior. They've got places for girls like you. It's either that or the work-house.'

Later that night when they were all in bed and Florrie was tossing with the phrase 'girls like you' searing into her brain, Rose decided that she would have to tell Tommy.

'Can't she stay here with us?' she asked, when the situation had been explained.

'How can she? Talk sense. It's bad enough her coming here for Christmas with her own family upstairs. What do you think Dermot would do with her livin' here? First Danny, now Florrie. And her in that state. Talk about shittin' on your own doorstep! He wouldn't put up with it. And I can understand why. Let her go to her own people. It's up to them to sort it out.'

'You know Dermot'll knock seven bells out of her.'

'He will anyway, when he finds out. And there's our Kate to think about. It only takes one rotten apple in the barrel to turn the rest mouldy. No. I'm sorry for the girl, but you'll have to get her out of here. Quick and all.'

So, on the day after Boxing Day, Rose took Florrie to the Sisters of Mercy and came back without her. Kate wrote to her and received one letter in return saying that she had been put to work in the laundry until nearer the time of the birth. After that no news came. In April, when she calculated the baby would be born, she wrote again. The letter was returned unopened.

Kate put Florrie to the back of her mind, being preoccupied with collecting for her bottom drawer and dreaming of Danny's return. As the summer of 1918 wore on, realisation began to penetrate, even in Bermuda

Street, that the war was coming to an end and the survivors would be coming home.

On the day the Armistice was signed, the island burst into exuberant life. Bunting appeared across the streets and the air rang with a jangle of sound from the craft on the river, fog horns, hooters, whistles and sirens blasting all day long in jubilation.

A few days later Kate was in the street painting – as many of the neighbours were – a sign on the wall. Assisted by Daisy she had written in large uneven capitals, 'Welcome home Danny'. She had started on the 'and' to go before 'Charlie', when a shadow fell across her work.

A young Ordinary Seaman stood behind her. She didn't know him but she seemed to be the one he sought.

'Is this number 71?'

'Yes.'

'Is Mr or Mrs Collins home?'

'Yes. They're both indoors,' said Kate, dread dousing her joy. 'Has something happened to Danny?'

'Danny? No. Not so far as I know. Can I speak to Mr Collins?'

She led him inside. Daisy tagged along and stood unnoticed by the kitchen door. Rose registered no surprise at a stranger coming into her house. She looked at him as though she had been waiting to receive his message.

'It's Charlie, isn't it?'

'Yes.' Tom in his armchair didn't stir. They waited. The young man went on.

'I'm sorry to tell you, he's dead.'

Rose took a long shuddering breath. 'When was he killed?'

'He wasn't killed exactly.' The young man was twisting his hat around in his hands. 'He'd been ill. Not seriously ill but he'd got the flu pretty bad. He was down in sick-bay. We was in Portsmouth when news of the Armistice come through. Anyway, there was a lot of shoutin' and cheerin' and someone on shore started lettin' off fireworks. Charlie come rushin' up on deck to see the fun. He must have caught another cold. He got much worse and that night, well . . . he just died.'

Rose sank into a chair by the table and covered her eyes. Tommy got cumbrously to his feet and amazed Daisy by laying an arm across his wife's shoulders.

'He got the flu and died on Armistice Day?' He sounded hoarse.

'Yes. You'll be gettin' a letter, but I'm on me way 'ome and the first officer said it was all right for me to come.'

Tommy remembered his manners. He thanked the young man and offered him tea. Daisy crept away. She felt stunned by what she had just heard but, with the callousness of extreme youth, could not imagine or share the experience of grief that was gripping Charlie's family. Outside, she took the paint brush and blotted out the 'A' of what was to have been the 'And'. The sign said 'Welcome Home Danny' and that was fine. Danny would still be coming home.

Out of respect, the street party was postponed until after Charlie's wake. The Navy brought his body home and the coffin lay with the lid beside it on the table in the kitchen. All week long, the neighbours called to pay their respects and offer what comfort they could, though Rose and Tom could not even share the bitter consolation of the bereaved among them, that their sons died defending King and country.

Normally, Rose would have been roped in to be on the committee organising the street party, but she was left in peace and meetings were held in one of the houses at the other end of the street. The ones with bay windows. Annie Carter was asked to help and Daisy was hoping she'd get a chance to go with her so she could get a look inside, but it didn't happen.

The women divided themselves into groups for making sandwiches, jellies, cakes and so on, while the men planned games and races. The Feathers donated beer and lemonade and loaned the piano. Jack Carter surprised everyone by revealing that he could play the piano accordion and actually had one that he was willing to bring to the party.

It was raining hard on the morning of the party. A stiff wind blew down the street, wound the bunting into strings and tore down the Union Jack that had taken four men all of one afternoon to stretch across the road. By four the rain stopped; by five the sun came out and the flag was reinstated.

Six long trestle tables were laid down the middle of the road, one slightly set apart from the others. This, it was made clear, was for the children from the blocks. Daisy, who always had a keen eye for a slight, noted that this table was being set with food that had gone slightly wrong. She spotted one of Dolores' contributions, her speciality, bread-pudding, cut into squares. She had seen it in the making and knew that the one placed on 'their' table was the one taken late from the oven. She herself had spent half an hour picking burnt fruit off the outside. The sandwiches too curled a little more than those on other tables.

A clown entertained them while they ate. Everyone

could see it was Mr Levene from the grocery and all the kids agreed that the make-up improved his appearance. His performance hardly distracted Daisy from her concern with the food. When the first stage of the meal was over, the women brought out the trifles and desserts. A bowl of unset jelly was set before her. She looked along the line and saw on the next table plates bearing jellies and blancmanges moulded to perfection. Her suspicions confirmed, she picked up the bowl and slung its runny contents into the gutter just as one of the women came by.

'Here!' she said. 'I made that jelly!'

'You didn't make it soon enough by the look of it, Missus.'

The woman spluttered in outrage. 'The cheek of you block kids!'

'Yeah!' Daisy yelled after her, 'any junk's good enough for the block kids!' Some of the others at the table yelled in agreement. 'There was more soldiers and sailors killed out of these blocks, Missus, than out of your end of the street!'

It was promising to develop into a brawl when the clown shouted, 'Quiet! This is supposed to be a peace party!' and the kids laughed. The party went on. They ran races for two white rabbits and danced until the morning.

Slowly, the young men who had survived returned. Some to Bermuda Street, some, like the boy from number 11, to the Star and Garter home for disabled servicemen. Danny got home at the beginning of December. He wasn't certain why, but Dermot welcomed him with surprising warmth. It could be, he thought, that the old man wanted to boast in the pub and show him off as a returned hero, or he could have been genuinely relieved that he had come back alive. Either way, he took him up on his offer to let him come back to live in the flat. It was taken for granted that he would pick up the threads of his courtship with Kate and her family were in mourning for Charlie, so he couldn't go there.

He had been home for about two weeks, during which he spoke little about his war experiences and lost a little of his pallor, when he began to look around for work. Dermot was disappointed at his reluctance to talk, but no amount of pressure would persuade him. He just seemed to want to be outdoors as much as possible and he did tell Sarah that he had been on a submarine.

Not much was on offer in the docks. Danny swore to starve rather than go back to cleaning bilges. For a while, he drove the greengrocer's donkey cart, picking up fruit and vegetables in the early hours of the morning from Covent Garden, but trade dropped off, and he had to go. Then he got lucky and was taken on at the sack factory, not making sacks, that was girls' work, but stencilling the name of the company and the contents of the sacks in white paint on the finished bags. Kate was satisfied. The money wasn't much but it was regular and he gave her a little to put by each week towards the day when they could marry.

He took to dropping in at The Feathers on his way home on Saturday nights for a drink with his father and Dry Dock Tommy. He was gradually, and without his realising it, assuming the life pattern of a Bermuda Street man. The whole neighbourhood was slipping into its pre-war habits, until a new plague came to threaten them. The influenza that had taken Charlie was claiming lives across the country. Bermuda Street didn't escape. Every other household had its victim. In the blocks, Tommy was the first to die.

Chapter 14

Royal Sovereign

As the 1920s began, the prospect of marriage for Kate and Danny seemed to recede. Danny was laid off by the sack factory. They kept Kate on and some other machinists at a reduced wage, but Danny spent most of his days tramping round every factory within walking distance hoping to pick up a few days casual work. Since he shared the hope with several hundred others, his chances were slim.

On the days he didn't call at factories, he went to the Labour Exchange. He detested these visits. They were gatherings of desperate men. Two policemen guarded the door and another patrolled inside. Every fifteen minutes a side door was opened to let in three hundred from the waiting crowd. A wide counter separated them from the clerks to make it more difficult for applicants, driven to violence when benefits were stopped, to seize them and choke them.

Danny had endured nine months on the dole, with no hope in sight, when he was tipped off that a pleasure ship, the *Royal Sovereign*, a large paddle steamer, was in dry dock for repairs and there was a chance they might be looking for a hand. He went at once to the dock and, not knowing who else to speak to, asked a workman if he had heard of any jobs going. The man looked him up and down. Months of unemployment had not helped Danny's appearance or self-confidence.

'You done a bunk out of the Navy?'

'No. I come out at the end of the war.' The question had undermined him.

'Well, the captain comes round every day to see how it's going. He'll be here some time this afternoon. I dunno when.'

Danny waited. When the captain appeared, he did not have to ask anyone to identify him, though he wore no uniform. His bearing and the way he paced the quay looking at his ship marked him out as the skipper.

Screwing up his courage, Danny stepped in his path. 'Excuse me, sir, can I speak to you?'

'Well?'

'I was hoping you might be needing another hand. I'm very strong and willing and I've had some experience.'

The skipper's face remained impassive, his eyes speculative but he appeared to be listening and Danny rushed on.

'Not on ships as big as this, but I was Captain Macfarlane's boy on the coastal barges for two years . . . well, nearly two years.'

This seemed to be of interest and he was questioned about his knowledge of the river, its bridges and tides.

'Hmm, well,' said the skipper, 'I'll let you know. What's your address?'

Danny gave his address feeling a sharp disappointment. He walked away telling himself to put the idea out of his mind.

Two weeks later, he was on the corner chatting with a

few lads when a young man approached them enquiring for Danny. He knew his mission before he spoke. The skipper had sent for him. He was to report to the old Swan Pier at eight the next morning.

Kate was less than delighted that his new job would take him away from home.

'It's only a day tripper,' he told her. 'I'll get home at least once a week, I should think.'

'You might not want to come home.'

'Course I will. You'll be able to come and meet me sometimes.' She was mollified. At least there would be money coming in.

Danny was on the pier at seven, his heart hammering. He could see the *Royal Sovereign* taking up most of the space between London Bridge and Cannon Street Bridge, her brasswork gleaming in the morning sun. He felt an absurd rush of proprietary pride. A few other men, obviously crew members, arrived and finally, the skipper. They were rowed out to the ship in a waterman's skiff.

The quartermaster and lamptrimmer took charge of initiating him into shipboard life. He introduced Danny to Evans who, as the other ordinary seaman, shared with him the lowliest position among the ninety crew. He was shown his detail of brasswork. All the brightwork on the starboard side.

The day began at four when the bosun shouted down the fo'c's'le hatch to muster the ordinary and able seamen on deck. There was just time to scramble into trousers and the new jersey and sailor's hat with *RSS co.* emblazoned on the front and swallow a cup of tea made by the AB on anchor watch before getting to work. The ABs scrubbed decks and the bosun hosed them down while Danny and Evans attacked the brasswork with a mixture of Colza oil and brickdust.

They worked with all speed possible without sacrificing thoroughness. The skipper came aboard at seven thirty and did his rounds, missing nothing. About seven, they dived down to the fo'c's'le for breakfast, dressed in clean jersey, hat cover and polished boots ready for the telegraph to ring 'standby' and passed any moments that might otherwise have been idle by peeling their quota of potatoes for the day.

Danny stood in line for inspection, quaking. His new mates had told him there were no second chances, but the skipper must have been satisfied. As new hand, Danny was detailed to make him a cup of tea while he went to the cabin to change into uniform. He emerged immaculate. On his cap shone the gold braid of a commodore captain. He wore a long frock-coat and a pair of kid gloves, which were replaced with new every Sunday.

One ordinary seaman was required to attend the captain on the bridge while the *Sovereign* came alongside Swan Pier to pick up the first batch of their complement of fourteen hundred and fifty passengers. The purser and the carpenter counted them aboard, then they were away with a blast of the whistle.

The mate took the wheel as they edged away from the pier while the captain supervised lowering the telescopic funnels and saw the mast swung down in its tabernacle. Only at the highest point of the tide was it necessary to raise the centre span of Tower Bridge. Today they slid smoothly beneath, then, with mast and funnels up, they piled on the steam to get to Greenwich ahead of ships from rival companies.

The river in the pool of London was crowded and

bustling with craft. If any threatened to impede him in his bid to get to Greenwich first, the skipper came as close as he dared with the great paddles, ordered 'full astern' and washed them clear. Danny laughed in exultation as the blistering language of the bargees floated up to him.

The ABs were ready to throw their heaving lines with practiced accuracy so as not to delay the getaway from Greenwich once the next batch had boarded. The first ship past a particular buoy in Thorpe Bay had its company flag hoisted by the piermaster at Southend and took precedence. Other vessels had to slacken speed and wait.

Passengers already aboard were hanging over the side and cheering wildly as the *Royal Sovereign* raced neck and neck with the *Golden Eagle* belonging to the General Steam Navigation Company. Danny, obeying the instructions he had been given, never allowed his eyes to leave the captain, interpreting his orders and ringing them down on the telegraph to the engine room. He knew a fierce joy as they passed the buoy, in front by a nose.

Casting off from Southend pier, the captain dismissed Danny with a nod and he was sent to join two ABs patrolling the decks, looking to the comfort and safety of the passengers. Some, he was told, travelled with them regularly. One young lady, who had her own seat just in front of the flagstaff, always dined at the captain's table, with a few other privileged persons.

That night, when the *Sovereign* was secured at her mooring between the two bridges, with an extra, stout hawser aft to withstand the rip of the ebb tide, the lower ranks among the crew lounged around on their bunks in the fo'c's'le discussing the day's events. One man in a bobble hat looked up from his knitting to remark that the young woman by the flagstaff seemed to have taken quite a fancy to Danny.

'Who, me?' said Danny in surprise. 'Don't be daft!'

'Oh, yes,' agreed an elderly AB, who was perched on the locker bandaging his gammy leg. 'Every time I come round she was looking at you up on the bridge. I go round the decks seeing to everybody and I come back, and there she is, still lookin' at you. Gazin' up, all adorin' like.'

'She must 'ave been lookin' at the old man.'

'Oh no. She only had eyes for you.'

There was a time when Danny's face would have burned, but two years in the Navy had toughened him, and he merely grinned.

'You want to play your cards right there, mate. They say she's an admiral's daughter.'

Danny was spared having to make a witty reply by a crash against the hull that shuddered through the length of the ship. A tug was towing four lighters under London Bridge on the flood tide. The end lighter had swung in a wide arc and struck their stern, almost breaking them adrift. Only one wire held. The men leapt from their bunks in the darkness – the impact had knocked out the oil lamp – and plunged towards the ladder. The old AB had got there first, trailing bandage behind him. The next man trod on it and all hands finished in a cursing heap at the bottom.

The damage was superficial. Under the captain's supervision, more wires were run out to the buoys and they were back in their bunks in time to snatch a little sleep before the four o'clock call.

There were no Friday sailings. On this day the crew painted the funnels and did fitting-out jobs that could not be done when they were steaming, after which, at around four, they were free to go ashore. On his first Friday as a crewman, Danny joined six of the other lads from the fo'c's'le for a night out in town. They caught a bus to the Holborn Empire, then rounded off their evening with another bus trip to the Elephant and Castle, for what was reputed to be the best pie and mash in London.

At the end of his second week – during which the only memorable event was the purser coming to him to tell him that the young woman sitting by the flagstaff had asked to be introduced – Danny was keen to go again. He had politely turned down the request, fearing that to be seen associating with her, however briefly, would put a barrier between him and his new mates. Anyway, she was obviously a lady. What could she want with him? He wouldn't know what to say to her.

He was laughing and chattering with the rest as the liberty boat nosed alongside Swan Pier, when he was a little dismayed to see Kate waiting for him. He had written a couple of times, but guilt, not pleasure was his chief sensation as he kissed her cheek.

'Why didn't you let me know you was coming?'

'How could I?'

This was true. It was also clear that he would have to change his plans for the evening. He took her arm and said to the ring of grinning faces, 'This is Kate, my girlfriend.' He felt himself flush and was annoyed.

'Hello, Kate,' said one. 'No wonder you don't want nothin' to do with the admiral's daughter, Dan. I wouldn't either, in your shoes.'

'Who's the admiral's daughter?' asked Kate.

'Oh, don't take any notice of him,' said Danny, steering her firmly along the pier. On Tower Hill they parted from his friends.

'Where do you want to go?'

'I don't mind.'

He found this reply irritating but kept his voice even. 'Let's go for a walk round the West End.'

Kate hadn't forgotten the admiral's daughter. She returned to the subject on the bus.

'Who is she then?'

'No one. That's what they call her. She comes with us to Margate a couple of times a week.'

'Don't she get fed up with it?'

'How do I know? I've never spoke to her. She's been ill. TB or something. Doctor said she's got to get plenty of sea air.'

'How do you know if you've never spoke to her?'

'It's just what the boys say. I don't know if it's true. What you worried about anyway?'

'I ain't worried,' said Kate, but she didn't say much for the rest of the evening.

Danny waited with her for the bus that would take her back to Poplar. She clung to him when she saw it coming.

'Danny, you do still want to get married, don't you?'

'Course I do.' He hugged her and stood waving until she was out of sight then made his way back to the pier. The lads were waiting for him. Someone struck a match and a few minutes later, a police launch came gliding silently out of the darkness to ferry them aboard. For this service, they paid sixpence each.

A couple of days later, nearing the end of the run, they were dropping the last passengers at Old Swan Pier when Danny was astonished to see Kate standing on the jetty, scanning the faces as they passed. He asked the purser for permission to step ashore for a couple of minutes.

'Go on, then, but you'd better look lively.'

He hurried down the gangway, trying not to push, and rushed up to her. 'Kate. What you doing here? Is something wrong?'

'No. I didn't think you'd see me. I just wanted to get a look at her.'

'Her? Who?'

'You know who I mean. The admiral's daughter. I want to be sure I'll know her when I see her.'

'You gone doolalley?'

'No,' she said, but there was a glint of madness in her eyes as she faced him. 'If she thinks she can get her hooks into you, she'd better think again. I'll have the 'air off 'er bleedin' 'ead.'

Danny had to go, the ABs were raising the gangplanks.

'How you going to know it's her?' he called.

'There ain't no mistakin' 'er. I've seen her gettin' into her Daddy's car. I'll know 'er again don't you worry.'

'Look,' he shouted. 'Don't come up on Friday. I'll come home.'

He was appalled. If Kate were to set upon the girl, he'd die of shame. She'd been working in that sack factory too long. She had picked up some rough ways. He was going to have to talk to her.

They didn't go to The Queen's that Friday as Kate wanted. The house turned out too late for Danny to get back for a few hours sleep. She was disappointed so he fell in with her second plan and endured a promenade up and down Poplar High Street, looking in the shop windows at things. they might one day have in their own home.

Danny raised the subject of the girl on the boat and tried to extract a promise that Kate would not approach her, but she was evasive and would make no promise. By the end of the evening, he was feeling quite dispirited and she more cheerful.

'I can get home by meself all right, don't worry,' she said to him.

'No. I ain't 'avin' you walk round the walls by yourself in the dark. I'll see you home.'

She put her arm round his waist, tucking her thumb through his belt loop and, each matching stride with the other, they set out, his arm around her shoulders. Halfway home, he stopped under a lamp to kiss her.

'You ain't still mad with me, then?' she asked.

He looked down at her face glowing in the lamplight, her eyes imploring. Sometimes she made him so wild he wanted to choke her, but now she seemed small and defenceless in his arms. He bent and gently nipped the end of her nose, his resentment slipping away.

'No. I ain't mad.'

They walked on and turned off the perimeter road into the street that led on to Bermuda Street. On impulse, as they were passing the laundry, Danny swung her off the pavement and pulled her into the concealing darkness of the deep porch. Kate giggled as he took her in his arms and pressed her against the wall.

She savoured his kisses responding when he nuzzled her neck by brushing her lips against his cheek, yielding like a dancer to his every movement. He began undoing the buttons of her blouse. She resisted then, pushing

164

against him, but he leant on her a little harder, tightening his grip, keeping his mouth on hers. She gasped when his hand found the smooth warm flesh of her breast.

'Danny no! Not till we're married.'

He didn't take his hand away. His thumb stroked her nipple.

'We're going to get married. What difference does it make?'

He kissed her again to keep her from protesting as he gathered up the material of her skirt, pulling it up above her waist. He felt a jump of excitement to discover that she was wearing loose-legged, French knickers.

'Danny, please, we mustn't.'

He took her hand and placed it over where his penis bulged against his trousers.

'I got to have you Kate. You are gonna be my wife.'

With his knee he parted her legs, holding her still with the great strength of his left arm as he fumbled to undo his flies.

'Oh, Danny, no,' Kate moaned. 'You might give me a baby.'

'It's all right. You can't get a baby if you do it standing up.'

At first, he couldn't penetrate her, so rigid she was and their bodies being at the wrong angle, but persistently and beginning with little thrusts, he entered her and was soon driving her back hard against the rough brick wall.

It was quickly over. Danny fastened his trousers and stood back while she rearranged her skirts.

'You ain't sorry are you?' he asked as he took her arm and they walked a little unsteadily on.

'I ain't sorry, no, but Danny, you're gonna have to marry me now.'

The *Royal Sovereign* carried no wireless, so there could be no advance warning of foul weather ahead. Danny was on the bridge with the skipper and the mate as, with a full complement of passengers, they approached Southend in deep gloom and driving rain. With great difficulty, they landed those who wished to go ashore then ploughed on to Margate with conditions worsening by the minute.

A beam sea was breaking over Margate pier. The skipper decided to come alongside with the stern to the swell. Putting her head to the shore, he edged her alongside at half speed, but a huge wave lifted them high above the level of the pier and would have smashed them on top of it, had he not ordered 'full astern'. Gradually, the ship picked up enough speed to clear them and swing them round. ABs stood by to help shaken women and children ashore and the voyage continued with only those who had paid for the round trip to Ramsgate.

The three on the bridge were getting a rough ride as the wings dipped and lurched through ninety degrees. Pieces of timber on the sponsons, the triangular platforms above the wheels, began to splinter and break away as the great paddle boxes rolled under. The skipper shouted to Danny to fetch a little brown canvas sack that was hanging in his cabin. Clinging to rails, banging against bulkheads, he obeyed and handed it to him, realising only at the last moment that it contained distress rockets.

With one hand the skipper tied it to the rail, hanging

on with the other. He shouted a warning to the mate to hold fast when they turned beam on to the sea to round the North Foreland. Until then, Danny had felt all right. He asked permission to go below to be sick and received a nod of consent.

He struggled through the forward cabin, stepping over prostrate passengers and wrenched open the door to the deck, not wishing anyone to see him being sick. He just had time to grab a stanchion, an upright post, when the *Sovereign* made her turn to starboard. She reared like a whipped horse then dived her head under. When she surfaced, all the cabin windows were smashed, stove in by the sea.

Danny forgot about feeling sick and forced his way back in through the door to a cabin in chaos. China and glass from the tea and beer bars lay everywhere smashed. Crates and loose furniture floated in the water that sloshed to and fro among the wretched passengers. Some were hysterical. The lad from the tea bar, a graduate of the Gravesend Sea School, was laying about him with a broom to keep people away from the lifebelt racks.

The *Golden Eagle* had reached Ramsgate ahead of them, having given Margate a miss. They had to wait while she pulled out, there being not enough room for them both, but they were able to turn their stern to the sea, stilling the motion of the ship a little, so that the crew could attend to those passengers in need of help. They used the top bar and the purser's office as dressing stations. It meant hoisting people over their shoulders and lugging them up to the top deck, where first aid was given.

Ambulances were waiting on the harbourside to take

the more seriously injured to hospital. About six hundred people were also waiting to make the return trip with them but this was impossible. The main saloon was under four feet of water and the sponsons were badly damaged. The skipper struggled through a crowd howling abuse, to telephone London to arrange a train to take them back to the city.

They stayed in harbour until the following afternoon, to make repairs and pump out. Some of the lads from the fo'c's'le decided to go ashore to the pictures. Danny was wet through, having been on the bridge for hours without a break; his spirits, too, were on the damp side. One of his mates lent him dry clothes and they stepped ashore for hot tea and reviving fish and chips. They missed the beginning of the film, but as they settled into their seats, the scene changed and there flashed on to the screen a scene of waves breaking picturesquely over the rocks. Without a word, the lads got up and walked out.

They left Ramsgate harbour the next day in bright sunshine and enjoyed an easy voyage home, having few passengers. News of their buffeting had got into the national newspapers and, as they made their way up the Thames, they were tooted by passing tugs. Entering London, they were cheered by crowds lining the bridges. Standing beside the skipper, Danny felt like a conquerer receiving the adulation of his armies.

Not long after this, as the season was coming to its close, Danny was summoned to the captain's cabin. Hastily, he brushed his boots and put on a clean cap cover.

'You asked to see me, sir,' he said, as he stood before the captain.

'Are you thinking of joining us again next season?'

'Yes. I very much hope so.'

'Hm. I've received a letter from a young lady who travels with us regularly; you've no doubt noticed her.'

'Yes. I think so, sir.'

'She has enclosed a letter for you.' The skipper skimmed a white envelope across his desk. 'Apparently she has been observing you and admires your devotion to duty.' No hint of a twinkle in the eyes. 'I must say, I've been pleased with your work. This young lady has asked me to see what can be done to advance your career.'

Danny was speechless. He picked up the envelope and held it stiffly by his side. The skipper went on.

'I have been discussing you with my son who is chief officer on the *Albatross*. How would you like to serve a five year apprenticeship with him, with the General Steam Navigation Company? You'd get ten shillings a week and then take your master's ticket. Think it over at the weekend, and let me know on Monday,' he added, when Danny still couldn't find his voice.

Back in the fo'c's'le Danny opened his letter. She had enclosed a photograph, otherwise there was nothing that could be seen as improper. She endorsed what the captain had told him. That she had watched him at work and thought he deserved a chance to better himself. She finished by wishing him well for the future. Nothing to confirm that she was the daughter of an admiral. Maybe, thought Danny, she was the company chairman's daughter.

He was wary of showing the letter to Kate; he considered keeping it to himself, but thought better of it. He would have to discuss the apprenticeship offer with her. It might make a difference to their plans and how else could he explain such sudden good fortune? He outlined what the skipper had said when he got home on Friday night. The photograph he kept in his pocket.

Kate was silent for a long time after she finished reading. Her eyes were fearful when she looked up.

'You don't really want to be stuck away at sea for years, do you?'

'It's a chance, Kate, a chance to make something of myself. I know it's not much money to start, but one day I could be earning really good money. Look, you'd get used to it. Lots of women marry sailors.'

'Well, I don't want to be one of them! I've seen women round here struggling on their own. Their men gone for years at a time, 'ome for a couple of months then soddin' off again, leaving the wife with another one up the spout!' She started to cry noisily.

'It won't be like that for us.'

'Oh no?' she snapped, 'Well, you'll have to tell your skipper you're turning it down, 'cos I haven't come on yet. I'm nearly three weeks late!'

Chapter 15

Captive

Rose could not organise a grand wedding reception, since Kate was 'married but not churched' – as the neighbours whispered behind their hands – and time was short. She didn't want her daughter walking up the aisle with a bulge a bouquet couldn't hide. The priest had raised his eyebrows at the fixture of a hasty marriage date, but Rose had quelled him with a look.

'You don't have to say it. She ain't the first and she won't be the last.'

It was to take place on a Saturday, after which the pair were to make their home with Rose. It made sense, now that she was on her own.

Everyone in the blocks lent a hand, every flat became part of the production line for sandwiches and sausage rolls. Room doors were taken off their hinges and propped behind the railings. Dermot was in charge of bringing in the beer. Crates were stacked in the yard and in the porch, a barrel bowed the legs of a trestle table.

Dolores didn't feel she could walk as far as the church. From first hearing about the impending wedding she had maintained that she would have nothing to do with it. She and Danny had carefully nurtured their hatred of each other over the years and had still not exchanged a word. Sarah coaxed her to change her mind.

'Come on, he's going to be living underneath us. He'll be your neighbour after this. Make a fresh start, for poor old Rose.'

So she was persuaded, and when the wedding party began to arrive back from the church, she was ensconsed in Tom's old chair in the back kitchen, making the first inroads into a pile of ham sandwiches.

It took an hour or so for the party to warm up. Rose's far-flung family arrived, adding the only strange faces to the throng that was beginning to fill the flat and spill out on to the pavement. At about seven, as dusk settled over the street, some untutored person flung open the parlour window and, for the benefit of revellers inside and out, began banging on the piano. A thumping, jangling sound issued, which bore no resemblance to the song started and taken up, but provided a cheerful background for the singing and the knees-up.

They ate and drank, danced and sang with lavish abandon, until the windows rattled and the ground was awash with beer slops. Not until after midnight did they begin to flag. Kate, still in the bridal dress her mother had run up for her from eight yards of white satin bought from a stall in Chrisp Street, was dropping from fatigue, but there was no hope of getting to her bed. Tired of pokes, suggestive digs accompanied by raucous laughter and suffering the dragging weariness of early pregnancy, she slipped out of the back door, up the back stairs and took refuge in Daisy's bed.

Danny didn't miss her for quite a while. Then, not seeing her in any of the rooms, he went in search of her into the street. He spotted Daisy sitting on the railings with

John two doors down and, being fuddled with drink, forgot what he had come for. He walked up to her.

'Why don't you bring your young man indoors?' Daisy looked at him in alarm.

'It's all right I've seen you together, down the Island Gardens. Bring him in. Sarah's got her boyfriend in there.'

'What about Dad? What'll he say?'

'Don't worry about the old man, he's merry. Anyway, he's got to know sometime. Might as well be now. I'll look after you. Come on!' He put his arm round John's shoulder and propelled him towards the flat. Daisy followed, but John turned back, took her arm and the three of them walked back together. Daisy's stomach contracted in fear when she saw her father in the porch, presiding over the dregs in the beer barrel, but John's step didn't falter.

'Good-evening, Mr Cavanagh,' he said, taking care to put the emphasis on the second syllable. Dermot looked up, bewilderment in his glazed eyes, and watched them march past and into the parlour.

The man with the accordion was playing a waltz. Daisy opened her arms and John held her and began to guide her stiffly round the floor. Sarah saw Dermot come into the room. She drew in her breath and held it. Colour, her boyfriend, picked up a newspaper from the chair and with trembling hands, held it upside down in front of his face. Dermot came and leant against the wall beside him, watching the dancers. After a while, he said laconically: 'Nearly time you turned a page, ain't it Colour?'

As Daisy turned she saw him and he beckoned her over. She went to him, prepared to defy him if she must.

173

'I'll tell you something, Nin.'

'What?'

'Your bloke's got two left feet. I'll show him how its done.' He slipped his arm round her waist and they waltzed round the room together.

'There you are,' said Dermot, bringing her back to John. 'It's as though me feet never touch the ground.'

John grinned. 'I'm more graceful with 'ammer and chisel.'

'Colour!' Dermot roared suddenly, making the boy behind the paper leap in his chair. 'Sarah wants a dance. Come on. Let's see what you're made of.'

'I'm hungry,' said John. 'Can we get something to eat? Why do they call him Colour?' he asked, as Daisy led him into the kitchen.

' 'Cos of the colour of his neck. When he washes his face, it leaves a black tide mark. They've always called 'im Colour, since 'e was a little boy.'

Danny was in the kitchen brewing tea.

'Have you found Kate?' Daisy asked him.

'Yeah, she's flaked out on your bed.'

'I see. I hope you don't think I'm going to give it up to make room for you.'

'No. When everyone's gone home, I'll go and fetch her down.'

'He's in no hurry.' Dolores piped up from beside the fire. 'There'll be no novelty in it for 'im. He's already tried the goods.'

Danny ignored her, but Daisy saw a muscle twitch in his jaw.

'Take no notice,' she said. 'She's drunk.'

'Drunk I may be, but I've got eyes in me head to see.' The eyes in question glittered and focused on Daisy.

'You're all the same, you Cavanaghs. Can't wait to be decently married before you're at the ruttin'. I see you haven't wasted no time bringin' a bloke indoors. Your father'll 'ave your hide if he sees you.'

'Dad's already seen us and he don't mind,' said Daisy hotly.

'He'll change 'is tune when you bring trouble home. He'll have you banged away, same as your sister. Won't think twice about it.'

Daisy couldn't look at John. She was red in the face with embarrassment, but it was Danny who rounded on Dolores.

'Shut up, you vicious, lying old mare! You've never got a good word to say for anybody. Florrie ain't here to speak up for herself.'

'No. She ain't here, is she? Where is she then? Ask yourself that! You ask Rose if you don't believe me. They cooked it up between 'em; 'ad her put away. Moral defective, that's what they said.'

She had shocked Danny into silence. Kate had told him about Florrie's pregnancy and that Rose had taken her to the sisters to be looked after, but that must have been five years ago. He had assumed that she was still in service in some distant place since she never came home.

'What do you mean? Where is she? Do you know what she's talkin' about?' he asked Daisy, when Dolores sneered and turned her head away.

'I dunno. We ain't heard from Florrie for years. Not even a Christmas card. She's turned her back on us and who can blame her?' said Daisy, casting a look of loathing at Dolores. She was more concerned about how John was taking this unseemly row. He had taken his plate to the yard door and was looking out with his back

175

to the scene in the kitchen. Oh well, thought Daisy. That's put the kibosh on that! He won't want to come round here no more.

Rose was ruefully viewing the wreck of her parlour when Danny found her. Most of the guests had gone. One snoring drunk was blocking the passage and a few others were slumped against the wall in the porch.

'Look at me piano,' she said to him as he sat down beside her. It stood forlornly skewed across the room, covered in mugs and glasses, beer trickling along the runnel of the lid and dripping on to the floor.

'Never mind. We'll all give a hand to clear up in the mornin'. Rose, Aunt Dolly's just been sayin' something about Florrie being put away. She said you know all about it.'

'Dolly and her big mouth!' said Rose. She closed her eyes wearily. 'Can't we talk about this tomorrow?'

'I just want to know where she is.'

Rose took a breath as though she were about to plunge into cold water. 'She's in Westbury.'

'Westbury? That's that lunatic asylum, ain't it?' He remembered the place from seeing it as a small boy, from the top of a bus when he was taken by his mother to see her sister in Clapham. A long cliff of grey brick, studded with rows of dingy, uniform windows. 'What's she doing there? She ain't a looney.'

'No, I know. But they don't just have looneys. Your Dad had her put in there. Old Tom let the cat out of the bag,' she said, seeing Danny's incomprehension. 'Your father wouldn't have known nothing about it, she could have gone in the convent – they got this place where girls can go, sort of home for fallen women – and come out when it was all over and no one any the wiser. Only

Tom 'ad to go and tell 'im. Thought he had the right to know, or else he was half cut. Anyway, that done it. Mind, he didn't tell 'im till after the baby was born. Florrie was workin' in the convent laundry and your father goes up there, makin' out he wants to bring her 'ome. Only he never.'

'What happened?'

'I don't know, really. I think Florrie must have give 'im a mouthful of cheek. The upshot was, he had her committed. Moral Defective.'

'He can't do that!'

'Oh, yes he can. He done it! Florrie was under age. Nothin' she could do about it. They come and took her away.'

'When is she going to get out?'

'I don't think they let you out of them places, once you go in.'

'But she's over age now. Why don't she just leave?'

'P'raps she can't. Anyway, where would she go?'

Danny pondered this question and the information he got from Rose, though he didn't act on it immediately. It was, after all, his wedding night and for a few weeks he devoted his time to pleasing Kate, painting the larger bedroom in the flat for their use. Rose moved into the small room.

He had been married a month or so when he stopped Daisy as she was about to go upstairs.

'Me and Kate's going to see Florrie on Saturday. Do you want to come?'

They got off the bus and walked along a long, unbroken run of wall, built from the small brown bricks much used in the past century, particularly in the construction of institutions. Danny had come by appointment. He rang a bell in a wooden door within a pair of high, wooden gates and after a few minutes, they were admitted by a man in brown jacket. Daisy had expected a white coat. She followed nervously as they were led through a wide marble hall into an aggressively clean room with two high arched windows looking out on to a quadrangle.

They were left alone and since there was no other furnishing, sat at the straight chairs drawn up to a centre table. In a little while the man returned, held open the door for Florrie, and went out, closing it behind him.

She walked a yard into the room and stopped, a colourless figure in a dark, shapeless dress that hung nearly to the floor, her black hair lank and tied untidily at the back of her head. Danny scraped back his chair and went over to her and kissed her on the cheek.

'Hello Florrie, come and sit down.' He led her to the table. She sat, looking round at them.

'Hello Daisy, I wouldn't have known you,' she said.

'Hello, Florrie. How are you girl?'

'There's no need to whisper,' said Danny.

There was an awkward silence, then Danny took a bar of chocolate from his pocket and gave it to her.

'Here, I remember, you used to like this.'

'Thanks.' She didn't smile, but took the chocolate and put it in a skirt pocket, then took it out again.

'Do you want some?' she offered.

'No thanks,' said Kate. 'You eat it.'

'You look as though you could do with a good meat pudden,' said Daisy. 'What do you do here? Where do you sleep?'

'There's a big dormitory at the back.' She gestured towards the deserted quadrangle. 'I clean mostly, and I help with some of the people they got in here. Wash 'em and dress 'em and that.'

'What, the looneys?'

'Some of 'em are just simple. There are some real nutty ones. You 'ear them sometimes, but we don't go near them. The staff look after them. They're all locked up.'

'Who's we, Florrie? Who else is in here? You got any friends?' Danny wanted to know.

'Some of them are the simple ones, what can still work. There's a few like me. You know, girls who went wrong. Some of them ain't girls anymore. Been in 'ere for years.'

'They don't lock you up then?'

'No. Well, we can't go out, but we can go in the quad sometimes and in the chapel.'

'What about the baby?' Kate asked softly. 'What 'appened to it?'

'He went to be adopted.'

'Do you miss him?'

'I don't let meself think about it. I didn't hardly see him. They take 'em away straight away. The nuns said that was best. I just seen it was a boy. I didn't hold him nor nothin'. Let's 'ope he's gone to someone rich.' She looked down at her hands. 'How did you find out where I was?'

'I asked the priest,' said Danny. 'He found out from the sisters at the convent. Then I wrote asking if we could come and see you.'

'Thanks. It was nice to see you.'

'We ain't going yet. I'm trying to get them to let you come home. Me and Kate's married now. You could come and live with us.'

Florrie shook her head. 'Dad would 'ave to sign a release paper.'

'I know. They told me. I've asked him.'

'And he said no.' She was telling him rather than asking.

'Yes, but I reckon I can make him change his mind.'

'He'll never change 'is mind. Not if you was to knock 'im black and blue.'

'Why not?' asked Daisy.

'Worried about what the neighbours think, I s'pose.'

'Sod what the neighbours think,' said Danny vehemently. 'I ain't finished with him yet.'

The door opened quietly and the man who had escorted them in waited without a word for Florrie to take her leave. She got up at once.

'We'll come and see you again,' said Kate, who was close to tears.

'If you like,' she answered, her face as expressionless as it had been throughout their meeting.

'Ain't you homesick?'

'I don't let meself think about it. Thanks for comin'.' She glanced down at Kate's rounded figure. 'I'm glad you and Danny are together.' She kissed each one in turn, then was gone.

No one spoke until they were standing at the bus stop, when Danny made a sudden outburst, cursing his father for a heartless viper.

'Here! Don't have so much of it!' Daisy was indignant. 'That's my father you're talkin' about.'

'He's mine as well! Gawd knows what our mother would say, seein' Florrie shut away in that place. It would break her heart.'

'Yes, well . . . it's her own fault. She shouldn't have been so bleedin' free hearted.'

'Free hearted? What do you mean?' asked Kate.

'She shouldn't have been quite so willin' to part with it. You know what I mean.'

'Per'aps she couldn't help it. Per'aps he forced her.'

'Forced 'er!' Daisy repeated contemptuously. 'I'd like to see a bloke try that on me. I'd make sure 'e didn't come out of it without a mark. No bugger's going to do that to me.'

Kate said nothing. They finished the journey home in a tense silence.

Chapter 16

Premonition

Daisy was nearly seventeen when she was laid off from her job at the sack factory. As a school-leaver she had rapidly mastered the machinist's skill and was a fast worker, so that with piece work rates of pay, she contributed more to the household budget than Sarah. Dolores was glad of it, except that her Saturdays were more than ever fraught with danger. Knocking-off time was not until five and now that Paddy had got a start in the coal merchant's office, there was no one to head off the debt collectors who liked to call early, before pay-day money was gone.

Notice of dismissal came on a typed slip in the pay packet. Daisy was not the only one. Dozens were laid off at the same time. She dreaded taking the news home almost more than having to go to the Labour Exchange to sign on. Hopes of finding work in other places were faint. Factories were reducing output. People were being laid off everywhere.

Matters were not improved when, two weeks later, Sarah was laid off too. Dolores dealt with the financial crisis by pawning every decent garment the girls had between them, leaving them with hardly a rag to wear. She ranted, wailed and cursed her luck all day without let. She followed Daisy into the scullery one night and stood behind her while she worked at the sink to pour on her more scalding criticism and complaint. Her subject this time was the quality of the meals she prepared.

'Don't be surprised if you come home to bread and marg. There's plenty round 'ere do. You've 'ad a good hot dinner every day of your life, but I can't work bleedin' miracles. How am I supposed to manage on the money you bring in? Your father's got to have meat slammed in front of him the minute he puts 'is foot in the door or there's murder. No good tellin' 'im I'm a bit short this week. He ain't like Jack Carter, put up with a tin o' sardines an' a drop 'o custard for 'is tea. Be more than my life's worth.'

Daisy's eyes glazed over as she tried to blot out the nagging but looked round when it stopped abruptly. Dermot had come in.

'You nearly finished at the sink, Nin? I want to get shaved.'

'Yes, Dad.' She wrung out the underwear she had been washing and moved past Dolores to hang it on the fireguard, but found she was rigidly blocking her path. Her face was set in an expression of apprehension. Without moving, she rolled her eyes towards the open door of the off room. Her meaning flashed upon Daisy at once and she changed track, went into the room and came out shutting the door firmly behind her.

She would have to hang up her smalls later. The sewing machine had gone to pawn so many weeks ago she had grown used to its absence and was becoming careless about keeping the door closed in case Dermot should notice that it was gone. He never had occasion to go into the room and, Dolores had reasoned, so long as the door was kept shut, he need never find out. Dolores relaxed and shot her a look of approval, but hissed in her ear as she passed, 'You get down Tate and Lyle's first thing in the mornin'. See if they're takin' anyone on.'

Most factories started work at eight. By a quarter past, if the gate was shut, it indicated that they were either not taking on any hands for the day, or that they had all they needed. Finding the gates of two or three closed against her, Daisy set off at a run to the canning factory. They had an eight-thirty start, she knew. She might just be in time. She flew along the road with all the speed she had gained with years of hard running but arrived just too late. A group of rejected men stood disconsolately on the kerb opposite. They saw her pant up to the gate and the sag of her shoulders when she found it locked.

'Knock on it,' one called to her. 'They've taken on all the girls that was 'ere. They've only just gone in. Knock on the gate. One of them will let you in.'

Daisy rapped on the gate and heard a bolt being quietly drawn. It opened a few inches and a girl looked out. Seeing Daisy she opened it wide enough to let her slip inside.

'Thanks, mate. Have you been taken on?'

About twenty women and girls stood in the yard. A man at the front was addressing them.

'We got about three weeks work,' said the girl. 'Some big rush order for Christmas, they got.'

'Leave your shoes in the shed,' the man was saying. 'Take a pair of clogs and collect your shoes when you knock off.'

They were led inside. A cavernous room with a stone floor housed a number of huge vats. Daisy took in about a dozen at a glance, in two rows, with large wooden barrels in the spaces between. A wonderfully sweet, sharp smell of citrus fruit hung in the air. The place seemed to be entirely peopled by women except for a couple of men patrolling the vats and another who was continuously hosing the floor.

The forewoman demonstrated what was required of them. They were to work in pairs, each pair to carry between them a large copper pan. They would take it to a vat, which was full of boiling syrup, and hold it while an operator pulled a lever and a stream of syrup, orange and lemon peel gushed into the pan. Lifting together, they were to carry the pan back to the apple barrel which served as a support. Lowering it with all possible care, they were to fit the ridge that ran round the base of the pan into the worn and ragged rim of the barrel.

'Now,' said the woman, when she had her demonstration pan ready, 'this is what you do next.' She took a pair of tongs in her left hand and a wooden bat in her right. With the bat she stirred the molten sugar into a froth.

'That's to stop it crystalising as it cools.' Taking the tongs, she fished out a piece of lemon peel, coated it in the froth and placed it on a wire rack to drain.

'Right. Let's see what you can do.'

Daisy was partnered with a girl called Lizzie. Her dazed expression inspired no confidence in Daisy and the first trip to the vat confirmed her suspicion that she had been paired with an idiot.

'Careful,' said Daisy as the sugar poured out. 'Lift it gently together.' Lizzie tried, but her wrists were skinny and they trembled in the effort. The sugar in the pan swilled dangerously from side to side as they edged

185

sideways to the barrel and, as they lowered it, the ridge did not fit smoothly into place but settled with a jerk. Some of the hot liquid slopped over Daisy's thumb. She was saved from a serious scald by the gloves they had been given, but the pain made her yelp.

'You silly cow! I said lower it together! You do that again and I'll knock your teeth out!'

They improved with practice. The forewoman came along to see how they were progressing.

'Have you made candied peel before?' she asked Daisy.

'No. I ain't done it before. I just watched what you done.'

'You're very good at it.'

The praise pleased Daisy and her pay at the end of the week pleased her even more. Thirty-five shillings. Ten bob more than she got at the sack factory. Nevertheless, she escaped on Saturday afternoon with a feeling of immense relief.

She arrived back at the factory on Monday morning in a black mood. She could not herself account for the intensity of her depression. Dolores had been no worse than usual over the weekend and her early morning chores of clearing the grate and sweeping the kitchen had gone without a hitch.

The men had been at work early and the great vats were brimming, ready for the girls to begin. Daisy worked hard, trying to keep her mind on the job but a sense of foreboding began to take hold of her. She avoided looking at Lizzie. That vacant expression filled her with venomous loathing. She felt an urgent desire to be outside, as though driven by toxic fumes to seek fresh air. The sensation grew steadily throughout the morning until she was in the grip of unreasoning panic. I've got to get out of here, she thought. No matter how she grappled with the fear, her own good sense refused to take command. She felt her heart begin to hammer in her chest. She looked at the syrup swaying in the pan and felt sick. Desperately, she signalled to the forewoman.

'What's the matter?'

'I want you to sign me out.'

'You look all right to me.'

'I ain't saying I'm not well. I just want to get out of 'ere.'

'Why?'

'I don't know why!' Daisy's voice was taking on a hysterical note. 'Just sign me out! I ain't staying 'ere. I've got to get out!'

'All right. All right. I'll give you a note. Don't be surprised if we don't want you in the morning.'

'I don't care!' Daisy snatched the note and bolted for the door.

As soon as the gate closed behind her, the panic vanished. She felt a fool. God knows what Aunt Dolly would say if they didn't let her in in the morning, but for now, she wasn't going to tell her. She followed the route she had often taken as a child when troubled and found herself sitting on the causeway. The reassuring bustle of the river had its tranquillising effect and, by knocking-off time, she was calm and ready to face going home.

Next morning, walking to the factory, she was apprehensive of her reception from the forewoman and from the other girls. She was embarrassed by the scene she had made. Sod 'em, she thought. Let 'em think what they like. She joined the scrum in the shed to change her shoes for clogs and heard the girl next to her whisper to her companion, 'Here she is.'

She bristled, but ignored it. The way Lizzie was looking at her really got on her nerves.

'What are you starin' at?'

Lizzie goggled at her and seemed to be going to reply when the forewoman came up.

'Are you all right this morning?'

'Yes. I'm sorry about yesterday. Something just come over me . . .'

'Don't worry about it. Ain't you heard what happened?'

'No.' Daisy realised that every face was turned towards her and every face wore an awestruck expression.

'What happened?'

'The girl I put in the line to take your place got a pan of boiling sugar all over her. You must have a guardian angel.'

The woman moved on. Lizzie started to speak but was drowned out by a chorus of voices all trying to tell her at once.

'It was awful.'

'Her screams were something terrible.'

'They had to cut the clothes off her before they took her to Poplar Hospital.'

She listened aghast.

'I s'pose it was you that done it.' She turned on Lizzie. 'You never come down nice and smooth with the pan. If you don't move together, it's no wonder the poor cow's copped it.'

'It wasn't my fault! She slipped while we was carryin' it. The floor was slippery. Her feet just went from under her.'

'She got it right in the face and all down her front,' said another girl.

'How is she now?'

'We went down the 'ospital last night but they wouldn't let no one see her. I reckon it's touch and go.'

'She ain't gonna have much of a face left, poor cow. Might be better if she does die.'

The accident had halted production for the afternoon. Daisy noticed that the floor had been scrupulously scrubbed and that another man with a second hose now worked ceaselessly to keep split syrup from congealing underfoot.

The news was shattering. Soberly, they worked through the rest of the day. Lizzie seemed to have cottoned on to the idea of moving in unison and for the two weeks that remained of the assignment, there were no more incidents.

The money from making candied peel came in time to provide a few comforts for Christmas but, since Sarah still had not managed to find work, had to be stretched as far as possible. Dolores directed that buying the 'oven buster' she planned to have for Christmas dinner should be left until the last minute. On Christmas Eve Daisy cleaned the house, prepared vegetables, then caught a late bus to Chrisp Street.

It was still crowded with shoppers. Stalls selling fruit, holly and mistletoe had been stripped of their wares, but butchers were desperately trying to rid themselves of remaining stock before the holiday began.

Daisy wandered along, enjoying the excitement and sense of carnival. She bought a small black rag doll dressed in brown velvet dungarees for Danny's baby daughter. She was in no hurry. She stopped at a china stall to listen to the lively exchange taking place between the costermonger and a woman trying to beat him down on the price of a big china jug.

'I can't knock it down no more, missus. What'll my old woman say? You should see what she done to me last week. Look. See this?' He snatched off his cap and displayed a cauliflower ear. 'It's shocking!'

'Yeah?' yelled the woman. 'What would shock you would turn a shit cart over!'

Daisy joined in the laughter. Farther on she joined the women ringing the butcher's stall like a pack of hyenas waiting for a stricken beast to breathe its last.

The stall-holder's banter had become a desperate pleading, but the women stood impassively waiting, knowing that he must close at midnight and prices would come tumbling down.

'Come on, gals,' he cried over and over again. 'Ain't you got any homes to go to?'

He began knocking shillings off the price of turkeys and chickens, flinging them unwrapped at the bidders. At five to twelve, those who stuck out the war of nerves to the end were rewarded. The circle of patient onlookers became a scrum as the last of the meat was sold off for a few pence. Daisy bagged her leg of pork and was lugging it to the bus stop when someone caught her by the elbow.

'Hello Daisy.'

John Fletcher took the bag from her. 'Here, I'll carry that for you. We're going the same way.'

Astonishment crossed his face when he felt the weight. 'What you got in there? How many are you going to be feeding?'

'Oh, we don't like echoes in our larder,' said Daisy. 'What you doing here?'

'I come up to see if I could get me Mum a puppy for Christmas. I've been up Club Row but I couldn't see one like she wants.'

'What sort does she want?'

'She's seen that dog in the Keystone Cops. She wants one like that. With a patch over one eye.'

'Shame you couldn't get it.'

'I have got it. They had one in that shop on the corner.'

'Where is it then?'

'In me inside pocket.'

John put the bag down on the pavement and, like a conjurer producing a rabbit, took a tiny black and white puppy from under his coat. It trembled miserably in his cupped hands.

'Oh! The poor little thing. You can't put 'im in your pocket, he'll suffocate. I'll carry 'im.'

'Go on, then. I didn't know you was so soft.' He handed the puppy over, surprised to see the tears that had sprung to Daisy's eyes. She laid it against her shoulder and covered it with a fold of her scarf.

'It's cruel! Poor little sod's too young to leave 'is mother.'

'Mind he don't pee down your neck.'

John boarded a number 56 bus with her.

'You want the 57 don't you?' asked Daisy. That bus took the route down the other side of the horseshoe that formed the island.

'It's all right. I'll carry this 'ome for you. I'm not likely to get a bridger this time o' night. You're not going to mass tonight then?' he asked, when they were settled in their seats.

'It's too late now. Besides, I'll have to be up early to get the fire alight. This is going to take all day to cook. I like to do it slow.' She looked ahead with relish to the smell of roasting pork wafting through the flat. 'My Dad likes the cracklin' just right.'

In the porch Daisy handed over the snoozing puppy. John hesitated as he passed back her shopping bag.

'Do you fancy going to the pictures one night?' He waited in suspense. She took a long time answering, considering how she would square it with Dermot. She would think of something.

'Yeah, thanks. I'd like to. When?'

'Saturday night? I'll call for you.'

'No. I'd better meet you outside. Seven o'clock?'

'Right.'

He kissed her on the cheek. 'Happy Christmas, Daisy.'

Chapter 17

Dolores Out

Disbelief numbed Daisy's brain. Her hands and feet were already devoid of feeling, frozen by the bitter January wind that lashed the line of workless people as they waited outside the Labour Exchange. On every other morning that week, she had walked from Millwall to Bow trying to get taken on, even for a day's casual work, but her efforts had yielded nothing. Now, when her turn had come at last to receive her dole, she had to ask the clerk to repeat what he had said.

'Money stopped.'

'What for?'

'Not genuinely seeking work.'

'But what about me lodgin' money?'

Dolores took fifteen shillings every week for board and lodging. There would be hell to pay if she went home without it.

'Money stopped. I'm sorry.'

'You ain't bleedin' sorry! I've got nothin' to get through the week! I'm entitled to me lodgin' money!'

The clerk raised his hand and a policeman stepped forward to take her arm and steer her away.

'Come on, love, don't make a fuss.'

The next applicant stepped forward to take her place.

No time was given for hearing arguments. She turned to shout over her shoulder as she was hustled along, past the queue of grey, dead faces that stretched to the door and out into the street.

That was where she found herself a moment later.

'It's all right for you,' she called after the policeman. 'You've got a job and a screw at the end of the week.'

Choking anger rose in her throat. She pressed her lips together hard to stop the gush of tears.

'Money stopped, love?' asked a woman in the queue. Daisy nodded and wiped her eyes on her sleeve.

'Go down the RO. They might give you something.'

'Yeah. Looks like I'll 'ave to.'

Pleading for charity was not a prospect to relish. It could take days if the matter was referred to a 'Board of Guardians'. In the meantime, she had three ha'pence in her pocket and no lodging money; but, as she could think of no other strategy, she set out to trudge to the Town Hall. She didn't think Dermot would let Dolores chuck her out, but the degradation was hard to bear. That morning Paddy had given her a bob for a sandwich. The gesture had made her cry. Hard knocks she could take. Kindness was harder to deal with.

While she was waiting to see the Relieving Officer, she thought she would enquire about a job scrubbing floors in the workhouse. She had been tipped off about it the night before and it had been her intention to go there after drawing the dole. She approached a woman sitting at a desk outside the RO's door, a smart woman, neatly dressed in quiet but good quality tweed. Daisy took in the pearl earrings and the brooch pinned to the lapel. A charity worker: one of those who knew all the answers to problems she could know nothing about. It was stamped all over her. The woman looked up, her expression kindly enough.

'Do you know anything about the cleaning job down Poplar workhouse?' asked Daisy.

'I'm afraid I don't.' The woman looked her over. 'You don't want to do scrubbing for a living, do you?'

'It's the money I'm interested in. Three pound a week I was told. That's as good as a man gets.'

'You're young and you look like a bright girl. Have you heard about the scheme to help young people to emigrate? The government are helping people like you to go to Canada; free and assisted passages. Why don't you think about it? There's a golden opportunity for a girl like you in Canada.'

'Look, missus,' said Daisy, 'all I want is me lodgin' money, not a trip round the bleedin' world.'

'But you really ought to think it over. You might not get a chance like this again. It really is a marvellous scheme.'

'If it's so bleedin' marvellous, what are you doing still sittin' there? Why ain't you in effing Canada?'

The woman blanched. She got up, tapped on the RO's door and went inside. That's buggered that, thought Daisy. I ain't gonna get no money now. But the woman returned with a note and handed it to Daisy. She was to take it back to the Labour Exchange and give it to the clerk. It was an instruction to give her money.

Having no work meant Daisy was free to be deployed in the porch on Saturday afternoons to meet the tallymen. As soon as Dermot got home, Dolores, with the merest motion of her head, sent her to keep guard. Some of the men were paid. When the money was gone, those that came after had to be told to call again. At all costs, they had to be prevented from knocking at the door.

She idled away the time between callers playing with Danny's baby who was taking an airing in her pram. Kate popped in and out to check on her daughter and to chat, but by the end of the afternoon Daisy was bored. She was stiff from sitting on the stairs and cold. She brightened when Danny came home from his work in the dock. He always gave her a warm greeting. They had been talking for a minute or two, when a sudden and violent uproar broke from the flat upstairs. Daisy shot Danny an imploring look, but he shrugged, picked up the baby and went into his own house.

She raced up the stairs two at a time and into the kitchen. Chairs and the table were overturned. Paddy was shouting at Dermot to leave Dolores alone. Sarah had hold of her father's belt, trying to drag him away, but she might have been an infant for all the effect she had. Dolores was on her knees, her head dragged back by the handful of hair he grasped in one hand, while he smashed punches to her face with the other.

Dolores was too fat to defend herself. Her short arms flailed and she cried out with every blow, but she could reach neither his hammering fist nor his pity.

'No more, Dad. She's had enough,' Daisy implored him, but Dermot didn't seem to hear. He went on, putting all his strength into the beating, sometimes kneeing her in the back, until he felt her sag and go limp. When he released his grip on her, she sank face down to the floor. He stood over her panting, then stooped to pick up the poker.

'I might as well finish her off,' he said, raising the knobbed handle above his head.

'No! Dad, don't!' Paddy caught his father's arm. 'You'll hang for it and she's not worth it!'

Dolores rallied. She raised her head an inch from the floor to gasp, 'You're all men and women now. Your turn's done!'

Dermot hesitated, then flung the poker back in the hearth. He righted his armchair and sank into it, breathing hard.

'All right. But out she goes! Now! I ain't 'avin' her in this house another night!'

'Oh, Dad!' said Sarah. 'She's ain't got nowhere else to go.'

'She should have thought o' that before.' He got to his feet. 'I'm going down the Feathers. If she's 'ere when I get back, I'll kill her.' He stood menacingly over Dolores and glowered down at her. 'And if I see you in the street, so help me, I'll stove your head in.' He lumbered from the room.

'What the 'ell started that?' asked Daisy, as she and Sarah helped Dolores to a chair.

'He went in the orf room lookin' for you and seen that the sewing machine was gone.'

'Oh blimey! Couldn't you have stopped 'im?'

'How could I? You know what he's like if he can't see you around.'

They washed Dolores' face and gave her tea. Sarah brought the brush and tried to tidy the tangled mass of her hair, but she whimpered with pain. She looked suddenly old and ill. The defiance had gone. She sat very still, then roused herself.

'Sarah, will you help me put me things in a bag?'

'What you gonna do?' Sarah was distressed.

'I'll sleep in the doorway tonight. See about gettin'

somethin' tomorrer. Orf the island, if I can.' She tried to get to her feet, but collapsed back into the chair, her lips blue in her swollen face.

'You stay there. We'll get your things together. Paddy, you got any money?'

'Yeah, I got a couple of bob.'

'I ain't got none,' said Daisy.

'I can give you some,' said Sarah. 'We'll see if we can get you lodgings somewhere. I'll come with you.'

They put her clothes into a bag. Daisy wrapped the remains of the boiled bacon they had had for dinner in a tea-towel and stuffed it in the bag and she was ready. Paddy and Daisy stood at the top of the stairs watching while Sarah helped her slowly and painfully to descend. Pity wrung Daisy's heart. 'Don't worry,' she called after her. 'We'll bring you some grub. We'll see you're all right.'

Dolores stopped and turned a face full of fear towards her. 'Don't let your father know where I am.'

She shuffled across the porch and was gone.

'She don't realise I said that about her not being worth it, to stop him killin' 'er,' said Paddy.

'She don't realise nothin', poor old cow,' said Daisy.

As she had so many times before, Daisy restored order, righting the chairs, propping up the table, feeling a strange sense of unreality. Aunt Dolly was really gone, yet the essence of her seemed to cling to the house, so that it was still a surprise not to meet her in the passage or find her in the scullery. Dermot had thrown her out many times but had always let her back in. This time was different. She had looked somehow defeated as she crept away, the defiance finally gone. She had taken her last beating.

Daisy had arranged to meet John outside the cinema. She wished she didn't have to go, feeling as she was, drained and depressed, but there was no way to let him know, so she washed and got ready to go out. Sarah came in as she stood in front of the looking glass, combing her hair.

'Did you get her in somewhere?'

'Yes. Dock Cottages. She's got a room for five bob a week. Don't tell Dad. She's terrified he'll find out and go round to do her in. I'll go round and see her tomorrer. She ain't well. He's really knocked the stuffin' out of 'er this time. I said you'd go Monday. Well, you ain't workin'. You ain't going out are you?'

'Yes, I'm going out with a couple of the girls from the sack place. There's a Charlie Chaplin picture on.'

'What about Dad's stout?'

'Oh! Can't you get it for once? I don't want to miss the end of the picture.'

'I'm going out meself. I ain't stayin 'ere. I'm going round Colour's house.'

'It's all right,' said Paddy. 'I'll go for the stout. Only for Christ's sake don't be late home. Either of you. We don't want to start 'im off again.'

'If you're going to be on your own with 'im, you might tell 'im about some of the talleymen comin' round. That's if he's not too drunk. He's going to 'ave to be told,' Daisy suggested.

'Oh blimey! No! Not me. You tell 'im – he might take it from you. Only make sure I'm out of the house when you do.'

'Oh, all right. I'll see if I can catch 'im in a good mood. Tell 'im I won't be long.'

*

John paid for the pictures. Daisy flopped into the cramped, lumpy seat, glad to rest her legs after the sprint from Bermuda Street. Her mind was churning but the lights dimmed, the screen leaped into life and she was soon absorbed. John sat beside her without touching her, embarrassed by the couples around them quite openly cuddling. He didn't attempt to put his arm round Daisy.

There was a lot of noise. Laughter, jangling piano music and a constant murmur of voices as poor readers among the audience spoke aloud the subtitles. Few managed to get to the end of a text before the next was flashed up, and John, whose own eye skimmed each line with ease, was finding it hard to concentrate. It was intensely irritating. Daisy enjoyed the Chaplin film hugely, laughing loudly, rocking in her seat. John's own laughter was more restrained, coming in small explosive bursts from between closed lips.

Action in the second film purported to take place in Limehouse, which brought howls of derision. Daisy joined in the shouts.

'That ain't Lime'ouse. Nothin' like it!'

'Take it orf! We seen it!'

John said nothing. There followed a scene in which a pretty, frail young girl locked herself in a shabby room to escape her drunken father who was intent on beating her senseless. The protecting door began to splinter under blows from the father's axe while the girl wrung her hands and paced desperately to and fro. It was too much for Daisy. She gripped the arms of the chair, leant forward and bawled at the top of her voice, 'Leave 'er alone, you rotten bully. Pick on someone your own size!' John was mortified. He slid his hand across to Daisy's thigh and pinched her hard. He had hoped to silence her, but her scream rang loud and shrill, above the voices around her.

John shrank back, trying to get his jacket to swallow him as heads turned to look at them. A minute later, a burly attendant was flashing a torch in his eyes.

'Oy! You! Out of it!'

Wishing to die, he got up and edged past the line of knees to the end of the row where he was seized by the scruff of the neck and frog-marched to the exit. Daisy grabbed her bag and rushed after him.

'What did you go and pinch me for?' she demanded, when they were in the street.

'I don't like you showin' me up like that.' John's face was scarlet.

'Showin' you up? I wasn't showin' you up.'

'Yes you was. Shoutin' and bawlin'. What would people think?'

'Who gives a sod what they think?'

'I do. I can't stick people makin' scenes in public.'

He strode off towards the bus stop, Daisy trotting to try to keep up. He didn't speak as they rumbled home. Daisy tried to ease the tension by telling him about her encounter with the woman outside the Relieving Officer's door. She thought it might make him laugh.

'She says to me, "There's a golden opportunity for a girl like you in Canada." One way to get rid of the out-of-works, I s'pose. Bung 'em all on a boat. I told 'er where she could go. Still, it makes you think. Maybe it wouldn't be a bad idea. There ain't much prospect for the likes of us here.'

John made a monosyllabic reply. He didn't laugh or even smile. She tried again.

'Would you go to Canada or Australia, if you got the chance? If they paid your fare?'

'No.' He seemed quite definite about it.

'Why not?'

He turned to look at her then. 'Because,' he said fiercely, 'I'm English, and England is where I want to be.'

'Ain't you s'posed to say "British"?'

'No. I got nothin' against foreigners, but I'm English, and I wouldn't want to be anything else!'

Daisy fell into a rather shocked silence, considering this entirely novel concept. Proud to be anything other than Irish? Glad to be English! She wanted to discuss it, but his head was turned away, his eyes on the grim brick of the dock wall running endlessly past the window. She gave up.

'You don't have to see me 'ome,' she said stiffly when they reached the stop.

'I got to go down your road anyway, ain't I? Now I've come on this bus.'

At the porch he said goodnight. There was no kiss on the cheek. Daisy looked after him, drew a long, shuddering breath and went miserably up the stairs. She didn't see John come back and stand listening under the window, checking that she was not in trouble with Dermot, before he stepped out for home.

Chapter 18

Curses

A week after Dolores left, Daisy called to see her. Her room, opening off a dark passage on the ground floor of a terraced cottage, was tiny. There was just enough room for a single bed, a chair and a washstand. Dolores was sitting on the bed, her hair hanging in one loose plait over her shoulder, bruises from the beating turning purple and green at the edges.

'I brought you some tea and sugar and a bit of pork pie,' said Daisy, looking round. 'Ain't yer got nowhere to make a cup o' tea? No gas stove?'

'I can use the landlady's kitchen, but she's been bringin' me tea. I ain't been able to get about much. By the time I been out the back a couple of times, that's me finished. '

'You'll soon shake it off. You always do.'

'What else you got me?'

'Just a bit o' bread. That's all I could manage.'

'No cribbins?'

Daisy flushed with annoyance. The selfish old cow knew she was out of work and taking a risk by coming here. It was time she understood, once and for all that she would no longer stand by and see her father deceived. She looked Dolores steadily in the eye.

'No. And there ain't gonna be any cribbins. You've robbed my father blind for years and I ain't doin' it. Soon as I can, I'm gonna get everything straight – when I get a job. Get a bit of decent home round us. You might as well get something straight. I ain't tellin' 'im no more lies for you!'

'You mare!' Dolores tried to get up, but sank down again, her breathing laboured. 'You wouldn't say that to me if I wasn't laid up. You're all grown up now. Got no time for me.'

'I'm 'ere ain't I?'

'How am I s'posed to get on for rent?'

'Sarah's workin'. She'll help out. Or you'll just 'ave to go down the RO.'

Dolores gave a snort of contempt. 'I can't get to the bleedin' door, let alone down the RO.'

'Well I ain't robbin' Dad, and that's flat.'

'I'll pay you back! Don't think I can't. I can still curse you!'

'You shouldn't curse no one. It's wicked!'

'I do curse you, you unfeelin' cow!' Dolores' dark eyes flashed with the fire of hatred. She spoke in a low, menacing voice, spitting the words with venom. 'May you melt away like the froth on the river! May you get run down by the first 'orse that comes along! May Gawd blind yer for turnin' your back on me!'

Daisy didn't wait to hear more. She was surprised that Dolores could still shock her. Her knees felt weak and she was trembling. It was dark in the street, with a mist rolling in from the river. Suppose she did have the power to curse people? Suppose I do go blind? Shut up, you silly cow! She tried to get a grip on herself, but hadn't there always been something a bit creepy about

Aunt Dolly? She'd always been very friendly with that gypsy down hopping. He could have taught her a few tricks.

She reached a wider, well-lit road and felt a little better. She hurried along the narrow pavement, keeping close to the wall. She neared the place where the pavement was interrupted in front of the fire station doors. As she stepped off the kerb the doors were suddenly flung open. She drew back.

A bell clanged and the fire engine pulled by two large horses tore out of the yard, their hooves slipping and clattering on the cobbles as they turned tightly into the street. Excited by the mad clamour of the bell, the horses were whinnying and snorting, their eyes and nostrils wide with fear. Firemen were clinging to the side and the driver cracked a whip, urging the horses to pick up speed. One nearside wheel mounted the kerb and rolled over the hem of Daisy's skirt as she crouched against the wall, her arms over her face.

Daisy had tried to muster the courage to tell her father about the debts, but in the rare moments when he was at home sober he seemed preoccupied and ill at ease, as though he too found it hard to get used to Dolores' absence. Then she had a stroke of luck which forced her hand. The sack factory took on a handful of girls and the foreman chose her from among the hopeful crowd at the gate, remembering her as a fast, skilled worker. With Dolores gone, and Sarah working, there was no one at home during the day to intercept the notices to quit which came regularly by the second post on Fridays, or to head off the talleymen. He had to be told.

She warned Paddy and Sarah that she would break

the news after tea on Sunday, so that they could make sure they were out of the way. The moment had to be picked with care: before he fell asleep and after his stomach was filled.

'Dad. There's a talleyman comes tomorrow.'

'What talleyman? What for?'

'Aunt Dolly was gettin' some things on tick. Clothes and that.'

Dermot pushed his chair back from the table and stood up angrily. Daisy cringed, thinking he might hit her.

'Where'd she get the money?'

'Pawnin' things, mostly. My stuff and Sarah's. Not yours, much. There's some more comes Saturday,' she added, taking quick advantage of the pause in which Dermot appeared to be knocked speechless.

'Look, you might as well know the lot. Here, 'ave a look at this.' She took the teapot brimming with dockets and pawn tickets from the sideboard and plonked it in front of him. Dermot sat down hard. Daisy stood silently behind him, biting her lip, while he went through them. It took him some time. When he had finished he looked sick and shaken.

'Why didn't you tell me? I'd have killed the mare.'

'Well. You've answered your own question, ain't yer? Thing is, what we gonna do? I can't keep on tellin' 'em "Not today".'

'I'll lose a day's work. See these blokes. I ain't payin' for this lot. I ain't responsible for 'er debts. You tell any more that come to the door that she's gone and we don't know where she is.'

'If you'll 'elp me,' said Daisy, putting into action the second part of the strategy she had been rehearsing all week, 'I'll try and get the stuff out of pawn, bit by bit.' She began sorting the tickets into date order. 'I'll start with the ones that's been in longest. Now I'm workin' we can get ourselves straightened out.'

Dermot took a day off and cleared the talleymen from the door. He handed over the housekeeping money to Daisy. The landlord was astonished when he hammered on the door on Thursday to have Kate pop out of the bottom flat and give him the rent, plus a little off the arrears.

A good many of the clothes in pawn belonged to Sarah but she was not keen to hand over money to redeem them. She was still smarting over Dolores' eviction.

'That's right!' she said. 'I've paid for 'em once.'

'Well, you can have the tickets for your stuff,' said Daisy. 'I don't see why I should get it for you.'

She grudgingly agreed, knowing it was cheaper than buying new. Gradually, over the next few months, the house took on a more comfortable look. Goods coming in, rather than draining out. Daisy was happy. John had asked her out again and there were no fights; until Dermot came home from The Feathers one Friday and found on the table, a parcel that Sarah had just collected from the pawnbrokers. He picked it up and read what was written on the label.

'Miss S. O'Lambert. Who's Miss S. O'Lambert?'

'That's mine,' said Sarah. 'I just got it out of pawn.'

'Your name's Cavanagh, not O' bleedin' Lambert. That's Dolly's name! I don't want to 'ear that name mentioned in this 'ouse!'

'They must 'ave made a mistake in the pawn shop. Thought I was 'er daughter.'

'And you never put 'em right.'

'I didn't know about it!'

'Don't tell me bloody lies!' Dermot's face was growing dangerously flushed. 'You're belyin' your own dead mother! Lettin' people think that fat cow was yer mother! And what about me?' He had his face close to Sarah's, bellowing. 'My name's Cavanagh! I'm your father, in case you've forgot! Ain't I good enough for yer?'

Sarah stood her ground as long as she could, not lowering her eyes, until her courage gave out and she shrank away.

'Nothin' to say? Well, I'll tell you this. If Cavanagh's not good enough for you, you can get out of my house! As quick as you like. Go on! Sling your 'ook!'

Sarah ran to the bedroom she had occupied alone since Dolores departed. Daisy found her there sobbing as she stuffed clothes into a pillow case.

'Go and wait out in the yard,' Daisy whispered. 'He'll be goin' out soon. You can 'ave your tea. You've paid for it. I'll talk 'im round when 'e comes back.'

'No. That's it! I've 'ad enough of that bastard. Aunt Dolly'll let me share with 'er.'

'She ain't got no room. There's only a single bed.'

'Well, I'll go round Colour's house.'

'Oh you don't want to go there!'

'Don't I? Anywhere's better than this hole! You want to watch out Daisy. You'll be next. He'll let you stay as long as it suits 'im, then you'll be out an all. He'll get rid of Paddy first, then you.'

'No, he won't.'

'Please yerself. Only if I was you, I'd clear out of here, before he chucks you out. I'm going to Aunt Dolly's.' Still snuffling, she picked up her bundle and left, slamming the front door with all her force as she went.

Sarah's going upset Daisy deeply, though it could not spoil her pleasure in the improvements taking place in the house. Dermot repossessed the bedroom after painting it and Paddy moved from the sofa to the folding bed in the parlour. Daisy herself enjoyed the splendour of having the 'orf' room all to herself. Dermot didn't notice Daisy was upset by Sarah's leaving and it didn't occur to her to question the laws he laid down, nor would she have dared.

Going to the sack factory and working with her old mates was a compensation. The work did not demand total concentration and the chatter and laughter that could be heard above the roar of the machines was tolerated by the management. It was good not to wake on Monday morning with a sinking dread. Daisy looked forward to going.

At lunch-time Daisy, her particular friend Mary, and a couple of others, having hardly a cent between them, wandered into the hat shop in search of amusement. They held their faces straight, so that the shopkeeper had to keep a rein on her suspicions, aroused by their unnaturally decorous behaviour.

They sat in a row in front of the mirrors, passing each other hats to try on. They paid each other lavish compliments and discussed how a hat might be improved by the addition of a few more feathers to hide the face, or a brim to dip over a mutton eye.

'Ooh!' said Daisy to Mary. 'That 'at really suits you. What with that veil an all, you can't see you've got one blue eye and a brown 'un.'

'Do you think so? 'Ow much is it?' Mary looked at the price tag and tossed the hat on to the pile of others they had discarded. 'No. I don't think so. Cheap gear don't do nothin' for me looks.'

They got outside and exploded with laughter, leaning against the wall and doubling over.

'I'm hungry,' said Daisy when she could draw breath. 'Let's go to Sid's and get some saveloys.'

They went into the grocer's shop they favoured for their lunch-time food. They had to wait to be served while a slow-spoken woman sent Sid ambling from shelf to shelf. In the periphery of her vision, Daisy saw one of her companions take a long German sausage and hide it under her jumper. She kept her eyes to the front. Poor sod. That must be intended for her family. They were stony broke.

Mary must have seen the theft, too. In the afternoon, she looked up from her machine and, winking at Daisy, called above the clatter: 'I just seen old Sid go in the office.'

'Oh my Gawd!' The girl paled. 'He must 'ave come about the bleedin' sausage! Here, quick, help me with this!' She took out the sausage and broke it into chunks, tossing a piece to every girl around the bench. 'For Gawd's sake, get rid of it!'

They stuffed their mouths and chewed as fast as they could, but there were still six or seven inches of sausage remaining.

The girl ran with it to the lavatory, threw it down the pan and pulled the chain.

'Oh no!' she whimpered as it bobbed back to the surface.

'Don't worry.' She looked round to see her mates grinning in the doorway. 'Sid'll think it's a turd!'

At the end of the shift, Daisy was crossing the waste ground in front of the factory, noticing with pleasure that the evenings were getting lighter, when she was surprised to see Sarah waiting for her.

'Hello! What you doin' 'ere? You ain't lost your job again?'

'No. I lost a day's work. Aunt Dolly's queer.'

'Well, what do you want me to do? I ain't goin' near her.'

'She's real bad, Daisy. I had the doctor. He said she ain't gonna last more than three or four days.'

'Blimey. That's a bit sudden, ain't it? You said she was all right last time I see yer.'

'She ain't been too bad this last couple of weeks. Mind, she never really got over that last bashin' the old man give 'er. But she's been goin' out. I give 'er the money to go to the pictures on Saturday. She likes Rudolph Valentino. Only when she come out, she see him in the street. Dad, I mean. It really put the wind up her. He never seen her, but it didn't half give 'er a shock.'

'I'll bet it did.'

'She ain't been able to get out of bed ever since. The doctor said she's had a stroke. I can't understand what she's sayin' an' she gets so ratty. She wants something and I don't know what it is. Would you come round and see 'er?'

'Yeah. Course I will. I'll 'ave to nip home and give Dad 'is tea. I got stew and dumplins doing slow on the back of the stove. That'll sweeten 'im up. I'll tell 'im I'm goin' round to see Mary. I'll come as quick as I can.'

It was easier to escape Dermot than she had anticipated. He wanted her to run to Poplar High Street with his betting slip for the dog racing. It meant a delay, but she skuttled along as fast as she could, arriving breathless at Sarah and Dolores' lodging at about nine-thirty.

Sarah opened the door to her tap.

'She's been watchin' the door ever since I told 'er you was comin'.'

'I'd 'ave been here before, but Dad sent me up the High Street. Blimey!' she whispered as she saw Dolores, 'What's the matter with 'er face?'

'That's the stroke done that. Left it all lopsided. She can't move 'er left hand, neither.'

Daisy crossed to the bed. Dolores watched her coming, recognition – and was it pleasure – in her eyes? She whispered something that Daisy could not catch and she bent her head lower. The sound was unintelligible, but she was looking earnestly into Daisy's face, then beyond her towards the foot of the bed.

'You want something at the foot of the bed?'

A small hissing sound, then the right hand came up and wavered towards Daisy's face. Slowly and gently, she traced a circle round her eye.

'You want me to wipe your eyes?'

The eyes closed in assent. Daisy looked around and found what Dolores wanted, a piece of white cloth hanging over the rail at the foot of the bed. She took it and carefully dried her eyes, then tucked the cloth into the good hand. Dolores' fingers closed tightly round her own and held them. The eyes closed again in thanks. After a minute, the breathing deepened and she seemed to sleep.

'I'll nip home,' Daisy whispered to Sarah. 'I can't leave you by yerself with this lot. I'll tell Dad I'm stayin' 'ere with you tonight.'

'S'pose he comes round 'ere?'

'He won't. Not if I tell 'im how things are.'

'I tell you what. You stay here, an' I'll go. I'll get

Danny to tell 'im. Better you sit with her than me. You can understand her. I won't be long.'

Sarah's footsteps ran along the street and Daisy was alone with Dolores, her rasping breathing the only sound in the room. Where had Sarah been sleeping? Daisy wondered. Then her foot came against a rolled blanket under the bed. She had no idea of the time; there was no clock in the room. Her back grew stiff. She tried to ease her hand from Dolores' clasp so that she could shift her position, but the movement roused her. She moaned and Daisy held still.

Sarah had been gone an age. She rested her head on the edge of the bed and tried to sleep. She wasn't sure if she had drifted off or not, but she raised her head, aware that something was different. Dolores' breathing had changed. It was shallower, her breaths coming at longer intervals. She watched, trying to time them. Several times she thought the last had come, when another came, deep and sighing. Daisy waited, holding her own breath. The chest rose and fell once more, then nothing. Dolores hadn't drawn breath for a full minute when Sarah came quietly back into the room. Daisy looked at her and shook her head.

'She's gone,' she said.

Chapter 19

Mistress

Daisy shook John's arm for the tenth time in half an hour.

'What's the time?' she whispered.

'I told you just now. It's only 'alf past nine.'

'I'll 'ave to go.'

'Just let me see this bit.' They were watching the last reel. The hero was galloping, guns blazing, down a dirt road.

'Come on, that's the third time I seen 'im go past that bush.'

'Shh!' Voices hissed at her out of the darkness.

'In a minute!'

'Well, you stay if you want. I got to go. The old man'll kill me if I get there after the pub shuts.' She got up and edged her way to the end of the row. John followed, stumbling, trying to keep his feet while his eyes were clamped to the screen.

Outside, in a thin drizzle, he turned up his coat collar and grumbled, 'We never see the end of a picture. Specially when it's a cowboy. Different when that girl was tied to the railway lines. You had to stop to see the end then.'

'Yeah. And I got into plenty of hot water. I had to tell

'im I stopped to watch a fight outside Charlie Brown's. If me Dad don't get his stout from the Jug and Bottle last thing, it puts 'im in a bad mood for days.'

'Why can't 'e get it himself?'

' 'Cause he just don't believe in gettin' it 'imself.' Daisy shot John a withering look. The idea was outrageous. What sort of man could his father be? 'Come on, or we'll miss the bus.'

The bus came into sight at that moment and they joined hands and pelted for the bus stop, but they were too late. It accelerated away before they got there.

'Oh Christ! Now I'll be for it!'

'No, you won't. Look! There's a five-two-five! He might stop for us!' Hurtling round the bend came a red double decker. It raced towards them and would have passed without stopping had John not stood in front waving his arms. It screeched to a stop and was off again when they had barely had time to climb aboard.

Pirate buses tended to be favoured by young people and avoided by the old. Rides could be hair raising. Daisy loved them. She clung to the seat in front, laughing as they were thrown from side to side in the break-neck race to pass the bus in front and reach the passengers at the next stop first. She could be fairly sure of getting to The Jug and Bottle in time.

The stop at the end of Bermuda Street came into sight and Daisy got up, ready to make the perilous journey to the platform at the back, ready to alight.

'I'll see you Saturday,' she told John through rattling teeth, clinging on with both hands and bracing her legs as the bus swayed and bumped madly over the cobbles.

'I'll get off with you, in case there's any trouble.'

'You don't 'ave to,' she shouted, but debate was difficult in these conditions. John struggled to the exit and leapt off with her before their conveyance catapulted away. She didn't know what John could do about it if there was trouble waiting; she'd most likely have to protect him. But it was comforting to have him loping along beside her.

All was quiet when they reached the blocks.

'Go and get the jug. I'll come with you to get the stout, if you like,' said John. He waited in the porch while Daisy ran lightly up the stairs.

Dermot was relaxed in his chair by the range, reading his *Racing World*. He seemed unusually affable.

'Hello, Nin. Good picture?'

'No. It was a cowboy. I don't like them much. I like a good laugh. I'll get the jug and go for your stout.'

'It's all right. Mrs Carter got it for me.'

Daisy stopped in her track to the scullery, astonished, 'Annie Carter?'

'Yes. She come in to see if you'd like a few eggs. Got a bit of a glut. She was going down the corner anyway, so she said she'd get me stout.'

It was very odd. The Carters had kept chickens in the yard for years and had never offered eggs before, as far as she knew. Perhaps she had, and Aunt Dolly had never mentioned it. Daisy shrugged it off. She was concerned now, about how to get out to tell John that she didn't have to fetch the stout. She took the coal scuttle and went to the little front room to refill it, hoping she might signal from the window, but he was still waiting for her inside the porch. She brought the scuttle back and turned for the door again. Dermot looked up.

'Where you going now?'

'Out the back.'

'Oh.' He settled back, but he watched her suspiciously. She had just reached the room door when there was a knock on the front door.

'Who the hell's that?'

'Dunno. I'll go and see.'

'You stop 'ere. I'll go. Could be anyone this time o' night.' Dermot threw down the paper and got out of his chair. Oh! God Help us! Daisy prayed and closed her eyes as Dermot opened the door. John stood there.

'Evenin', Mr Cavanagh. Is Daisy there?'

'Who wants to know?'

'I'm John Fletcher. I just want to ask her something.'

'Try askin' me first.' Dermot's jaw was jutting belligerently, but Daisy appeared beside him.

'Hello Daisy,' said John. 'You all right?' She nodded dumbly. 'I wondered if you want to come for a tram ride Sunday?'

'Where to?' growled Dermot.

'Oh. Up Blackheath. Just for a walk. We might 'ave a cuppa tea out somewhere.'

'Yeah, thanks,' said Daisy. 'I'll see you then.' She started to close the door.

'Wait a minute.' Dermot stopped her. 'Don't you want to make arrangements? You'd better see the young man to the foot of the stairs. Only don't be long. Just a couple of minutes.'

'What did you do that for?' Daisy dragged John into the sheltering nook of Danny's doorway away from Dermot's line of sight.

'Well, when you didn't come out, I thought he was cuttin' up rough. I couldn't 'ear nothin'. It was all quiet and I got worried.'

'You'd 'ave heard 'im all right, don't you worry. You and the rest of the street. It's a wonder he didn't choke the life out of you!'

'I'm a bit too quick on me feet for that. An' a bit too fly. One good punch in the middle of his pot belly, I reckon that would take some of the fight out of 'im.'

'You wouldn't try an' hit my Dad?'

'As a rule I wouldn't, no. But I ain't gonna stand by doin nothin' while he knocks you about, am I?'

Daisy didn't know what to say, or how to respond when John slid his arms round her and drew her towards him. He was himself unsure of how to proceed with finesse, but he had been watching closely the techniques of screen lovers. He tilted her head and planted a lingering kiss on her mouth while she held herself woodenly in his embrace.

Neither actually enjoyed the kiss, but both were pleased with the effort. Daisy was panting a little when they drew apart from having held her breath for so long. She giggled, closed her eyes and held up slightly pursed lips as John moved in for a second attempt.

They were given no chance to improve. Dermot flung open the front door and bellowed down the stairs.

'Daisy!'

'Comin', Dad!' She pushed John away. 'Where'll I meet you Saturday?'

'I'll come round for you.'

'No!'

Dermot bellowed again, making discussion impossible. 'Daisy! I won't tell you again!'

John stepped to the foot of the stairs and looked up at him. 'Goodnight, Mr Cavanagh. I'll call for Daisy after dinner on Saturday.'

Daisy elatedly took the stairs two at a time. She brushed hurriedly past Dermot, but the expected clip on the ear didn't come. He sat down and picked up his paper.

'Daisy.'

'Yes, Dad?'

'When I say a couple of minutes, I mean a couple of minutes. Not bleedin' ten.'

'Yes, Dad.'

'Daisy.'

'Yes, Dad?'

'You want to hang on to 'im. He's all right.'

Daisy redeemed her blue silk dress with the pleated skirt to wear on the outing with John. It wasn't next on the list of things to be reclaimed, but on the only occasion she had ever worn it, Dermot had complimented her and she looked forward to seeing it again as though it were an old friend. She turned into the porch with the parcel under her arm, her face bright with anticipation.

Rose was outside her door, sitting on a chair brought from her kitchen. She was rocking the pram, minding Danny and Kate's second baby. Their firstborn was chalking a picture on the tiles. Daisy bent to admire the drawing.

'Goin' out tonight, love?' asked Rose.

'Yeah, later on. John's comin' round for me about six.'

'He looks a nice chap. I'm glad you got someone decent. Known 'im long?'

'Off and on, about five years.'

'Oh. You'll be startin' your bottom drawer, then.'

'I don't know about that. It'll be years before we can get married. He ain't asked me, anyway.'

'Well, you don't want to be in too much hurry . . . Enjoy yourself while you got the chance. You don't get much chance after.'

Daisy laughed. 'You make it sound like a real Beano.'

'I just mean, once you start 'avin' kids, you can't get out and about like you used to.'

'Kate and Dan are lucky. They can still get to the pictures now and again. They got you to mind the kids for 'em.'

'That'll soon 'ave to be knocked on the 'ed. Danny'll 'ave to put in some overtime. And I don't know that I can manage three on me own any more. I'm gettin' on a bit.'

'Three? She ain't havin' another one already?'

'I thought she would've told you. She's five months.'

'But he's only eight months!' said Daisy, pointing to the infant in the pram. 'She wants to send 'im back on the pleasure boats. That'd keep 'im away from home six nights out of seven.' Daisy was scandalised, but tried to keep it out of her voice. Disgusting, it was, having one baby after another.

'It'd only make him more eager, love. They're all the same. They don't 'ave to 'ave 'em. Still, he's a good boy. He don't go out drinkin' an' he brings his money home reg'lar.'

'It's nothin' to do with me, how many they have. I ain't got to feed 'em. Anyway, I gotta go. I got to change the beds and get the sheets in soak before I go out.' She turned for the stairs.

'I think it's all been done for you,' said Rose.

'What?' Daisy stared at Rose in disbelief.

'Your Dad give Annie half-a-crown to help you out a bit. I seen her hangin' out the washing this mornin'.'

Dad? Paying out good money for someone to do the washing when he could get it done for nothing? What was coming off here? Last week she'd missed the end of the picture to rush home to get the stout, only to be told again by Dermot that Annie had already got it. He was calling her Annie now, not Mrs Carter.

Rose had followed her to the foot of the stairs and was looking up at her.

'Nice for you,' Rose was saying, 'not to come 'ome from work and find another lot waitin'.'

There seemed to be meaning in her look, but Daisy couldn't make out what it was.

'Your Dad's home,' Rose called, when Daisy didn't answer. 'He's been in about a half-hour.'

It dawned on her then, that Rose was trying to prepare her for something. She guessed what it might be and, dreading she might be right, crept up the last few stairs and quietly pushed open the front door. Unusually, the door to the living room was closed. She stood outside, listening: Quiet, and then a chair creaked. Daisy opened the door.

Annie Carter leaped guiltily to her feet, her colour draining. She was not quick enough. Daisy had seen her cradled in Dermot's lap, her face close to his, stroking his moustache. Shock robbed her of speech and she stalked by them into the scullery where she leant against the sink, gripping the edge, trying to steady herself. Presently, Dermot came in behind her.

'Listen. It ain't what you think. We ain't done nothin' wrong. But you ought to use your noddle. She could be a great help to you. She could teach you right from wrong.'

Daisy rounded on him, her voice trembling with fury.

'Her! Teach me right from wrong? It seems she don't know the bleedin' difference herself! An' who's helpin' 'er kids while she's in 'ere sodding about with you?'

Dermot's tone had been quiet and reasoning until then, but his control was never far from breaking point. He raised his hand to strike her but held back and jabbed his finger into her shoulder.

'That's enough of your bloody sauce. Any more of it and you'll find yourself outside. I'm not havin' it!'

He backed to the door, keeping his eyes on her, daring her to answer back. 'I'll do as I like in me own house. If you don't like it, you know where the door is.'

In a little while she heard the front door slam as he went out.

Daisy wandered into the kitchen. Annie Carter had gone. She took the blue dress out of its wrapping and shook it. Anguish was giving her a physical pain, gripping her chest so that she felt a need to press her closed fist against it. She sank into the chair, buried her face in the carefully pressed pleats and howled.

She cried herself dry, then got up to fetch pork chops from the scullery. There was Paddy's tea to get ready. She'd better do some for Dermot, though God knew when he would be coming back. She put the chops into the pan and began to mash cold potatoes and cabbage together to make bubble and squeak, sniffing and brushing away tears with the back of her hand as she did so. She was more composed by the time Paddy arrived but he wanted to know the reason for her red, swollen eyes. They sat and ate together while she told him.

Apparently Paddy had been aware of the situation for some time.

They were discussing their less than rosy predicament in low tones, when Daisy suddenly gripped Paddy's knee. She had heard Dermot's footfall on the stairs. She jumped up from her chair and brought his plate from the lower oven and placed it on the table seconds before he opened the door.

He fixed on them a look of bitter contempt as he slowly placed his cap on the door. Oh, Jesus, thought Daisy. He's had a skinful.

'Well?' he demanded of Paddy. 'I s'pose she's told you all about it. What 'ave you got to say about, it then?'

'Nothin', Dad.'

'Nothin'?' His fist smashed down on the table, making the plates and cutlery jump. 'I bet you've had plenty to say behind me back.'

'No, I ain't.' Paddy cringed as Dermot seized the front of his jacket and hauled him to his feet.

'No. You ain't got the guts to say nothin'. Not to me face, yer yeller-bellied little git!'

'Leave 'im alone!' Daisy shouted. 'He ain't done nothin'.'

Dermot let go and glowered down at Paddy as he dropped back into the chair.

'Well, this is my house! I'm master here! You can piss off if you don't like it. Go on. Clear out! And you can go with him. Get your things together and piss off out of it, the pair of yer!'

'I ain't finished me tea!' said Daisy and would have defied him by sitting down again, but Paddy put his hand on her arm.

'Come on, Daisy,' he said quietly. 'Let's go. We'll be better off out of it. I can't eat this now anyway.'

Daisy went into the off room and in a few minutes

had collected her clothes into a paper bag. She went to the parlour to see how Paddy was getting on.

'Make sure you only take what belongs to you,' said Dermot as she passed his chair.

Paddy was ready. They were about to leave when Daisy remembered the lock of her mother's hair. Dermot, looking in, caught her with her hand in the jar.

'Put that back! That don't belong to you.'

'No. You're right, it don't. You robbed us of the rest of her, you might as well keep that bit. Come on, Paddy.'

Together they walked to the end of the road.

'What we gonna do?' asked Paddy. He looked white and shaken.

'We could go round to Sarah bunk in with her till we get sorted out. P'raps we could get a place together.'

'There won't be room for all of us at Sarah's. I think I'll go to Aunt Edie's in Clapham. Why don't you come with me?'

'I can't chuck me job up. Anyway, we ain't seen Aunt Edie for years. We don't know 'er.'

'No. But she might take me in. Just for a little while. I just want to make a fresh start. Away from 'ere.'

'You go, then. Let us know how you get on. I don't know what I'm goin' to do. I think I'll go and find John.'

In an unusual display of affection, they clung to each other briefly, before they walked off in opposite directions, Paddy to seek the charity of his mother's sister, Daisy to put John to the test. To see if he really would stick up for her.

Chapter 20

Photograph

Crossing the bridge from Cubitt Town to Millwall, Daisy remembered that this was the night John went to watch the boys boxing at the Dockland Settlement. Having seen his mother only at a distance, she did not want to turn up on his doorstep when he was not at home. She hitched the deadweight of her bundle higher and went back the way she had come. Unlike her heart, her head felt light and she passed familiar landmarks with no clear recollection of how she got to them. Everything looked the same, yet everything was different. The terraced cottages with their dark parlour windows seemed aloof, indifferent to her existence, and there was a hostility in the shuttered shop fronts.

A cheerful thumping and roaring still came from the settlement building. She couldn't go in. Females were excluded and her appearance there would have been embarrassing for John. She settled to wait in the street until the evening's entertainment was over. Propping her bag against a wall, she sank to the pavement to lean against it.

It was good to be in the shadows. She closed her eyes and drifted into a dream-like state, though she knew she wasn't sleeping. Music came to her from a long way off, soft music gently played, yet it smothered the noise from the hall. She knew the tune: 'Ramona'. Where had she heard that song? A white figure floated into her vision. A young woman in a white dress, sitting on a wide swing tied to the stout, lower branches of a tree. Up and down with the music she swung, the white skirt billowing. On each slow surge towards her, Daisy struggled to see her face. Each time the woman came a little nearer but the face receded before she could make out the features. She knew with certainty that it was her mother. She stretched out her hand but couldn't reach the vision, called to it, but no sound came.

The music died away and the vision faded. Daisy was staring at the rows of lighted windows on the other side of the road. John was standing beside her.

'Daisy! What's the matter? Has your old man chucked you out?'

She tried to get up but the pavement tilted crazily and she sank back again. 'Yes,' she whispered. 'Me and Paddy.'

'He ain't hit you, has 'e?'

'No, he never 'it me.'

'You look like you just done ten rounds with Wag Bennett. You're white as a sheet.'

'I just want a drink o' water. I'll be all right.'

John ran back into the hall and brought a cup of water. He knelt by her, steadying her hand while she drank. By the time he came back after returning the cup, Daisy was on her feet, dusting herself down. He picked up her bag and put an arm round her shoulder.

'How d'you feel now?'

'I'm all right. I 'ad a funny turn, that's all.'

'Come on.'

'Where we going?'

'I'll see if me Mum can put you up for a couple of days, till we can work somethin' out. If you go to Sarah's place you'll 'ave to sleep on the floor and you ain't very well. I can sleep on the sofa. You can 'ave my bed; Mum won't mind.'

'You sure?'

'Don't worry about it. Tell me what happened,' said John.

'There was this woman on a swing . . . I couldn't see 'er face.'

'What?'

'Oh, you mean what started the barney at home? Well, there ain't much to tell, really.' Daisy was hedging. She was still a little dazed by what seemed to her a supernatural experience. She was not ready to speak of it and she found it difficult to tell anyone what her father had done, but she owed John the truth, however shameful.

'I walked in on me Dad and Mrs Carter. They was canoodlin'. It's been goin' on a long time, only me, silly cow, didn't twig. Paddy knew all about it. Apparently Jack Carter found out about it an' all. He chased her up the road with an 'ammer.'

'Blimey! What happened then?'

'The soppy sod didn't catch her,' said Daisy with a flash of her usual vigour. She came to an angry standstill when John laughed.

'It's nothin' to laugh at! He's too scared of the old man to do anythin' about it. That two-faced cow will be movin' in next. She goes to church mornin' noon and night but it don't stop her cheatin' on her husband! That's why Dad wants us out the way. Paddy's got no

227

one. Poor little sod. He never said a word an' got chucked out just the same.'

'I bet you had plenty to say.'

'I reckon church should be used for the glory of God, not a cloak for people's sins! We was just gettin' everythin' nice an' comfortable. I could choke Annie Carter!'

They were coming to the corner of Cuba Street, when Daisy faltered.

'What's your Mum gonna think, you turnin' up with me?'

John was a bit worried about that too. His mother was herself a regular churchgoer. She had been known, when severely tried, to exclaim, 'Christ Church!' but beyond that, strong language never passed her lips. John was hoping Daisy would be moderate in her choice of expression, but he didn't dare make the suggestion. Daisy would, he knew, prefer to sleep in the street, if there was any hint that she might not be welcome.

'She'll be all right. She wouldn't see anyone left out in the cold.'

Later, Daisy lay wakefully in John's bed, thinking over the events of the turbulent day. The meeting with John's parents had been strained. His father had greeted her kindly, but afterwards hardly spoke. His mother's questioning had been sharp and penetrating. Daisy couldn't blame her, but she had found herself having to make evasive replies in response to enquiries about how she came to be without a roof for the night. She wasn't going to run her father down to a stranger. John had come to her rescue by pointing out that she wasn't well.

Mrs Fletcher bustled about then, putting clean sheets on the bed, despite Daisy's entreaties not to bother. Now she lay, unable to sleep in these strange surroundings. The house was like a thousand others on the island, but posh by Daisy's standards. There was a fringed lampshade and china ornaments!

She started when John came softly into the room, and raised herself on to her elbow.

'I just come to see if you're all right,' he said. 'I thought you might be upset.' He sat on the bed and touched her face in the darkness, finding her cheeks wet. 'Don't cry. Your Dad'll be sorry for what he's done when he's sober.'

'Don't matter if he is. I can't go back there. Not if she's gonna be there. And I can't stay here either.'

'Yes, you can.'

'No. It's very nice of your Mum to take me in, but she don't like me, I can tell that. It's because I'm a Catholic. On Saturday I'll go and see Paddy at our Aunt Edie's. See how he's gettin' on. She might let me stay there an' all.'

'I'll come with you. But Clapham's a long way. Be a long way to come and see you.'

'We'll have to get round that best way we can. That's if she'll have me.'

Edie's was not one of the larger houses in Clapham but it was substantial, having three floors and steps running down inside a railed area to a basement. Daisy stared so hard at Edie when she opened the door to their knock, that it was John who had to explain the reason for their visit.

'This is Paddy's sister Daisy. Is he 'ere? We just wanted to see how he's gettin' on.'

'Oh. Hello, Daisy.' She was clearly not overjoyed to

see them, but she stood back and held the door open for them to enter. They were shown into the parlour. Edie went to the foot of the stairs and called Paddy.

He came bounding down, his face alight with pleasure.

'Oh, Dais!' he said, flinging his arms round her. He seemed unable to say anything else and stood with his face buried in her neck.

'Well,' said Edie, 'I'll make some tea. Sit down, I won't be long.' She pulled out a fat horsehair chair for John and went out to the kitchen.

'What's it like here?' asked Daisy when she'd gone. 'Are they gonna let you stay?'

'Yeah. I've got a room right at the top. It's a bit funny. I miss sittin' round the stove with everybody. They ain't really used to havin' somebody livin' with 'em. So I stay upstairs most of the time. But they been good to me. Uncle Albert's gonna try an' get me a start in the bank. What about you?'

'Oh, I ain't found lodgin's yet. I been stayin' round John's house. I wonder if she looks like her.'

'Looks like who?'

'Aunt Edie. She's our Mum's sister. I wonder if she looks like her.'

'I dunno. Listen, Dais, there's another little room next to mine, at the back. I'll ask Aunt Edie if you can have it if you like.'

Teacups rattling on a tray were heard coming along the passage. Edie set down the tray and put a plate of chocolate biscuits on the table. The only time Daisy had seen such delicacies was when she was packing them into boxes at the provisions factory. The tea-set filled her with awe. Fluted china with a pattern of roses. The saucers matched and so did the teapot. All intact!

She handled her cup with extreme care, afraid it would crush in her grasp, but the biscuits she attacked with enthusiasm, finding them much to her liking. Edie hid her consternation and refilled the cups.

'Paddy tells me Sarah has left home as well,' she said.

'She didn't 'ave much option either,' said Daisy.

'I can't believe you're all so grown up.'

'Well, we ain't seen a lot of you, 'ave we?'

John judged that it might be wise to attempt a tactful remark.

'What a nice house you got, Mrs Kemp. Right near the common, too.'

'Yes,' said Daisy. 'Lovely lot of room an' all. You never had no kids, did you, Aunt Edie?'

'Er, no. We wasn't blessed.'

'I often wondered why you never kept more of an eye on us. I would if Danny's kids got left with no mother.'

Edie was flustered.

'Well, I've never been strong.'

'Ain't yer? You're all right now, though? You gonna let Paddy stay?'

'Yes. Albert thinks he could do very well in the bank.'

'Yeah. He was always good at readin' and writin'. Mind, he never 'ad to bunk off school to do the bleedin' washin'.'

'I was wonderin', Aunt Edie,' Paddy broke in. 'There's that other little room next to mine. I wondered if you could let Daisy 'ave it. In return for her keep.'

'I could give you a hand with the housework and the shoppin',' said Daisy, but she sounded doubtful.

Edie put her cup down. 'Oh, I don't think so,' she said, addressing Paddy. 'It's one thing having you, your

Uncle Albert doesn't mind that, but Daisy's a young girl. He wouldn't want the responsibility.'

There had seemed no point in lingering. John steered Daisy to the door before she said something that might put Paddy's position in jeopardy. He glanced down at her. Her eyes were bright and she walked down the front steps with her head up, looking straight ahead, 'That's that, then,' she said. 'I don't know what I'm gonna do now.'

John slipped his arm through hers. 'I been thinkin',' but he didn't finish. The front door opened again and Paddy pounded down the steps after them, calling their names.

'I just remembered. Aunt Edie give me this. You can 'ave it if you like.'

He pushed a piece of stiff card into Daisy's hand.

'What is it?'

'It's a picture of our Mum and Dad.'

She didn't look at the picture straight away, but held it against her.

'You sure?' she asked.

'Course I'm sure. Aunt Edie ought to know. You can see it's Dad, anyway. Like he must 'ave been years ago.'

It was a sepia print, mounted on thick card. A young Dermot, wearing pinstriped trousers and a dark jacket was seated, balancing a bowler hat on his knee. Standing a little behind him, resting her left hand lightly on his right shoulder was Charlotte. The other hand held a heart-shaped fan in front of her tightly cinched waist. The collar of her jacket, it seemed to be of velvet, stood up a little, to frame her face. They both looked serene against a backdrop of trees.

'They must 'ave both been about nineteen,' said Paddy. 'There's a date on the back. Aunt Edie said they 'ad it took when they got engaged.'

Daisy devoured the picture, taking in the line of her mother's chin, the eyes and the dark, piled hair.

'She does look like Florrie, or Florrie looks like 'er. Can I keep it, Paddy? She give it to you.'

'No, you 'ave it. She's prob'ly got some more knockin' about. You can get a copy done for me, if you like.'

'I will. I'll get it enlarged. Thanks, Paddy.'

'That's all right.' Paddy bent and kissed her cheek. 'Look after yourself.'

Daisy tucked the picture inside her coat. Every few yards as they rumbled home on the bus, she took it out to study it. Gifts had been rare in her life, but never had she been so thrilled to receive one. To look on her mother's face at last!

'You look as though someone's give you 'undred quid,' said John.

'It's better than 'undred quid. There ain't no money could buy it.'

'Ain't you seen a picture of 'er before?'

'No. We went to my granny's house once, when we was little. There was a photo of all of 'em on the piano. Edie and some of her other sisters – my granny. I asked which one was my Mum, but she said she wasn't in the photo. I didn't really believe her. Dad must 'ave told her not to tell me.'

'Why would he do that?'

'He always said it's better to forget her. I don't even know where she's buried.'

'Ten to one she's up Leytonstone. We'll go and look if you like.'

233

'I'd like to know where she is, but I ain't one for vis-
itin' graves. It don't do no good.'

'You comin' back to our house tonight?'

'No. Thanks love, but I don't think so. I been thinkin'.
I could go to Sarah's, but she's courtin' Colour strong
now. He's there most of the time an' it could be awkward – you know, when I want to get washed an'
dressed an' that. So, for the time bein', I'm gonna ask
Danny an' Kate.'

'But that's right on yer Dad's doorstep.'

'I know. But he's the one that's in the wrong, not me.
An' he don't own the street. I can't get off the face of the
bleedin' earth just to suit 'im. He'll 'ave to put up with it,
same as I will.'

Daisy took out the photograph again and gazed at
Charlotte's image.

'I'm gonna save up an' get a really nice frame for this.
It's somethin' I can do for the poor cow. You know, John,
I thought she come to me the other day.'

'How d'you mean?'

'When I 'ad that funny turn. I seen this woman on a
swing. She was singin', I think. I couldn't see her face,
but I'm sure it was her. She must 'ave known I was in
trouble. She must 'ave seen Dad chuck us out an' she
was trying' to let me know she was near me.'

'Well, I don't know nothin' about things like that.
Maybe you did see her. But p'raps she'd rest easy if she
knew you'd got me to help you. I ain't got no money, but
I've got a steady job. Now your Dad's chucked you out,
we ought to start savin' up to get married. I reckon we'd
rub along all right together.'

234

Chapter 21

Coventry

Danny and Kate made room for Daisy without rancour. A packing case from the greengrocer's had to serve her as a repository for her collection of pots, pans, and linen, the big bottom drawer of the chest in Rose's room being occupied by the youngest Cavanagh grandchild. His older brother and sister shared with her the double bed in the off room. This was immediately below its counterpart in Dermot's flat and was no bigger, though slightly better decorated.

Often she found herself straining her ears for Dermot's footsteps above her head, visualising what she knew he must be doing. At eight o'clock, he went into the scullery to get washed ready to go out, then into his room to change out of his working shirt. Despite knowing his habits so well, she came face to face with him one Friday night, as she knew she must, sooner or later.

She was hurrying down Bermuda Street, her newest acquisition under her arm, when Dermot came out of the porch and walked towards her. He saw her at once, but did not change his step or look away. He kept his eyes steadily on her face and as they drew near each other, she too kept her gaze firmly on him. She was determined not to let the old git outstare her.

They drew level and, when his eyes could swivel no more, he flicked them to the front, allowing only contempt and never recognition to register. He passed her without speaking. If he had hit her in the face, the pain she felt could not have been more acute. It made her gasp and bite hard on her bottom lip.

Kate was busy poking tiny garments through the mesh of the fireguard to dry when she went into the kitchen. Rose was in the chair by the range giving the baby his bottle. She looked up.

'What's the matter with you?'

'I just seen Dad. He walked past me like he didn't know me. Never said a word.'

'Never mind, love, you'll get used to it,' said Rose.

'I s'pose you get used to anythin' in time.'

'You should worry,' said Kate. 'He don't have much to say to us. Danny wants to keep it that way.' She dragged the toddler out from under the table, plonked him in the high chair and began spooning mashed potato and gravy into his round red mouth. 'Let's see what you bought then.'

Daisy put the parcel on the table and undid the wrapping.

'It's a frame for Mum's picture.'

'Ooh, look Mum,' said Kate, holding up the frame for Rose to see. 'I'n't' it lovely?'

It was oval, ornately carved and heavily gilded.

'Lovely,' said Rose. 'That must 'a cost you a few bob.'

'I been payin' it off for ages. Do you think John'll like it?'

'Course he will,' said Kate, but it was Rose's approval that Daisy wanted. She looked at her hopefully, but she was looking down at the baby, her lips pursed.

Rose did not approve of mixed marriages.

'If you like it, he'll like it. He's a nice bloke,' Kate said stoutly.

'He's nice enough,' Rose conceded. 'I just think we should stick to our own. Still, I dare say you'll get on all right, once you're married.'

'Yes, well! if I can find a hammer, I'll put this up on the wall in the bedroom.' Daisy picked up the frame and went through the scullery to the off room.

'Leave it till the mornin', will yer?' Kate called. 'I just got 'er to bed. She's been a little bugger all day.'

The eldest child was sound asleep. Daisy gathered her sprawling limbs and tucked her under the blankets. Coming so soon after the encounter with Dermot, Rose's attitude depressed her. Even Kate, who seemed surprised to find John likeable, despite his being non-Catholic, assumed that he would come over to their side once he was married. It was not going to be that simple.

John had no objection to a Catholic wedding, but he had made it quite clear that he absolutely would not agree to have any children brought up as Catholics.

'Why not?' Daisy had been dumbfounded.

'I been findin' out about it. There's lots of things I like about it, but there's some books they try an' stop you readin'. Well, I ain't 'avin' that.'

'What books?'

'Well, there's one, I can't remember what it's called, but I know there is one.'

'Do you want to read it?'

'Not particular. It's in French or somethin', but that ain't the point.'

'Well, what is?'

'One of my kids might want to read it. And there's

other things.' John had sensed her irritation and had gone on, treading warily. 'It's all that stuff about the bread and wine being the real body of Jesus.' He had broken off, the stress of trying to find words to express what he felt proving too agonising. He knew the word for what he could not accept, but could not bring himself to use it: transubstantiation. She might scoff at him. 'And I can't see what good it is 'avin the service all in Latin. No one can understand it.'

The Latin mass was one of Daisy's joys. She didn't understand the words, but she felt their uplifting majesty and always came out of church feeling strengthened and purified.

'You don't know what you're talkin' about! You can't just talk straight at God!'

'Why not?'

'Oh, I can't explain it. You'll 'ave to see the priest.'

'No,' said John mulishly, 'I got me mind made up.'

'Oh, I don't want to talk about it any more!' Daisy had been exasperated. 'It always ends up in a fight an' I don't want to fight with you. But I tell you this. I ain't standin' up in front of no priest makin' promises I got no intention o' keepin'.'

An angry silence had fallen between them. Daisy sighed at the memory. She knelt and dragged the packing case out from under the bed and delved into it to find the enlargement of her mother's photograph. It lay on the bottom, wrapped in tissue paper and protected by a layer of linen sheets. She positioned the picture behind the mount and fastened the clasps at the back of the frame. She held it up and gazed at her mother.

'You look lovely in there,' she told her. 'I'm gettin married soon. It's gonna 'ave to be St Luke's. I know it's not what you would 'ave wanted, but I can't help it. It's not hurry-up affair, or nothin' like that, but he's a Proddy, so I can't get married in St Edmund's. But he's a decent bloke.'

The picture looked wonderful. Good enough to grace a town hall. She laid it back in its place without addressing any remark to the image of Dermot. One day, she would have a wall to hang it on.

She had reluctantly agreed to marry in the Church of England, since the only other way out of their dilemma was to marry in a register office and she had put her foot down about that.

'Might just as well live in bleedin' sin!'

'It'll have to be St Luke's, then.'

'I won't be married in the eyes of our church.'

'You will be, in the eyes of God.'

So it was settled. She hadn't told anyone about it yet. The wedding was still too far in the future to be worth upsetting anyone over the issue. The prospect of being married in England's church robbed the occasion of any appeal. Still, it would put a ring on her finger and give her the right to a home, and a bed, that she could call her own.

It was about six months later, when Kate was beginning to have trouble persuading the newly mobile baby to stay in the bottom drawer, that she asked Daisy when she thought her wedding might take place.

'About 1932, the rate we're goin'.'

'It ain't gonna take you that long to get the money together, is it?'

'P'raps not as long as that. They kept me on in that last lay off. Why?' Daisy asked sharply, suddenly suspicious.

Kate didn't look at her. 'Oh, I was just wonderin'.'

'Oh no! Don't tell me! I thought I heard you spewin' this mornin'. I thought I was dreamin'. You ain't fallen again, 'ave you?'

'Yeah.'

'Good Gawd! What's the matter with you? Can't you say no?'

'It's easy for you to talk. It ain't that simple. You wait. You'll find out.'

'I'll make bloody sure I don't end up with a house full o' kids I can't feed.'

'Yeah? That's what I used to say.' Kate wearily pushed her hair back from her forehead with the back of a damp hand. 'Anyway, I don't want you to think I'm tryin' to get rid of you. It ain't for a long time. Danny don't even know yet. I'm just tryin' to work things out. Rose'll just have to have one of 'em in with her.'

Pity for her gripped Daisy. She looked so worn and defeated.

'That's all right. You've got plenty to be gettin' on with, without worryin' about me. I'll have a look round for some different lodgin's.'

'That's why I'm tellin' you now, really. There's half a house goin' up the other end of the road. Upstairs, number 126.'

'That'd be too big for me. I couldn't manage that on me own.'

'No, but if you and John got married sooner, you could move in there together.'

The notion took hold of Daisy. She put on her coat and went in search of John, deviating so that she could pass number 126. On impulse, she knocked and found out from the ground floor tenant, the name of the landlord.

'I couldn't 'ave a quick look, could I?'

'Go on, then.'

Four rooms! The one at the back overlooked the railway line that ran from the great flour mill into the dock. It had a sink, so was clearly meant to be the kitchen. John would like that. He could watch the trains while he was having his tea. The gas cooker was out on the landing, standing in a recess, next to what appeared to be a cupboard, She opened the door. A lavatory! Inside!

She ran along the passage, her feet clattering on the bare boards. A tiny boxroom lay to her right, its window staring into its exact copy in the terraced house next door. Another room, also overlooking the railway, opened off the passage. It had a small black fireplace with a pattern of yellow flowers in tiles on either side. Daisy caught her breath when she saw it. She could get one of those half-round mats to go front of that. Best of all, the room at the front with the bay looking on to the street! She'd seen the frilly curtaining in Chrisp Street that would be the very thing to drape round there.

She ran downstairs to the waiting neighbour.

'Can you make sure, if anyone else comes to look at it, to tell 'em that someone's already took it?' The woman looked doubtful. 'I wanna bring my bloke to see it. If he likes it, we'll get the banns called Sunday.'

'All right, love. I'll tell 'em it's spoke for, if anybody comes.'

Daisy was off again, excitement adding to her speed. At the bridge she had to take a flying leap to get across before a chasm opened in the road and held her up, causing the operator to shout after her. She didn't care! She wanted to get to the landlord that night before it

241

was too late. She wanted confirmation that the flat would be hers.

There was surprisingly little opposition from John's mother. His father, as far as Daisy had ever been able to make out, never expressed an opinion about anything. John was difficult to convince. He listened to the rapturous description of the flat and the pressing reasons for taking it.

'But we ain't got no money for furniture,' he protested.

'We'll 'ave a roof. That's the main thing. Furniture can wait. We can kip on the floor. Rose'll find us a couple of chairs. I can put a cloth over an orange box. That'll do for a table. Just for a start. Oh, come on, John.'

'The girl's right, John,' said his mother; she had so far been unable to bring herself to call her Daisy. 'You might not get another chance like this. And with four rooms, you can always take a lodger when money's short.'

'We ain't even got enough saved up for the weddin'.'

'I'd rather spend the money we 'ave got on takin' these rooms. I can't see the point in savin' up for a weddin' party for some sod to upset as soon as they got enough drink inside 'em.'

She wore him down. He agreed to come with her to see the flat. Outside in the street he grumbled. 'I wish you wouldn't swear so much. My Mum don't like it.'

Daisy bit back the retort that sprang to her lips. She must try to sweeten him up a bit if she was to get him to sign up with the landlord.

'I know your Mum don't swear. And I know she don't like me. I don't like her much, but she's honest, I'll give her that. And she wouldn't think much of me pretendin' to be somethin' I ain't. She'd see through that straight away. She'll 'ave to take me for what I am or do the other thing. Cheer up!' She slipped her arm through his. 'You wait till you see the flat.'

'I don't want to go round there now. It sounds all right from what you tell me. If you like it, it's all right with me. Let's just go and pay the deposit.'

Going home to Bermuda Street, Daisy was walking on air. It was late by now. She passed The Three Feathers and saw Annie Carter coming out of the blocks, jug in hand, making for The Jug and Bottle. Timing her assault carefully, she waited until they were within touching distance, then spat at Annie's feet.

Annie didn't retaliate. She closed her eyes and passed on. Never mind! It would have been lovely to have an excuse to smack her in the mouth, but nothing could spoil her elation.

The banns were called on the next Sunday and the wedding arranged for four weeks later. Kate offered to lend her wedding dress but Daisy regretfully turned it down.

'It wouldn't look right without a bouquet and we ain't brassy enough for that.'

She looked down at the calculations she was making on the back of an envelope. We can have buttonholes for John and the best man. They're 4d each and a special one for me for a tanner. That'll have to do us. There's only John's Mum and Dad, you and Danny, Sarah and Colour comin'. We'll 'ave enough for a drink in The Pride afterwards.'

'Ain't Paddy comin'?'

'He's workin' in the bank. They work all day Saturday. Mind, I think he's glad of the excuse. He don't like the idea of goin' in a Proddy church.'

Danny didn't like it either, but swallowed his objection

243

because there would have been no one to give her away if he had refused to come. On the day, Daisy wore her pretty pink crêpe dress with the bugle bead trimming and handkerchief hem. John surprised her by sending a white car to collect her and drive her to church.

She didn't feel like a bride as she walked up the aisle on Danny's arm. No wedding march to sound her progress, only the heels of her court shoes rapping on the flagstones. She gazed about her as the vicar intoned the rites. So strange and unfamiliar it seemed. Not the reverent hush of a holy place, only sepulchral cold and gloom. No sanctuary lamp burning near the altar. She made her vows in a voice that seemed to belong to someone else. In a moment it seemed, it was over, and she was in the street again.

There was not enough money to pay for a return journey in the white car, so after a short celebration in the pub, during which the Fletchers sat at a table while the Cavanaghs stood at the bar, they walked back to the new flat.

Walking up Bermuda Street for the first time as Mrs Fletcher, Daisy was mortified to see, arriving ahead of them, a coster's barrow being pushed by the boy from the greengrocer's. Her mother-in-law had given him a tanner to deliver her wedding present. It was an old striped mattress.

Chapter 22

Pregnancy

With so much evidence of fecundity around her, Daisy could not fail to have a clear idea of the sexual duties of a wife. What surprised and dismayed her was the frequency with which she was called upon to perform it. You got married on the understanding that he would be allowed to do it to you now and again, she knew that, but she hadn't bargained for two or even three times in one night.

John's approaches had been clumsy and tentative at first. His calloused fingers hard and awkward but he gained in experience and now, whenever he felt the need, he took her quickly and with confidence.

At night it wasn't so bad, but he seemed always to wake with an erection and want to pester her when she was still cocooned in sleep. She hated it but didn't refuse him, laying beneath him with her eyes shut tight, thankful that the mattress was on the floor. The woman downstairs might have heard a bed creaking and guessed what they were up to. As it was, she dreaded meeting any one she knew, fancying that they looked at her with prurient curiosity.

She could hardly bear to look herself in the face. Combing her hair in front of the little mirror next to the sink, she avoided her own eyes, fearing her new knowledge showed in them and she appeared somehow depraved. Her body looked the same, she washed it down every morning after John left and before she set off for the factory, but she couldn't get it clean on the inside.

It wasn't that John repulsed her. Affection for him deepened with every day. As the sheets grew warm when they first got into bed, she might have initiated the cuddles, had it not been for what was likely to follow. She saw to it that she went to bed first and could feign sleep when he came to join her. She never let him see her naked if she could help it. Her body was slim and shapely. The sight of it always aroused him. On Sunday mornings, when he didn't have to get up early, she tried to slip out of bed before he woke, taking her clothes to dress in the lavatory.

Realisation that she was pregnant coincided with the news that John had been laid off work. They had been married for six months. John tramped round the whole area looking for work but he was one of a vast legion, the unemployment figure having reached three million.

They were lucky. Daisy's job in the sack factory kept them out of the soup kitchens, but with so many hungry workers waiting at the gates, there was no need for bosses to molly-coddle the ones on the inside.

As her pregnancy advanced it got harder for Daisy to lift the bales of sacks on to her head to load on to the barges or to bring them to her machine for repair. The foreman caught one of her mates bringing her work to her and came storming along the row of benches. He shouted and bellowed at the girl until she slunk back to her machine and resumed her work. He moved along the line and came to Daisy.

'You! You don't get special favours round here. I ain't havin' you takin' gals away from their machines. Nobody leaves their machine unless I say so!'

Daisy might have withstood the onslaught and vented her feelings later by blowing a raspberry at him when he turned his back, but he hadn't finished. He came closer and jabbed his finger into her shoulder.

'Women like you think you can get away with murder. Well, not while I'm in charge!'

It was more than she could bear. Her hand closed round one of the large whetstones placed at intervals along the bench for the girls to sharpen their knives. She was shorter than him by six inches but hot fury lent her strength. She pushed back her stool and advanced upon him until he was leaning backwards over the bench.

'Piss off!' she hissed. 'If you don't want to see murders done, piss off while you're in one piece!' The temptation to crack him over the head was strong, but she resisted, the weight of the stone above her head causing her hand to shake. He retreated, but the summons everyone expected came from the office soon after. She was to collect her cards on the way out.

John had arrived home ahead of her. He had a fire burning and seemed quite cheerful. Her instinct was to put off telling him she'd got the sack, hating to dampen his spirits, but he saw at once that she was upset.

'What's the matter gal?'

She could never cope with sympathy. She burst into floods of tears and poured out the story.

'Never mind,' he wiped her face. 'You couldn't have gone on there much longer anyway. And I got a bit of good news. I got a start next Monday over Woolwich.'

Daisy brightened at once.

'How much?'

'Well it ain't a lot. Thirty bob a week, and the fare's three shillings. I was workin' it out. If I pay off for a bike, that'll cost me two bob a week so we'll save a shillin' and when I finished payin' for it, we'll save three!'

'What if the job don't last?'

'The bike'll have to go back. But I reckon it's worth takin' a chance.'

They reviewed their resources. Daisy had her wages and she had five shillings put away in a jar towards the gas bill. On the strength of the wage that John would bring home next Friday, they decided to splash out on some pie and mash. She got her coat. It would no longer meet at the front.

'Come on then.' John hesitated.

'What's wrong?' she demanded.

'Nothin' . . . well you stay 'ere. You don't want to go out in the cold. I'll go and get it. We'll 'ave it indoors.'

'But I'd like to go out.'

'You go then. I'll stay 'ere and keep the fire goin'.'

'You're ashamed to be seen with me ain't yer?'

'Not ashamed no. But it's a bit embarrassin'.'

'What d'you think it's like for me then?' said Daisy, her temper flaring. 'I can't just walk away from it!'

'All right. Keep your 'air on. I'll come.'

They put up the fireguard and set out for Chrisp Street,

As the day of her delivery neared, Daisy began to worry about what was going to happen to her. There had always been an abundance of babies in her life but she had never actually seen a birth. What few questions she had dared to ask of Rose or Kate had been met with smirks and evasion. A conspiracy seemed to exist between mothers, a determination not to impart information.

She had begged Rose to tell her what she might expect. Her reply had unnerved her.

'Oh. It's different for everybody. You hear all sorts of stories. But it's only one or maybe two days out of your life. And you soon forget it. Till the next time,' she said.

For the first time in her life, she found herself with time on her hands. Long hours and a long bike ride kept John out of the house until late in the evening. She busied herself sewing scraps of flannel into baby clothes, but she was restless. She called on John's mother.

Over a cup of tea, she asked her how she would know when the baby was about to be born.

'How will I know when to go to the lyin'-in home?' She looked beseechingly at her mother-in-law.

'Oh. Mother Nature tells you.'

'Bloody good job she does. No other bugger will.'

The first pain, when it came, was so faint that she wasn't sure she felt it, but it alerted her and for the rest of that afternoon she was tuned in to her abdomen, on the look out for the smallest spasm. Definitely, she was feeling something unusual. This must be it. It was starting. She wrote a note for John, telling him that she had taken herself off to the lyin'-in home and that there was rabbit stew to be warmed for his supper. She was confident that she had allowed plenty of time, but was relieved when she reached the home in Stepney. She had dreaded making a spectacle of herself on the bus.

The midwife examined her.

'You've got a long way to go yet. We won't send you

home again as you've got such a long way to come, but I wouldn't get into bed. Walk about a bit.'

John arrived at half past ten, looking weary and white-faced. Daisy was smitten with guilt. The pains had disappeared. Poor sod had cycled all that way for nothing. He came again the next night. Her labour was underway. Pain searing across her belly every few minutes making her thresh and writhe. John couldn't stay. He had to be up at six.

She seemed to be no farther advanced by the next morning. She was worn out. She thrashed about with less energy. The midwife came.

'Put your knees up and let them fall apart,' she commanded. Daisy obeyed, gritting her teeth, bearing the humiliation and pain of fingers probing between her legs because she was powerless to do otherwise.

'You're coming on nicely,' said the midwife.

'How long?' Daisy asked.

'That depends on baby. Baby will come when it's ready.'

It would have helped to know how long. There was no clock in the ward, but a shaft of sunlight striking the opposite wall in the corner told her it was still morning. You could bear most things if you knew how long the torment would go on. You could tell yourself, that's another hour gone. Only so many to go.

The pains grew in severity. It seemed to Daisy that every few minutes a hot knife sliced into her vitals, was withdrawn a little , so that the pain subsided then was plunged in again. The midwife appeared beside her and told her not to make so much noise. She was upsetting the other mothers. She hadn't realised she was making a noise. She was sorry.

The sunlight travelled slowly across the wall and came to rest by the door. Presently it dimmed and faded away. Shadows filled the room. John came and went. Other midwives rustled in, shaded the lamps, rustled out. Daisy lay stifling her groans until the light returned.

By morning pain possessed her. She paid no heed to sunlight or to probing fingers. The world was pain. Nothing existed beyond it. A sudden gush of fluid soaked her bed. She was only dimly aware that she was being moved, wheeled along a corridor into another room. A midwife held a cup to her lips.

'Come along dear. You must drink this. You still have lots of hard work to do.'

She sipped, not seeing the hand that held the cup or the face beyond it. Another wave of pain consumed her and she felt a slithering sensation between her legs and a wetness against her thigh. She raised her head. The midwife was bent over the baby, working swiftly. It looked very blue. Daisy saw the midwife free a loop of cord from round the baby's neck and slip it over the head; saw her clear its mouth and wipe the tiny, angry face.

A thin wail pierced Daisy to the heart. The midwife held up the baby for her to see.

'There she is: a pretty little girl. What's her name going to be?' Daisy flopped back against her pillow, swamped by unbelievable happiness.

'Erin,' she said.

John looked almost as exhausted as she did when he come to see her at visiting time. Daisy had been bathed and had her hair brushed by the time he arrived. He gazed down at his three-hour old daughter with an expression of faint astonishment.

'Ain't she lovely?' said Daisy.

'Yeah, lovely. I went round to Kate and Danny's for me dinner, Sunday. Kate sent this in for you.'

Out of the bag he passed her, she took a shawl, much washed and dingy grey in colour.

'Thanks.' She tossed it aside.

John drew a chair near the bed.

'Kate said, she don't know for sure, but she thinks Annie Carter's gone. She seen 'er goin' off with a couple o' bags last Tuesday and she ain't seen 'er come back.'

'What's happenin' to Dad?'

'Dunno. She ain't seen 'im either. Must be there on his own.'

The news disturbed Daisy deeply. How would Dermot manage on his own? He couldn't do it. She couldn't bear to think of him returning to a cold empty flat at night, with no dinner ready. Who would see that he had a fresh shirt and keep his boots polished? She fretted so that the midwife scolded. her.

'If you go on like this, your milk won't come in and you'll have a very cross baby.'

The news got worse. When John came again he confirmed that Annie had indeed departed. Dermot had been to Danny and Kate to ask to be taken in. He had put the tenancy of the flat into Annie's name and now he was under notice to quit.

'Where's Kate goin' to put 'im?' asked Daisy. 'She's already got a houseful.'

'She ain't gonna put him nowhere. Danny won't take him in. He said if he had a row of houses he wouldn't give him a room in one of 'em.'

'Poor old sod.'

'He might be a poor old sod,' said John. 'But he's

brought it on 'imself. You can bet your life, he give Annie a beltin'. You can't blame her for not stayin' around for another dose when she don't 'ave to.'

'Yes, but I know what it's like to be out in the street with nowhere to go.'

'And who put yer in the street? You was only a kid when 'e chucked you out. He didn't care what 'appened to you. He ain't spoke to you for years.'

'I know. But I got to remember the fix he was in when Mum died. He could 'ave put us all in a home, but he didn't, he kept us together.'

'You might 'ave been better off if 'e had. You wouldn't 'ave come up against Aunt Dolly.'

'Just the same, first thing I'm gonna do when I get out of 'ere is go and see 'im. No. The first thing I'm gonna do is get a decent drop of suds and wash that shawl properly.'

Daisy didn't risk taking the baby with her to see Dermot. She took her to Kate.

'Will you mind her for a minute while I go upstairs? Just in case Dad shows off.'

She thought at first that he was not at home. The front door was open as always but there was not a sound from inside. She glanced into his bedroom as she passed the door. The bed was rumpled and dirty. At the kitchen door she paused listening, then opened it a crack. The table was covered in unwashed crockery. A pair of dripping long-johns hung crookedly over the airer. Dermot was hunched in his chair. The range was just flickering into life but was generating no warmth.

Daisy stepped into the room and stood looking down at him.

'Hello, Dad.'

He looked up and nodded, showing no surprise. 'Hello Nin.'

'Look, you can chuck me out again if you like, but I come round to see if you're all right. Have you got anything for your dinner?'

'I got some fish and chips on the way home.'

'They tell me you've got to get out of the 'ouse. Is that right?'

'Yeah. I been a bloody fool Nin. I made it all over to her and now I got to clear out. Thirty years I been here. Now I got notice to quit.'

'How long 'ave you got?'

'Another week. New people comin' in dinner-time Saturday.'

'Have you found yerself some lodgin's?'

'Not yet. I can always go down the workhouse. But they don't let you take nothin' with you.' He got up and went to the sideboard, shuffling his feet as though he had suddenly grown very old. 'I hope I don't 'ave to part with me tobacco jar.'

'You can come home with me.'

'What? What about John?'

'He won't see you with nowhere to go. We're gonna 'ave to get a move on if the new people are comin' in in a week. We'll 'ave to get rid of most of the furniture.'

Dermot gripped her by the shoulder with a trembling hand and sank his head on her shoulder. He wept.

'Oh, Nin. If only your mother was 'ere.'

Daisy stood still, letting him weep. 'She done 'erself a favour, dyin' young. Spared 'erself a lot of grief,' she said softly.

When he had control of himself, she pushed him

away. 'Snots and tears ain't gonna do us no good. We gotta get on with it. You'll 'ave to bring your single bed with yer. We ain't got one. You can 'ave that in the little room. Me and John'll 'ave to sleep in the front room. We could do with your bedstead. What we gonna do with the one in the orf room?'

'Sarah can 'ave it. She's gettin' married ain't she?'

'Yeah. We might as well let her and Colour take what they want and give the rest to the rag and bone man.'

'You'll 'ave to clean that bedstead up a bit, if you're gonna give it to Sarah.'

'Look Dad,' said Daisy. 'If Sarah wants the bedstead, she can bloody well clean it up 'erself!'

Chapter 23

Mosley

The midwife had been right. Erin was a cross baby. She hardly slept and, for most of her waking hours, she cried. Nothing seemed to pacify her. At times her screaming went on for so long her face became discoloured, reminding her mother of mottled grey and white stove enamel.

Most afternoons were spent trying to pare vegetables with one hand, the other supporting the baby slung over her shoulder. Erin's screams became so urgent and insistent when she was laid in her Moses basket that Daisy couldn't stand it and had to pick her up.

One of the things that amazed her about John was that he didn't seem to mind if his dinner was late. It had taken her a while to get used to his preference for sitting with a cup of tea, quietly rolling a cigarette, before he tackled his meal.

'I don't mind if you ain't got it ready yet,' he repeatedly told her. 'So long as I get me cuppa tea when I get in. And you don't 'ave to run to open the door. I'll wait till you get there.'

Gradually it dawned on her that she had nothing to fear from him. He would even take the baby from her and walk about talking to her in soothing tones. In gratitude, Daisy saw to it that at about seven thirty in the evening, the time of John's return, the kettle was on the point of boiling, the teapot warmed and cups laid out with a dash of milk in each. She was beginning to learn how to exist in peace when Dermot came to live with them. His coming changed everything.

At sixty, Dermot was still reasonably well. Caring for him should have meant little more than an extension of the housekeeping: another mouth to feed, more washing, another bed to make, but Daisy soon found herself slipping into her old role of winged messenger. Midday, she took his horse-racing bets to the bookies in the next street; in the early evening she was back with his bets on the dogs. Whenever she went to Poplar she was expected to go to Pennyfields to pick up the papers from the Chinese man who ran the Pucka Poo.

She might just have managed, especially as Dermot seemed to like Erin. As the months went by and the baby seemed less fragile, he didn't mind if he was left to mind her for the few minutes it took to run to the bookies and back, but Dermot's short-term memory was beginning to slip. She arrived back breathless one day, anxious to give the finicky Erin her lunch to be greeted, not for the first time, by her father in a state of agitation.

'You'll 'ave to nip back quick! I forgot to put me *nom de plume*!'

'I ain't runnin' all the way back there. The baby wants 'er dinner.'

'You'll 'ave to go. I'll lose me stake money else!'

'It'll 'ave to wait till I've fed the baby!'

'It can't wait! The race starts at two o'clock!'

'That means a double journey. I'll 'ave to bring the slip back 'ere for you to sign, then run back with it in time to get it on for the two o'clock race! Go your bleedin' self!'

'You know I won't get there in time. Your legs are younger than mine. Go on. I'll keep the baby quiet.'

Daisy swore and ran back down the stairs. As she opened the front door she heard Erin set up a fresh wail at seeing her mother disappear so suddenly. All the way, as she pounded along the pavement she could hear her baby crying. It took the bookmaker a few minutes to locate Dermot's betting slip. He had signed it. Fuming, Daisy raced home again.

Erin had stopped crying. Dermot had quietened her by handing her a large, over-ripe tomato which she was busily demolishing, her clothes soggy and stained. She wanted none of the carefully minced food her mother had prepared for her. Daisy was angry and anxious.

'Now look what you've done. She won't eat nothin' now. If she's lost weight when I take 'er down the welfare, there's gonna be hell to pay.'

Dermot was unimpressed. He didn't hold with welfare clinics.

'What do they know? She'll be all right. She's got small bones, that's all.' He put his cap on, ready to go back to work. 'You want to get 'em to 'ave a look at you while you're at it. You're like a rasher o' wind.'

Daisy wasn't convinced, especially as Erin was violently sick after he'd gone. The baby just didn't seem robust enough to her and she grizzled all the time. All afternoon she whined, until Daisy gave her sugar to suck through a wet handkerchief. At last, she snoozed.

Daisy tiptoed about her kitchen, enjoying this rare moment of peace, making certain that everything was at the ready to place the evening meal on the table the moment Dermot walked in. Coming up to five-thirty, the table was laid and the kettle singing at the back of the hob. Daisy prowled about on the alert for the first knock. It wasn't possible to leave the street door open in this flat because the tenants downstairs objected. As soon as the knocker dropped, she hurtled down the stairs as fast as she could go. Best to get there before the second knock. If he had to knock a third time you could guarantee you were in for trouble.

His expression boded no good. She stood aside to let him in and he passed her without speaking, stamping up the stairs so she feared he would wake the baby. He flung his coat over the bannister and went ahead of her into the little side room they were using as a living room.

'That's a roarin' fire you got there,' he said acidly.

'I didn't want to make it up yet in case the noise woke the baby up. I've only just got 'er off. It ain't cold, Dad.'

She should have made up a different excuse. To even hint that someone else's needs took precedence over his was enough to enrage him. He brought his fist crashing down on the mantelpiece, making the clock jump and the baby wake with a scream.

'I pay my way in this 'ouse. I'm entitled to be looked after properly!'

Daisy snatched Erin up and faced him.

'This is my shanty! If you don't like the way you're looked after, find someone else to do it!'

He wasn't listening. He was still shouting and waving his arms. Daisy raised her voice to drown him out.

'Find some other bugger to run round after you, if you can find anyone daft enough to do it!'

Dermot brought his hand up as though he would hit

her, but thought better of it. The baby stiffened as Daisy instinctively flinched and she redoubled her screams.

Daisy turned her back on Dermot, carried the baby through to her bedroom and shut the door. Sod him! Let him get his own dinner! She lay on the bed, cradling the baby, kissing the hot little head and trying to soothe her. After a long time, she was calm enough to suck her thumb and eventually fell into an exhausted sleep.

John put his head round the door.

'You all right? It's not one of your funny turns, is it? You been gettin' a lot o' them lately.'

'No. I 'ad a headache that's all.' He must not know that Dermot had been throwing his weight about. He'd give the old man his marching orders. 'It's gone now. I 'spect she give it to me. She ain't stopped bawlin' all day.' Gingerly, she eased herself off the bed. 'Sorry. I'll come and get your dinner now.'

'Don't worry. I've made a fresh cuppa tea. Come and 'ave one.'

She went into the kitchen, hardly glancing towards Dermot, where he sat hunched behind his newspaper. John felt the obvious tension between them and asked sharply: 'What's been goin' on 'ere?'

'Nothin',' said Daisy. She dished up a plateful for John. 'Do you want any more of this?' she asked her father.

'Yes, I'll 'ave some more, if there's some left, and if it's not too much trouble,' he replied with heavy sarcasm.

The atmosphere in the tiny kitchen was oppressive. John tried to engage Dermot in a discussion of the news, but for once, he wouldn't be drawn. They lapsed into a silence which did not deter Daisy from tackling her food with relish. She wouldn't let the old sod ruin her appetite.

The silence was broken by the sudden blare of music. The wireless in the house next door had been turned to full volume. John and Daisy looked at each other, guessing the probable meaning. In a moment the unmistakable sounds of a domestic fracas came to them. Furniture being overturned, thumps and cries. It went on for a full ten minutes, when abruptly the wireless was turned off and a door slammed. A woman could be heard moaning and a child crying. Daisy had pushed her plate away, unable to take another mouthful.

'That's what I like to hear,' said Dermot. 'A man who's master in 'is own house!'

'Do you?' said John. 'Well, that ain't my idea of a man. Knockin' some poor cow half 'is size round like an old hat. Scarin' the poor bloody kids. I'd like to take 'im outside for half an hour. See if he'd take me on.'

Dermot looked thoughtful. Later, when John was settled by the fire and Daisy was doing the washing up he came out to speak to her.

'I'd ask John to come up the pub and buy 'im a pint, but I don't want to get 'im started on bad habits. D'you think he'd like it if I was to buy 'im a cigar every Sunday?'

Erin was about three years old when Paddy brought his wife to visit. He caused a sensation in Bermuda Street by drawing up outside number 126 in an old Daimler. Daisy was delighted to see him and to meet Kathleen. She sent John up to the stall outside The Feathers to fetch cockles and winkles while she opened a tin of peaches and made custard. Paddy helped her carry the table from the kitchen into the living room where they could all sit around it.

Kathleen seemed to be extremely shy. Daisy smiled at her encouragingly as she spooned peaches into a bowl for her.

'You workin', Kath?' she asked.

'Er, no.'

'She don't need to,' said Paddy. He leaned back in his chair displaying a neatly tailored waistcoat. 'I'm gettin' good money at the bank. They might be movin' me to another branch soon. Promotion. I could get to be assistant manager one day.'

'That's really good, Paddy. I'm glad for you. It's about time he 'ad some luck,' she said to Kathleen. 'Poor little sod never 'ad much when he was comin' up. He was always in trouble for somethin'. If it wasn't Aunt Dolly givin' 'im a good hidin', it was Dad.'

'Where is the old man?' asked Paddy.

'He's gone down the dog track,' said John. 'Pity you missed 'im. He would 'ave loved your motor.'

'It's lovely i'n't it?' said Daisy. 'Can we 'ave a ride in it? Just round the island. Show the neighbours.'

'We could have a run round the West End if you like,' said Paddy generously.

'No! I know. Let's go up that new picture palace in Stepney. 'Ave you seen it? They just built it. The Troxy it's called. You never seen nothin' like it. All carpets, and plush. Danny and Kate went. Kate said they got these big, spangly curtains. You'd like to go wouldn't yer, Kath?'

Kathleen's eyes brightened. 'Yes, but what about the baby?'

'We'll 'ave to take 'er with us. She'll be all right,' said Daisy.

'Won't she cry?'

262

John laughed. 'No. She only cried once. Trouble was she didn't stop for eighteen months. Then she seemed to make up 'er mind it wasn't gettin' 'er nowhere and she ain't cried since. Well, only if she hurts 'erself. She don't make a sound. Wouldn't know you had a kid in the house.'

'She's a lovely little thing.' Kathleen stretched her hand towards Erin, who responded by shrinking away, lowering her brows and scowling.

'That's one thing that will start 'er off,' said Daisy. 'She can't stand it if strangers talk to 'er.'

She wiped Erin's sticky fingers, put on her coat and led her down to the car. Paddy beat off the crowd of small boys who were swarming over and under it and opened the door with a flourish, holding it while they all climbed in.

'Coo er,' said Daisy in excitement. 'I'n't it smashin'!'

She breathed in the smell of leather, settled back with Erin on her knee, revelling in the luxurious softness of the seat. As they pulled away, she raised her hand graciously, its back towards the little boys on the kerb and waved to them with a small circular motion, as she had seen the Queen do on the newsreels.

The Daimler swept over Glengall Road Bridge and, cushioning them over the cobbles, on up the West Ferry Road and off the island.

'It's marvellous!' shouted John from the front passenger seat. 'Where d'you learn to drive, Paddy?'

'Oh, the bloke I bought it off showed me the gears and give me a run round the houses. I soon picked it up.'

'Don't let's go to the pictures. Let's just go for a ride round. You don't mind, do you, Kath?' John leaned over the seat and looked at her entreatingly.

'No. It's all the same to me.'

They sped through the East End and were soon bowling along the embankment towards Westminster. They stopped to look at the river and the Houses of Parliament.

'Chokes yer, dunnit?' said John. 'Makes yer proud.'

'Let's go up Buckin'am Palace!' said Daisy.

'Well, I would, Dais, but we got to get back to Clapham and I got work in the mornin'.'

'Course, sorry. It's been lovely. Let's go 'ome along the river.'

Paddy swept the car round in a circle and made his way eastwards again.

'I can't stick by the river all the way. There's warehouses on the front after Blackfriars. I'll go down by the Tower and cut through Cable Street.'

A contented silence fell on them. The soft purr of the engine and the car's slow sway soon had Daisy's head nodding over Erin's. They both slept. She woke when the car stopped with a jolt and John said sharply: 'What the 'ell's goin' on?'

'There's crowds of people in the street,' said Paddy. 'They're all over the road. I can't get through.'

As they waited, the car became an island in a sea of humanity. Men of all ages, working men, without ties, in mufflers and flat caps were thronging the street. They walked quickly and puposefully, their eyes on some goal ahead of them. Some glanced into the car, none touched it. They all passed by, unsmiling.

'I'll find out what's happenin',' said John.

'No! Don't get out,' Daisy was alarmed. 'I don't like the look of it.'

'We can't just sit here. I won't be a minute.' He got out

and was soon swallowed in the mob. The others sat in growing apprehension. Daisy looked down at Erin. She was still asleep. Please God, let her stay that way, then she wouldn't be frightened. She peered out through the window and was relieved to see John coming back. He slid into his seat.

'You'd better back out of here quick! Oswald Mosley and his blackshirts are gonna march down here tonight. This lot's the anti-fascists. They've put a bleedin' great barrier across the road to stop 'em gettin' through. We're drivin' right into the middle of it.'

'Who's Oswald Mosley when he's at 'ome?' asked Daisy.

'He's a bleedin' turncoat, that's who he is. Come on, Paddy! There's gonna be murder 'ere. I want to get my kid out of it.'

'I don't know how to go backwards!' Paddy was agitatedly jiggling the gear lever. Outside, the men marched by in an endless stream.

'Christ Almighty!' John opened the door again. I'll push. You steer her back round that corner.' He leant his weight against the bonnet and pushed with all his strength. 'Let the bloody brake off!' he yelled, when the car budged not an inch.

'Here,' said Daisy. She pushed Erin into Kathleen's arms. 'Try not to wake 'er up. I'll help 'im.'

Together they pushed, until their combined might got the car rolling. They had almost trundled it out of the way, none of the marching men offering help or hindrance, when Daisy gave a cry of terror. In a cacophony of neighing and clattering hooves, a troup of mounted police charged into the crowd, laying about them with their batons. John dragged Daisy into the doorway of a shop in the sidestreet. She struggled to free herself from his arms.

'The baby! The baby's in the car!'

'She'll be all right! Hold tight. I'll get us back to 'er when this lot's gone past.'

The main onslaught thundered past them, along Cable Street, scattering the demontrators. Some ran past the place where they were hiding. Daisy could see the car, a few yards from her, rocking and swaying as fleeing men cannoned against it. One boy was not quick enough to get out of the path of a horseman and received a crack on the skull that felled him. A colleague gripped him by the coat collar and dragged him into the porch. John helped to prop him against the wall. Four now shared the protecting shadows.

Paddy must have discovered his reverse gear. The car suddenly shot backwards up the street. Daisy cried out and John put his hand over her mouth.

'Shh. It's the best thing! Paddy'll come back for us.'

For an hour they cowered there, anxiety for Erin making Daisy want to scream, but she prayed and waited. They heard the hooves of horses returning at a walk and shouted orders as the troupe regrouped farther along the street. John ventured to put his head out.

'You stay there, I'll go and find Paddy.'

'Not bleedin' likely! We stay together.'

'Come on, then. If we find our car, we'll come back for you,' he said to the man who was bending over the injured boy. 'We'll drop you off at the 'ospital.'

They could see the barricade clearly now. Several old pianos, trestles and odd lengths of timber formed a solid wall across the road which men were now beginning to dismantle. All around cobbles and paving stones had been torn from the road, some to hold the structure in place, some stacked up, no doubt for ammunition. Heads were appearing from upstairs windows.

They walked in the direction in which the car had disappeared, scanning the sidestreets, Daisy fighting her rising hysteria. They passed two or three turnings, when she shouted: 'There they are! Paddy!'

The car was slewed across the road but appeared to be undamaged. It started to move and drew up beside them. Paddy wound down the window.

'Jump in quick, before there's any more trouble.'

'It's all over now, mate. I just want to give someone a lift to the 'ospital. He's down in that doorway.'

There wasn't room for both young men so they helped the injured one into the car. He sat with his head lolling against Daisy. Erin was still sleeping in Kathleen's arms.

'We'll take 'im to the London 'ospital,' said John.

'Better not take him there,' said his companion, 'It's the nearest hospital to here. The police'll be rounding up anyone who's had a crack on the canister.'

'Right. Well, we'll take 'im to Poplar, then.'

They drove without saying much back to Poplar. The young man was conscious by then and they bundled him out.

'That's where you go, mate. Through that door there. They'll look after yer. I'd come with yer, but I got to think about me wife and kid.'

John pointed the boy in the direction of the accident department and closed the car door with a sigh of relief.

'Let's get 'ome out of it. I wish we'd gone to the pictures now.'

'What I'd like to know is what they want to go

marchin' along Cable Street for in the first place. What good does it do 'em?' asked Daisy.

'Lots o' Jew boys got shops in Cable Street,' said John. 'That's what they want. To frighten the shits out of the poor sods and get the mob to chuck bricks through their winders.'

When they were safe indoors and Paddy and Kathleen had gone, John put the kettle on while Daisy put Erin to bed.

'Bleedin' Mosley,' he said when she joined him in the kitchen. 'First he was a Tory, then Labour, now he's started with these Blackshirts. I got no time for a bloke who don't know his own mind. It might be all right for the I-ties, but it won't do for us. Old Mussolini. Him and the Germans, they're tryin' to cook up another war. Here's your tea, love.'

He held out a cup for Daisy, but she didn't take it. She had flopped into a chair and was staring fixedly at the wall. John looked at her closely.

'Oh blimey, not again,' he said softly. He put down the tea and fetched a glass of water. He stood beside Daisy while she remained in her trancelike state, her face drained of colour. After a minute, she blinked rapidly, three or four times, sighed deeply and turned to look vacantly at him.

'Here you are, love,' he said gently, holding out the glass. 'You've been 'avin' one of your turns again.'

Chapter 24

Evacuation

Erin could not remember a time when she couldn't read. There were no books in the house. Her early reading matter was a cartoon strip in the *Daily Mirror* about the exploits of a small girl named Belinda, and her Scottie, Witch. The adults sometimes discussed the news but it was above her head and her mother's interest seemed to centre on the Live Letters column. Erin had to wait until everyone had finished with the paper before she was allowed to have it.

She was still too young to realise that the momentous events taking place were anything other than usual. She felt the heightened tension when she heard that the Troxy had been closed down and that the street lamps were to be blacked out, but none of it affected her. It was only when her mother bought her three new vests all at once and began to write her name in black ink on pieces of tape before sewing them into her clothes that she had any sense that her personal circumstances were about to change.

Daisy explained to her that all the children from her school were going to be sent away to live in the country. A war was going to start and the Germans were going to drop bombs on London. It wouldn't be safe to stay. They were going to be taken by train. Her teacher, Miss Morgan, would be going with them. Mothers would follow later.

On a very hot August day, the day of evacuation, the children were taken to school early. They were lined up in the crocodiles they were used to forming before marching into class. They were excited. Each child wore a luggage label with the name and address and had a new gas mask in a box suspended round the neck by string. Each had a bag of some sort containing lunch and a change of clothes. Erin's was a tiny brown attaché-case that John had found for her.

She stood in line wearing a freshly washed overcoat, passed down to her from one of Kate's offspring, feeling excited and proud because in the little suitcase there were, for her personal consumption, biscuits in a brightly coloured box. She had never seen such a luxury in the house. Only broken biscuits from the grocer, sometimes, when there was company for tea.

She could see Daisy outside the school gate, waiting with the other mothers to see them off. The buses were a long time coming. It grew hotter as the sun climbed. Some of the children behind her were growing fidgety and asking for drinks. The children were lined up in height order, smallest at the front; Erin's position was two places back. Miss Morgan, patrolling her queue of charges, said that no one was to drink, because there would be no chance to go to a lavatory. They must wait. Mothers had been instructed not to pack drinks for that reason.

The overcoat was heavy. If she took it off, she would have to carry it. Erin opened her case. She knew the coat wouldn't fit in there, but she could have another look at the beautiful box of biscuits.

There was a stir of excitement among the mothers at the gate. The buses were coming! Three double-deckers. Erin would have liked to go upstairs, but the older children were allocated those seats. There was much waving and calling out. Only when one of the women could contain herself no longer and broke down in tears, was there any crying among the children. Then it began. It took all Miss Morgan's considerable power of command to keep order as they pulled away.

They had no idea where they were going or when they would be back. Had they been given a place name, it would have meant nothing. They only knew that they were going to 'the country' where there were fields and cows. Such a place was beyond imagining. Erin knew that her mother would come to her as soon as she could. She held on to that.

The train had no corridor. Miss Morgan travelled with the very youngest, promising to see Erin and the other little girls riding with her whenever they stopped. There were many stops on that long, slow journey into nowhere. Once, the train was shunted on to a siding to let a troop train through. Boy scouts came along the length of the train with buckets of water, and handed a tin cup through the window to be passed around, making the problems of no access to a lavatory extremely acute, when the journey resumed.

It was growing dark when they arrived at the final station, and was dark with a black totality never experienced in London, when the waiting buses deposited them at the village hall in Street, Somerset. A committee of village ladies was waiting for them.

271

Inside, they sat on benches ranged along the walls, while people from the village came to make their selections.

'I'll have that one,' or 'I can take two, girls, not boys.'

'Has anybody got room for three?' A plump woman seemed to be in charge. 'These are brothers and a sister. Let's try to keep them together.'

Their number dwindled and it was growing very late. The children were white-faced with tiredness. Some of the little ones slept, lolling against their neighbours. Erin opened her case and looked at her box of biscuits. Not many children left. She was almost the last. She started to cry.

The plump woman put her arms around her.

'What's the matter, my dear?' She talked funny, but her face was kind.

'Nobody wants me!' The tears came in a flood.

'Oh, no. I've left you to last, because I want you for myself. I'm going to take you home with me. I've got a little girl of my own, same age as you.'

She lay on the bench and slept while the evening's business was concluded, then Mrs Wynne led her stumbling the few yards along the street to her cottage. She was washed, put into a strange nightgown and tucked between snowy sheets. She was just aware of a girl looking at her from another bed before sleep claimed her again.

When she woke, she looked for her suitcase but couldn't find it. She asked Mrs Wynne for her box of biscuits.

'I had to throw them away. They were all soggy. I'll get you some others.'

It was a sharp disappointment. She would have liked to keep the box.

Erin liked the Wynnes, but her stay with them was short. For reasons never explained to her, she was moved again after a few days to be billeted with an elderly, childless couple in Wells.

Declaration of war with Germany came a week after the children were sent away. Those left behind braced themselves for the expected air attack but it didn't come. Kate went to join her children in Northampton and Sarah joined a group going to Banbury in Oxfordshire. Daisy wavered. John was due to be called up any day. She wanted to spend the remaining days with him and besides, she couldn't leave Dermot.

The house seemed empty without Erin. Even Dermot asked after her repeatedly, but the postcard Daisy had packed in the little suitcase, to be posted when she arrived at her new address, didn't come for ten days. It came in the same post as a letter from Sarah saying she was planning to come home. Nobody wanted to have a pregnant woman billeted on them. That's that then, thought Daisy. I'll 'ave to stay 'ere now. Her second baby was due in February.

In November, she made the journey by coach to Wells to see Erin, taking her a new pleated tartan kilt and a red jumper. Erin wanted to show her the jousting knights on the clock in Wells Cathedral, so Daisy quelled her misgivings about entering a non-Catholic church and took her. They walked about the sunlit grass hand in hand but under a strange restraint.

The child had grown spindly and rather withdrawn. They sat on the low wall feeding the goldfish, waiting for the swans to ring the bell at feeding time.

'It's lovely here,' said Erin. The sounded aspirant hit Daisy with a shock. The kid had only been here a couple

273

of months and she was sounding her aitches!

'Yes, lovely,' she agreed. 'Do you like it 'ere, love? Do they treat you all right?'

Erin didn't meet her eye. She trailed her hand in the water, a frond of bobbed, dark hair falling forward across the pale cheek.

'Mr Yeo is nice. He brings me here on Sundays to see the clock strike and feed the swans, but I don't think Mrs Yeo likes me. She won't let me speak. I have to change my clothes when I get in from school and sit in a chair reading a book till supper time. Then I go to bed. She won't let me play with the doll you sent me, in case I break it.' She looked up, the grey eyes grave and curiously adult. 'I want to go home, Mum.'

Daisy's heart was wrung. 'I'd take you 'ome if I could, love, but it's better for you to stay 'ere in case the air-raids start. It won't be for long. The war will soon be over.'

Erin nodded and seemed to accept what she'd been told. Daisy reflected, going home on the coach, that the kid hadn't smiled once all day. She hadn't cried at their parting, but waved her goodbye from the top of the house steps, her small face set and composed.

She had planned to go again before Christmas, but John's call-up papers came and she couldn't spare one of his last ten days. January brought her last chance to go before the baby came. She was really already too far advanced in pregnancy to travel comfortably, but it was easier to make the journey with the baby in her belly than to have to carry it in her arms. God alone knew when she'd be able to go again after the birth.

She arrived at the house soon after lunch. She was shown into the parlour. Daisy looked about her with curiosity. It was not so different from the parlours on the island. There was the piano, the three-piece suite, a bureau with books in a glass-fronted cupboard. Only here everything stank of money.

Erin came in, followed by Mrs Yeo. Daisy held her arms open. The child didn't throw herself into them but kissed her sedately on the cheek and stood back, her eyes lowered.

'Where's the nice kilt I sent you? Don't you want to wear it?'

'I'm only allowed to wear it on Sundays.'

'Well, come on, get your coat. I'll take you out. 'Ave you 'ad your dinner?'

'I'm afraid you'll have to spend your visit to Erin here, Mrs Fletcher,' said Mrs Yeo. 'Erin is being punished. I have said she is not allowed to go out.'

'Oh yeah?' said Daisy with a note of real interest. 'What's she under punishment for?'

'Disobedience.'

'What did you do, love?'

'I came into the parlour without Mrs Yeo.' The voice was barely a whisper. Erin hung her head. 'I only wanted to look at the china dog.' She glanced up at a porcelain figure on the mantelpiece.

'Erin is not allowed in here unless she's with me or my husband. We have some valuable things. I caught her in here last night.'

'She sent me to bed without any supper,' said Erin.

'Did she? Well, I tell you what, love. Never mind what this old cow says. You go up and get your coat. While you're at it, get the rest of your things. You're comin' 'ome with me.'

Joy suffused Erin's face and she fled.

'You can't do that!' Mrs Yeo glared at Daisy.

'Who says I can't? You? She's my kid and I'll do as I bloody well like.'

'What kind of mother are you? Taking the child into danger!'

'You wouldn't know nothin' about what kind of mother I am. The nearest you ever got to bein' a bleedin' mother was when you bought yourself this.' She picked up the china dog and plonked it in the startled woman's hands. 'Erin can take 'er chance with me. If 'Itler's got a bomb with our name on it, we'll go together. I don't want 'er left in the world by 'erself. I come up without a mother an' I know what it's like to be at the mercy of tight-arsed old cows like you.'

They were delayed on the journey home. The coach pulled into the station too late for them to catch the connection back to the island. Daisy settled on a bench to spend what remained of the night, making Erin as comfortable as possible. Among the posters on the wall warning against careless talk and reminders to carry gas masks at all times was a picture of an anxious mother with three children, In the background hovered the ghostly outline of Hitler. Below the picture was a message which seemed to have been designed specifically for her. 'Don't do it, Mothers! Leave the little ones where they are!'

Daisy put her arm protectively across Erin where she slept, her head on her knee. The other hand she rested on the bulge of her abdomen. Everything she'd got left in the world was here. Sod you, she thought. We're all together. Please God, we'll stay together. Sod 'Itler. My biggest problem is going to be the old man. I'll 'ave to stand up to 'im, now John's not around.

Dermot himself solved the problem. In the week that Daisy was due to be confined he stayed late in The Feathers, drinking with those who had been left behind or not yet caught by the conscription net. He had taken a good deal of drink even by his standards and was having difficulty weaving his way along Bermuda Street, cursing at the lack of lighting, when the doom clock which had been ticking quietly inside him for a number of years, struck his last moment. An aortic aneurism ruptured and felled him. He was dead before he hit the ground.

Daisy waited up to let him in, her mind on the impending birth, longing for what she most dreaded. She looked at the Christ figure thinking that now she had some idea of how he must have felt in the Garden of Gethsemane. There was no way round the ordeal to come. Only through. Where the bloody hell had her father got to? She wanted to get to bed. After an hour, her irritation turned to alarm and she slipped out to find Danny. On her way to his door in the blackout, she passed Dermot's body without seeing it.

Danny sent her home and took charge. His father was clearly dead when he found him, but an ambulance was summoned and, in deference to Daisy's condition, he was taken to the morgue in Poplar Hospital. There could hardly be a wake, with family and friends scattered around the country.

Underlying Daisy's grief was a sense of outrage. It was bloody typical of her Dad to go and die without warning a few days before the baby was born, when it was difficult to get about. There was so much running around to be done when someone died.

She dragged the box where Dermot kept his personal

belongings from under his bed, looking for the insurance policy that would pay his funeral expenses. She had never been permitted to look at the contents. She sat on his bed turning them over. Several paying-in books to insurance companies; a membership certificate of The Grand Order of Buffalo; memorial cards and death certificates of her long-dead siblings, and birth certificates, including her own.

She spread out the birth certificates. Paddy's wasn't there. He must have taken it. Here was a strange one. Michael John, born August 22, 1894. Daisy frowned. She'd never heard of a Michael. She shuffled through the memorial cards. No Michael John. 1894? She found Dermot's marriage certificate: Charlotte Mary to Dermot John, July 20, 1894.

The shock hit her like a douche in cold water. Anger against her father mounted in her. Poor cow! The poor cow! He kept her hanging on till she was eight months gone before he married her. No wonder her family would have nothing to do with them. He must have promised to marry her. Why else would they have had that picture taken? She would never have let him have his way unless she was promised to him. There was no sign that she was pregnant in that picture.

Daisy went on with her search, looking for something that would give her the date of Michael's death, but there was nothing. He couldn't have lived long. Danny didn't know about him, she was sure of that, and Danny was born 1896.

She was reaching the bottom of the box. Her hand touched an old brown envelope. She opened it and drew out what must have been the original of her enlarged picture of her parents on their engagement day. Daisy dissolved into tears. The old bastard! All that pleading she did as a child to know what her mother looked like, and he had a picture of her all the time.

Daisy's face was still swollen and tear-stained when the midwife called and ordered her to bed. For the first few hours she fretted about Erin, but the child was resourceful. School was not functioning, so she whiled away the time crayonning in a picture book and making herself jam sandwiches when she was hungry. At the end of the first day, the midwife found an elderly neighbour across the road who had refused to leave her home. She took Erin in and fed her.

At the end of a second, bitterly cold day, Erin was taken in to see her mother.

'Here's your new baby sister,' Daisy said. 'It would 'a been nice to have a boy, but I would 'ave had to call 'im Dermot. Now I don't have to. Her name's Verity.'

Chapter 25

Blitz

Sarah didn't like the name Verity. Her own carroty-headed infant, five weeks older than Verity, was called Tom. She expressed her opinion plainly to Daisy as they walked home together, pushing their prams, from the welfare clinic.

'Bleedin' crackjaw names – Erin and Verity. What's wrong with names like Mary and Emma? Or call 'em after people in the family. Call 'er Charlotte.'

'No. I don't believe in namin' 'em after aunts an' grannies. Nice unusual names. Gives 'em a fresh start.'

Daisy looked down with satisfaction at the baby sleeping in the shade of the elaborate canopy she had paid for over several weeks. Dark head and delicate limbs against the pale pink and lace of the pram pillow. Tom presented a much less pretty picture; his linen not so pristine, but then his mother hadn't much experience as a washerwoman. The heat of the afternoon was making his skin as red as his hair.

Both women ignored the air-raid warning when it wailed out over the streets. There had been many in the past months, but nothing had happened. People had got used to them. At first, when war was first declared, they'd gone round expecting to be bombed any minute, but that had worn off. Now, nearly a year later, they took no notice.

'Must be gettin' on for five o'clock,' said Sarah. They had reached the corner of Glengall Road where their ways parted. 'You comin' in for a cuppa tea?'

'No thanks,' replied Daisy. 'I left Erin playin' out in the street. I got to get back to 'er.' Daisy bore down on the handle of her pram to negotiate the kerb, when she stopped, her eyes widening in frightened astonishment.

'Gawd, blimey, what's that?'

Towards the south-east the sky had darkened and the air was filled with a droning sound that swelled by the second. At first Daisy thought it was smoke, that one of the factories in Cubitt Town was on fire, but then she saw that the substance of the great black cloud that threatened to blot out the sun was planes, flying low, in close formation. The distant thud of falling bombs, followed by the flash of fire and pluming smoke was growing rapidly closer. In the moment that it took them to gather their wits, the formation broke and changed. The big, black bombers fanned out, spreading, like a biblical plague, long tentacles of death over south and east London.

'My Gawd!' Sarah was aghast. 'We ain't got time to get 'ome. We'll 'ave to get in the school!' She turned her pram and started to run towards the gates of the school, which had been designated a Public Shelter. 'Come on, Daisy! Run!'

'I can't! I've got to find Erin!'

She didn't look back, but set off at a run. bumping the pram over the cobbles, so that Verity woke and set up a wail. Erin and another child, whose mother was running towards her from the opposite end of the street, were standing uncertainly in the road, staring up at the sky. By the time Daisy had scooped her up and got both children to the Anderson shelter in the back yard, the first peppering of bombs had hit the island.

She cursed herself for not keeping the corrugated iron shelter in better condition. She'd hardly been down here since the men came to sink it in the ground. Now, she and the children and the old woman from across the road crouched in the dank darkness, listening to the whistle of falling high explosives, puddles of water swilling round their feet.

With each explosion the ground shook. Some were so close it seemed their little haven must be plucked from the ground like a tooth from a gum, so much did it shudder and sway. The violent movement of air in their confined space seemed to suck in the walls and blow them out again. With each whine and shriek, Erin fell on her face, her fingers in her ears and her mouth open, as she had been taught to do, so that her eardrums would not rupture. She didn't whimper or cry, being too intent on waiting for the next bomb to drop.

At about nine in the evening there came a lull and Daisy ventured to open the door. She pulled the twine that undid the latch and looked out, expecting the deep blackout to which they had become accustomed, but was surprised to find it bright as day, lit with an eerie red light. Red smoke and smuts filled the yard, so that even in the glow of the thousand fires ringing the island, she could only just make out the shape of the house. Acrid fumes filled her lungs and she began choking and coughing.

'Gas!' she shouted to the old woman who had not spoken a word since the raid began. 'And I've left the baby's respirator indoors! I'll 'ave to go and get it.'

'No!' The old woman roused herself to protest. 'Don't go out there.'

'I'll 'ave to. You stay 'ere with the kids. Put your gas masks on. I'll only be a minute.'

Daisy hauled herself out of the dugout and ran to the back door. Glass crunched underfoot. The windows had gone, but otherwise the house was still standing. Upstairs, she found the respirator, like everything else, covered in grit and dust. She spared a moment to look out of the gap where the front windows had been, to see that where the houses opposite had stood, there was now a pile of smoking rubble. Hearing the low roar of returning aircraft, she grabbed the respirator and ran.

All through the second wave of the attack, Daisy pumped the respirator, not daring to stop, even when Verity began to writhe and squall with hunger. At about five in the morning, the ferocity of the bombardment seemed to ease, but she willed herself to go on. Erin had fallen into an exhausted sleep, her head in the lap of their neighbour; grotesquely comical in her Mickey Mouse mask. Just before six, someone dragged the door open. Daisy looked up in alarm, half expecting to see a German, but a familiar island voice asked: 'Is everyone all right in here?' It was a member of the auxiliary fire service. He had been working his way along the back yards checking the occupants of the shelters. 'You're all right for a bit now, love. The all clear's gone.'

'I didn't 'ear it. What about the gas?'

'There ain't no gas, love. The paint factory got a direct hit on the ammonia store. That's what the smell is. You can take your gas masks off. It's all right to go indoors. Get yourself a bit o' dinner. We don't know when Jerry will be back. Make yourselves a cup o' tea, if you got any water. The main's been hit. If not, go over the school. There's a relief station set up there.'

Shakily, they emerged into the defiled September morning and stood in dazed bewilderment, looking about them and at each other. Black smuts floated thickly in the foul air. Above the wall at the end of the yard, they could see cranes in the docks, standing red against the pall of thick black smoke that rose on every side. Daisy turned to her dirt-streaked neighbour and said gently, 'You'd better come indoors with me. I think your house 'as gone.'

Danny heard the warning that sent Sarah scuttling for shelter into the school. It was knocking off time in the dock, so he unhurriedly collected his tea-can and set out to stroll across to his mate, thinking they would go together to the rescue station where they had spent many evenings in the preceding months, standing by, ready for emergencies. Everyone who had not been conscripted into the forces volunteered for one of the auxiliary services. Danny, because of his phenomenal strength, had been designated a member of the heavy rescue squad. There had been a couple of weeks basic training followed by almost a year of eventless stand-bys.

He hadn't gone more than a couple of paces when his attention was dragged, rudely, to the skies above Woolwich. A solid mass of black aircraft that filled the south-eastern sky was screaming towards him. Hundreds of them, flying low, as unheeding of the shells and tracer bullets streaking to head them off as of a summer shower. Danny's heart sank. All the guns were bashing away but they were flying right through it!

Close by, the big gun on the mudchute, that area of land raised to a high point by the dredging of the dock, barked, adding its fire to the barrage from the ships and gun emplacements along the river, but the advancing horde did not falter or break formation. As he watched, a handful of British fighters rose to intercept and were soon smitten by the enemy, spiralling down, with flame and smoke pouring from their tails, to crash somewhere to the south.

Danny looked about him for cover and decided on the bottom of the dry dock. He reached the base of the vertical ladder just as the first stick of bombs hit the Millwall Docks. One after the other, in rapid succession, ships, barges, cranes and warehouses spurted fire and smoke. Danny ran and squeezed himself between the hull of a ship from Argentina and one of its supporting baulks of timber.

How long he crouched there, listening to the rush, roar and shatter of bombs, he couldn't be sure. At what he judged to be about nine in the evening, though it was impossible to be accurate in the false darkness, he heard the throb of aircraft receding and came out of his hiding place. He could hardly breathe. Smuts and ammonia fumes borne on the rolling red smoke fouled the air, making him choke. When he had gained level ground at the top of the ladder, he took his handkerchief and tied it over his nose and mouth.

Toppled cranes, fallen masonry and timbers littered the landscape he had known since he was a child, turning it into an alien battle field. Amidst the devastation, only one person was near. A man was wandering in a dazed way towards the inner dock, picking his way over and among the debris. He seemed to be unhurt, so

Danny left him. It was hard to get his bearings but he set course for the main gate. Beyond it he could see firemen struggling to climb a crane with a hose so that they could play water from above on the inferno that was the tobacco warehouse.

He hadn't far to go to the rescue station. All fire crews had been mustered. He passed several engines and a pump being drawn by a taxi. He heard weary men cursing at the lack of water. Hoses had been run into the river, but the tide was out.

The control room was lit by candles, the first blast having taken out the electricity supply, but everywhere telephones shrilled and clamoured. The officer in charge didn't pause to greet Danny or comment on his late arrival but at once directed him to go as relief to a crew working in an area where several small streets had been laid flat.

There was not much left standing for some distance. Danny found the warden in charge and asked for instructions.

'There's not much chance of finding survivors,' said the warden. 'It's going to have to be a bare hands job, though. Can't very well use picks and shovels in case there's anyone left alive. They wouldn't be much good anyway. The brickwork seems to have just disintegrated. It's all fine rubble. Just do what you can. There must be somebody underneath.'

Working with a piece of wood and his fingers, Danny toiled for a couple of hours without finding anything. About twenty yards away another gang of men were sifting through the rubble. Now and again, a limb was found and placed in a sack. Not until dawn was breaking and the all clear was sounding did the shout go up:

'We've got one 'ere!'

It was a body, not a survivor. An elderly man, still sitting in his armchair, completely encased in plaster and rubble. They dug him out and put him in a sack ready for despatch to the temporary morgue set up in the school which also housed the rescue station and the mobile hospital unit. The armchair came out intact.

At seven, Danny was relieved. He turned for home, feeling a surge of thankfulness to see the blocks and most of Bermuda Street still standing. A deep crater in the road outside The Feathers had been cordoned off, but the policeman on guard let him pass.

At twelve, he got up and washed and shaved, surprised to realise that he had slept for three hours despite the buzzing in his brain. He made his way to the dock, but was not allowed to go in, so he returned to the rescue station in time to see the mortuary staff shrouding the bodies so far recovered.

Smoke and haze had cleared during the morning and it was another day of fine, warm weather. The doors to the shed that served as the mortuary were open, and the bodies, about ten of them, were lying on the ground. A screen had been erected, a pointless nicety, Danny thought, because of the remote possibility that there might be casual passers-by, who must be shielded from the sight.

An official from the Poplar coroner's mortuary was instructing the men detailed to assist him. He had them strip off what clothing remained on the corpses.

'Now,' he said. 'Give them a wash.'

A man picked up a bucket and a sponge and began gently to wash the face of a corpse.

'Not like that,' said the official. He ordered that two

men kept the buckets of water coming. 'We can't have the job taking four hours,' he said. 'Do it like this.'

With a long-handled mop, well wetted, he gave the body a good wash down, back and front. Then he showed the men how to wrap it in a shroud and stow it inside the shed ready to be coffined. It took about three minutes. The official looked round at the shocked faces. He passed the mop to the nearest man. 'You'll soon get the hang of it,' he said.

At the end of the tenth day of continuous bombing, a rough pattern to the attacks began to emerge. Often, there was a break during the morning. In the afternoon the raiders came again and continued their work until about five o'clock, when, sometimes, there was a lull. They would return at about seven to pound the docks and the surrounding areas all night; it could be absolutely relied upon.

The all clear sounded at six one morning in late September and Danny went home to rest and eat. He found the bed from the unoccupied flat above dangling through what remained of the ceiling; most of the rest of it reclined on the mat in front of the stove. He turned the tap. No water. He would go to Daisy's. She always managed to make a cup of tea somehow.

She was glad to see him.

'I been down your 'ouse every day to see if you was all right, but I've never managed to catch you in. You poor sod! You look terrible.'

'You don't look so good yourself. Where are the kids?'

'I put 'em into my bed, to finish their sleep out. They don't get no sleep down the dugout, what with the bleedin' noise and the damp.'

'You shouldn't keep 'em 'ere, Dais. You ought to get 'em away. Why don't you go over to Paddy's?'

'What, Clapham? That ain't much better than 'ere.'

'It's away from the docks. 'Itler ain't gonna leave us alone till there's nothin' left. You'd be all right there. Paddy's got a shelter in the back.'

'No thanks. I'll take me chances 'ere. I've 'ad enough of lodgin's. Besides, Kathleen's got enough troubles without me addin' to 'em.'

'What d'you mean? Paddy's in a reserved occupation. She's luckier than you, she's got 'er man at home.' .

'She might not think she's so lucky. I reckon he knocks 'er about.'

'No! Did she tell you that?'

'She don't 'ave to. I know the look in the eyes well enough. I don't want my kids goin' into that, I'd sooner put up with ol' 'Itler. We'll be all right down our shelter, unless it gets a direct hit, then we won't know much about it. I've bailed all the water out and put some decent beddin' and some night lights down there. We've 'ad some near misses, but they say lightnin' never strikes in the same place twice.'

'That's what they all say, but I know different. That's what that poor old gal in Stebondale Street thought. She's sittin' up in the watchman's hut that they put in the big hole the land-mine made. She's been there three days. Won't go to the centre. She's waiting to see if they bring anybody out of the rubble. Four of 'em she's got under there somewhere.' Danny rubbed his red eyes and took a swig of tea.

'Is Sarah all right?' he asked. 'I ain't seen 'er.'

'I seen her yesterday. She's sleepin' over the rope works at night. It's too crowded in their Anderson. It's damp and the baby's got a bad chest. She likes it over the rope works. The Salvation Army got it all cleaned up. They give you nice sheets and blankets and they 'ave a sing-song to drown out the noise of the bombs. It keeps people cheerful. Look.' She touched his arm. 'Why don't you get some kip 'ere? If you wake up before the warnin' goes, I'll get you to come round to John's mother's with me. Sometimes, if there's craters in the road, the policemen won't let you through. They're more likely to let us through if you're with me. I heard there was some houses down in their road. I ain't got no time for the old gal, but I ought to see if they're all right, for John's sake.'

She woke him at one with tea and toast and dripping. When he had finished eating, she put on her coat.

'What about the kids?' he asked.

'Erin'll look after the baby. I told 'er we'll be back soon. She knows to take 'er down the shelter if the warnin' goes.'

'She's a bit young to be left, ain't she Dais?' Danny said. He was pushing his bike, lifting it over obstacles as they picked their path towards the bridge.

'I know. But kids 'ave to grow up fast these days. They can't even play in the street no more. Erin's a good kid. She can mind the baby as good as me. I tell you what. John wouldn't 'alf be proud of 'er. She ain't gettin' no schoolin' to speak of. Only what Miss Morgan can fix up in people's 'ouses a couple of days a week, but she reckons Erin won't 'ave no trouble passin' the scholarship. She'll walk it, she says. Mind you, I don't know where she's gonna go to school. Still, it makes you feel funny to think there's brains in the family. Must get it from John.'

They crossed the bridge and Daisy fell silent, trying to digest the changes about her. They were passing along a road still almost intact, but entirely deserted. Where only a few weeks before had been the bustle of an East End street with carts, hawkers, children playing, people walking to and fro to the pubs and shops, now, there was only dust and desolation.

They turned a corner and found their way blocked by a heap of rubble. Three houses had been taken out of the row, leaving a grinning gap. Pictures still hung drunkenly on the inner walls and a piano was sliding gently down the slope. Behind the heap could be seen the little gardens. Surprising how many trees there were, hidden away behind the houses.

'Funny, i'n't it? The way the stairs always seem to stay put,' said Daisy. 'I reckon that's about the safest place to be. Under the stairs.'

They reached John's mother's house. The windows had gone and the front door had been blown off and was lying flat half-way up the passage. Daisy called out but no one answered.

She stepped in, her feet crunching on the soot and plaster. There was no one in the little parlour. Daisy knelt on the fallen door and rat-tatted.

'Anyone in?'

Her father-in-law appeared at the top of the stairs, carrying a broom. He began to sweep the stairs, raising a thick cloud of dust.

'Got to get this cleaned up,' he said. 'It would upset mother to see it like this.'

They learned from him that John's mother was safe. She had gone to relatives in Essex. Danny persuaded the old man to go to the rest centre and to join his wife when he could. He went, telling them to salvage what they could of his possessions.

'Here,' he said, thrusting a large clock into Daisy's hands. 'Mother would want John to 'ave this.'

They collected an assortment of things, tying as much as they could to the bike. Daisy carried what she could in her arms and they started the walk back to her flat. With every step the clock clanged and chimed. The siren wailed out and they walked on more quickly through the deserted streets. Into the blue sky across the river rose a thick column of smoke. Their situation suddenly struck Danny as ridiculous. Here he was, with a broom lashed to his bike, Daisy carrying a chiming clock and all as black as Newgate's knocker! He started to laugh; Daisy joined him. They laid down the bike, sat on the kerb and laughed till they cried.

Chapter 26

Flight

Until Spring, 1941, Daisy remained steadfast in her determination not to leave the island. The bombing had continued relentlessly for seventy-six consecutive days and nights except for one, in early November, when the weather was too severe for the enemy to take to the air. After that, Hitler changed tactics and the raids became more sporadic, though they continued with great intensity until mid-summer.

By late March, the blocks were down and Danny had moved in with Daisy. The little terrace of bay-windowed houses was shorter, having lost four of its number closest to the stonefield, but hers was still standing. It was used mainly as a store and place of respite between the raids. Everyday life was played out in the Anderson shelter. They never slept in the house.

On the day she changed her mind, Daisy came up out of the shelter in the chilly dawn, to see if she had the means of making tea and preparing breakfast. Danny might be in soon, but the night had been loud with bombs and gunfire and there was no knowing when he might be relieved. He came in, dirty, red-eyed and hungry as always, just before seven.

She gave him tea and put the kettle back on to heat

water for his wash and shave. He seemed too tired even to speak.

'I got two letters from John yesterday,' she told him. 'Don't 'ear nothin' for weeks, then I get two at once. Still, I don't know how the poor bloody postman finds anyone. Door numbers don't mean much any more. You heard from Kate?' Danny nodded.

'Yeah. They're all all right. The kids like Northampton.' He stirred his tea, not looking at her. 'I wish you'd get away. It only wants the bridges to go west and there's no gettin' off the island.'

'You keep sayin' that. We've come through so far. If one o' them bombs 'as got my name on it, well, that's it. You can only die once.'

'Yeah, but what about John? Don't you think you should make sure he's got somethin' to come back to?' His voice had an unusual edge. 'How are them poor sods expected to carry on over there, fightin', if their wife and kids ain't safe? Poor ol' Colour . . .'

'Colour?'

'I didn't know how to tell you this. There ain't no easy way. The rope works bought it last night. A thousand pounder right through the roof. Ninety dead. I was on another job, but I 'eard about it when I got back to the station.'

There was a short, stunned silence, then Daisy said: 'We don't know for sure Sarah was in there.'

'We do. My mate seen 'er.'

'And little Tom?'

'They ain't found 'im. But there's no chance, Dais, no chance.'

Daisy absorbed the news without immediately feeling grief.

294

'I told 'er she'd be better off in the Anderson. I don't trust Public Shelters,' was all she said.

During the morning, while Danny slept, a sense of outrage grew in her. Sarah was dead. All that struggling to keep the family together, for what? All this time she had clung to her home, believing that one day people would come back, kids would play in the street and everything would be as it had been. She saw clearly now that it could never be the same. The bombs had burned and blasted away more than just rows of houses.

She told Danny when she woke him that she would leave as soon as the all clear went in the morning. She would pack their essential belongings on the pram and walk as far as the underground, then get to Paddy's place. That would do for a start.

'Look for somewhere a bit farther out, if you can. There's plenty of empty 'ouses. You just have to apply to go in 'em. I'm gonna look for a place out Chigwell way after the war, if I'm still 'ere.'

'What about you, Danny? I don't like leavin' you by yourself.'

'I've gotta stay 'ere, ain't I? Maybe, when things quieten down a bit, I'll see if I can get Florrie home. Now Dad's gone, they ought to let her out. I don't mean just to look after me. They'll probably make her go in the munitions factory, but if she wants to come 'ome, I'm gonna give her the chance.'

'Funny,' said Daisy. ' I can't 'ardly remember 'er. I'll come back if they 'ave a service for the people in the rope works. I'll come back for that.'

Daisy did not stay long with Paddy and Kathleen in the house in Clapham. Paddy welcomed them and Kathleen was a dutiful hostess, but there was something between the two that made Daisy tense. Nothing happened to confirm her suspicions that Paddy beat his wife and she was not close enough to her to ask and get a truthful reply.

In fact, Paddy lost control only rarely, not more than two or three times in a year, and when he did beat Kathleen, he took great care not to mark her face. The blows and kicks, though savage, were landed in places that could easily be covered by her clothes. Once he had gone too far and cracked a rib and she had had to explain her wincing pain on drawing breath as a 'touch of pleurisy' and stay close to the house until she healed. Usually, there was no problem. She saw few people other than the ones she spoke to in the shops and apart from her pallor and dead, expressionless eyes, there was no outward sign of her suffering.

At the first opportunity, Daisy left the children with Kathleen and took a bus going east, to see if she could find a place to live. She chose the place at random. The bus stopped in a broad, tree-lined road outside a pub. It had been some time since they passed a bombed building so Daisy got off and walked back, past a row of small shops which gave way to terraced houses. Several had 'To Let' signs in the windows, but she walked on until she found one with a tiled front path and a bay window. A bit bigger and more recently built than the house in Bermuda Street, but with a comfortingly familiar look. She was standing at the gate looking at it when a woman went by, a shopping basket over her arm.

'Excuse me, love. Do you know if these are council houses?'

'No. These are private. If you want to look at that one, ask the lady next door. She looks after it for the landlord.'

The arrangement was quickly and simply made. It was as good a place as any. Daisy moved her children into the house a week later, having established that there was a functioning school a few blocks away, or at least, half a school, the boy's section having been commandeered for use by the auxiliary services. There was already an air-raid shelter in the long garden behind the house. Once she had raked up a few basic bits of furniture from a second-hand store and hung the picture of her mother and father in the front room, they had everything they needed.

They had lived there a couple of months before John's letters found their way to her and for nearly a year when news came through that Erin had won a place in a grammar school.

Erin herself accepted her success in a matter-of-fact way, as being no more than she expected, but Daisy was beside herself with joy and pride. She rushed into the street holding the letter, to show the first neighbour who passed, but she got to the gate and stopped. The only person walking by was on the other side of the wide road where traffic swept past. She didn't know her anyway. There was no one to tell. She wrote to Danny, returning from the pillar box feeling deflated and heartsore.

Daisy's pleasure in having a daughter at grammar school began to evaporate in the first few weeks and by the end of the first term had disappeared. In the first place, Erin had to take a long, expensive bus ride to the ancient institution when there was a modern elementary school just round the corner. Girls there were not required to wear a uniform. Having spent so many precious clothing coupons in providing the outfit, Daisy was furious when Erin ripped her gym slip during a hockey match. She nagged her about it, but Erin didn't sew it up for weeks and when she did, she cobbled it together so that she still looked scruffy.

It was such a job, trying to keep clothes on the kids' backs and shoes on their feet. When Verity passed her third birthday, Daisy put her into one of the state-run nurseries and got a job in a factory making the trays that were used for holding maps in aircraft.

She enjoyed being at work again, loved being with a crowd of women; singing with them when 'Workers Playtime' was relayed over the loudspeakers from the wireless. It was everything else that got her down. Still, everyone was in the same boat. Queueing for food. Trying to make the rations stretch.

It would have been easier to cope if they weren't constantly robbed of sleep. Daisy had given up using the beds in the house. It was too nerve-wracking getting the kids out in the night when the warning went, to hustle them down the garden path in the cold and dark to the shelter. Better to settle down there for the night and get what rest you could.

At the beginning of Erin's second year, Daisy got a letter from the headmaster, asking her to call to see him. It was not easy to arrange for Verity to be picked up and looked after or to get the time off work, but she presented herself at his office on time, wearing her best coat and, as she thought of it herself, with her fighting irons on. She tended to be aggressive when she felt out of her depth.

The headmaster was a courteous man. He looked ill at ease. Daisy was sharp enough to know why. He wasn't used to dealing with her sort. The other mothers would all be very pound-notish. He came to the point. He was concerned that Erin was not making the progress they had expected of her. She was under-achieving.

'It's her homework that's really the problem, Mrs Fletcher. It's not up to the standard of her other work. Sometimes she doesn't even complete it. Er, where does she sit to do her homework?'

'She clears a corner of the kitchen table. It's the only table we got.'

'Is that where the rest of the family sits? She's in the same room as you, with the wireless on?'

'Yes.'

'Couldn't she go into another room?'

'What, and burn another light? You don't 'ave to pay the bleedin' bills. And it's cold in the front room.'

'Her bedroom, perhaps?'

'There ain't no light in there, 'cos of the blackout, and I only go in there to clean it. We're all down the dugout by nine.'

The headmaster looked weary. 'Well, see what you can do to help her, will you, Mrs Fletcher? Did you know Erin has said she'd like to be a doctor?'

'A doctor?' Daisy had heard of lady doctors, but had never come across one. The idea was preposterous.

'She has the ability,' the head was saying, 'but it will require hard work on her part. She will have to be more punctual, too. She was late for school twice last week.'

There had been fractious rows on most mornings last week. Erin couldn't find her socks, or there were holes in the heels. It drove Daisy mad when she was rushing round, trying to get Verity ready and off to nursery by eight. She couldn't work miracles, New socks cost coupons. She felt angry with Erin for letting her down, for putting her in this embarrassing position, but she would stick up for her in front of him.

'What do you expect? The kid gets woke up every night by them square-'eaded bastards, then gets the cane for bein' late for school!'

'Erin hasn't been caned. We are all anxious that she should make the most of her opportunity here, but it's not entirely up to us. She has to do her part.'

'Don't you worry. I'll make sure she does 'er 'ome-work!'

For a couple of nights after the interview, Daisy took a closer interest in Erin's work.

'What you doin'?'

'History.'

'I 'ated bleedin' 'istory. King Alfred burnt the cakes,' she said contemptuously. 'Who the bloody 'ell cares?'

'We're not doing King Alfred. I've got to learn the dates of accession of the kings and queens from 1066 up to the Tudors. We've got a test tomorrow. Will you test me on them?'

Daisy took the book and followed the dates as Erin recited them. She was impressed. The kid got them right.

'Henry the Eighth, 1509 to 1547,' said Erin.

'That old git,' said Daisy with a vehemence that startled Erin. 'He 'ad six wives, didn't he? Chopped their 'eads off.'

'It was hundreds of years ago, Mum, and he didn't chop all their heads off.'

'He started a new religion, didn't 'e? Chucked out the

Pope! Everyone was Catholic before 'e started the bleedin' proddies.'

'He started the Church of England.'

'The Church of England!' Daisy's voice was raised in a sneer that couldn't express the anger and loathing she felt. 'They ain't like our lot. Bleedin' vicars! You read about 'em every week in *The News of The World*!'

'It's the same religion.' Erin groped to find an explanation from her own scant knowledge. 'It's just that he didn't agree with some things. That's why they're called Protestants. Protesting, see?'

'What did they 'ave to protest about?'

'I don't know. They used to make people do penance. Walk round with stones in their shoes, things like that.'

'Don't be silly! It's the Protestants who wrecked poor bleedin' Ireland! Bloody English are always on the grab! It was peaceful till they stuck their oar in.'

Erin was out of her depth, but patriotism stirred in her.

'How do you know? You've never even been to Ireland.'

Daisy wasn't standing for that.

'Who do you think you're talkin' to?' she demanded. 'I'm your mother, not the bleedin' 'ouse cat. You're gettin' too big for your boots, my gal. That school ain't doin' you no good. Why don't they learn you somethin' useful?'

Erin gave up. She was close to tears as she put her books back into her satchel. She was beginning to learn which subjects it was best not to mention in her mother's presence: Germans, of course; the Salvation Army, religion and the monarchy; particularly not Henry the Eighth.

It was more difficult to know what path to tread when

301

it came to talk of England. Daisy didn't seem to know for sure whether she was English or Irish, switching from pride in the forces fighting overseas to hatred of them in the context of Ireland. Erin knew without doubt that she was, herself, English.

A rash appeared on the inner surfaces of Daisy's elbows. She ignored it at first but the patches of hot, itching skin began to spread along her arms and she went to see the doctor. There was a long wait in the waiting room and when she got in to see him, he was distracted and pressed for time. He gave her ointment.

'It's your nerves,' he said.

'I don't suffer with me nerves, never 'ave.'

'We all suffer from nerves these days.'

She thought about that on the way home. The worry had to come out somewhere, she supposed. She had noticed that those turns, when she heard the music and struggled to see the face of the woman on the swing, seemed to happen when she'd been worried or frightened.

There was that time about a month ago. She had stuck to her place in the queue at the fish-shop when the siren sounded. She wasn't going to give it up after standing there for more than an hour, and had just come out, lucky she had, when a German fighter, straggling behind the others, had dived on the row of shops and machine-gunned the women in the street.

No one was hit. Daisy and another woman had thrown themselves flat in the little patch of scrubby bushes that ornamented the wide pavement. They had picked themselves up and gawped at the row of neat round holes in the fish-shop window.

302

That must have shaken her up a bit. She had felt queer that night. Erin had been good. She was standing beside her with a glass of water when she came to. Daisy always felt calm, almost disembodied afterwards. She knew why. It was her Mum trying to get through to her, to let her know that she was near by, watching over her. It was very comforting.

There had been no news of John for nearly three months. That must be why she had come out in this rash. Still, no news was good news. The butcher's was quiet. Daisy nipped in and picked up her ration. She was in luck; there was a bit of offal. So far, she'd managed to give the kids a hot dinner of some sort, every night.

Her next-door neighbour came out to speak to her as she reached the front gate.

'There's no gas or electricity. Can't even make a cup of tea.'

'I didn't 'ear the warnin'.'

'No. It's not a raid. There's an unexploded bomb round the back of the library. They're trying to defuse it. They've cut everything off.'

'Oh well. We mustn't moan, then. Poor sods are riskin' their lives.'

'Have you got enough bread for the kids?'

'I ain't gonna give 'em bread. I'm gonna cook 'em a dinner.'

'How will you manage?'

'There's always a way round it.'

Daisy considered the little grate in the back room, then rejected the idea. Couldn't get a decent-sized pot on that. She went into the back garden and dug a hole. She lined it with stones and fixed a shelf from the oven above the

303

fire she lit in the bottom. On this she placed her big, iron pot, satisfyingly full of meat, onions and potherbs. When she had everything prepared, she called over the fence to her neighbour.

'Give us your kettle, love. I'll make you a cuppa tea like the ones we used to 'ave down hoppin'.'

The letter from John, saying he was coming home on leave, arrived on the day the V2 rocket knocked down the cinema in the high street, killing forty people. In a strange way, both events brought a mixture of relief and dread.

It was her first experience of the V2 and mingled with the sorrow for the dead was a thankfulness that this newest weapon was more merciful than what had gone before. At least you couldn't hear these rockets coming. The V1 had kept whole neighbourhoods transfixed with terror as they coasted along the roof-tops after their engines cut out, to choose victims according to the whim of the wind. The V2 flew faster than sound. Once the crash was heard, the danger was over.

Anticipation of John's homecoming was tinged with fear. They had not seen each other for nearly five years. He had never seen Verity. Letters had been infrequent and inhibited, with any real information scored out by the censor. Sometimes they had gone astray and several arrived together after months of non-communication. A stranger was coming to take his place in her home and bed. Sometime in August or September, he had said.

In July, Daisy made the last payment on the twenty yards of old-rose brocade she had been paying off at the linen draper's. She had in mind dressing the bay window, in time for John's return, as she had seen the window of the Kent farmhouse dressed, so long ago.

It caused ructions with Erin. She watched her mother smoothing and handling the folds of rich fabric with an expressionless face.

'What's the matter? Don't you like it?' asked Daisy.

'What do we want new curtains for? What's wrong with the ones we've got already?'

'I want everything to look nice when you father comes home.'

'Did you get it on the black market?'

'No. I paid off for it in Newman's.'

'You paid coupons, as well?'

'Course.'

'Is that why I couldn't have my summer uniform?'

'The coupons won't stretch to everything, and there's nothing wrong with wearing your white shirts and no jumper when the weather's warm.'

'All the other girls have got uniform dresses. I'm the only one in the whole school that hasn't got one. They had to lend me one so I could be in the school photo.'

'I don't give a sod what the other girls 'ave got. It's up to their mothers 'ow they spend their coupons. I'll spend mine 'ow I like.'

The kids seemed determined to spoil things. Daisy finished the new curtains and got them hanging a couple of days before John was due home. The night before he was expected, she discovered that Verity had wiped her nose on one of the hems. It made her very angry. She shouted and raged for a while and put a tearful Verity to bed early. The mess was easily cleaned up, but it was just another example of how her wishes were always denied her.

Her head swam and the music in her brain started almost as soon as she sat down after clearing away the supper things. She struggled hard to see the lady's face but, as always, she was not still for long enough and she floated away. The spell could not have lasted long. Erin was standing beside her with a glass of water when her surroundings came back into focus.

'That's funny,' she said when she had taken a sip. 'I wonder what brought that on.'

'Was it the same as always?' asked Erin.

'Yeah. It's always the same lady. On a swing. I keep trying to see 'er face, but I can't. I really believe it's 'er.' Daisy turned her eyes to where the portrait of her mother looked back at her. 'She's tryin' to tell me somethin'.'

'I don't think it's that, Mum. I've been reading about it. I just happened to be reading about epileptic fits and I came across it.'

'Fits?'

'Yes. There are two sorts. Two sorts of epileptic fit. There are minor fits and major fits. Major fits are called *grand mal*, where the person falls down shaking and frothing at the mouth.'

'I ain't got no bleedin' epilepsy,' said Daisy listlessly.

'I know you don't fall down and have major fits, but I think you've got *petit mal*. That's when you just lose consciousness for a short time. Sometimes it's only a couple of seconds. Some people hear things, some don't. It's a minor sort of epileptic attack.'

Daisy smiled and closed her eyes. The kid thought she knew everything.

'No,' she said. 'I know what it is all right. It's me mother, lettin' me know she's still around.'

When Erin had gone to bed, Daisy looked round the room. She had made it as nice as she could. Good job John was coming home tomorrow. Erin still had ideas about being a doctor. He'd have to talk some sense into her. Reading up about epilepsy! The kid was getting to be too much for her to handle.

All next day Daisy prowled the house, unable to settle, afraid to go out in case she missed John's return. The late spring afternoon was almost gone and still he hadn't come. At least it was warm enough to stand outside. The sun was low, making her screw up her eyes as she scanned the road. John might come by bus or he might come by train, in which case he would come from the other direction. She turned her head to look eastward. No sign of a returning traveller. A bus rounded the bend and she watched it trundle past her down the hill to the stop at the bottom, keeping her eyes on it until it had deposited its passengers and receded out of sight. She turned and went indoors to stir the stewpan and turn the gas to the merest glimmer, wishing she knew what time he would come. It would be nice to have dinner ready to put in front of him.

She went back to the gate. The horse chestnut trees lining the road were in blossom. Daisy was glad of it. If this were the East End, the neighbours would have hung the flags out, but they didn't do things like that round here. Still, the trees made a bit of a show. John would like the road; she hoped he'd like the house. Look out for a bay window at the end of a row, with pink brocade curtains, she had said in her letter. Not that John knew brocade from hopsack. Unless he'd changed a lot.

She had laid her arm against her forehead to give shade, staring at the little parade of shops at the foot of the hill where the bus had stopped, when she caught a movement at the periphery of her vision. Much closer than the shops; only ten houses away, a man wearing a baggy brown suit and carrying a holdall, was walking towards her, not looking in her direction but with his head turned to look closely at each house as he passed.

Daisy started to run but checked herself. She wasn't absolutely sure it was John. So many men were coming home and this one was a bit too thin. He had passed the house next-door-but-one before she saw him full-face and doubt vanished. He saw her at the same instant, grinned and lengthened his stride. As she took a step towards him he dropped his bag on the pavement and clasped her firmly in his arms.

Heedless of the stares of passers-by, they clung to each other. Daisy, her arms about his neck pressed her face against his, awkwardness banished by the joy of seeing him. As he tightened his hold, planting kiss after kiss on a cheek reddening from contact with his day's growth of stubble, Daisy remembered and felt again the dear, sweet essence of him. John sought her mouth but, mindful that they were in the street, she pushed against him.

'Let's go indoors.'

Over her shoulder John saw the child by the gate, watching them with a wary expression.

'Erin!' he shouted.

Daisy turned and laughed. 'That ain't Erin. That's Verity.'

'Oh. Course! It must be.'

He crouched until he was at the child's eye level. 'Hello, Verity. You going to come and see your Dad?'

Verity dropped her eyes but did not cringe away and John gathered her up in his arms. Daisy picked up the bag and, with John's free arm across her shoulders, they walked together up the garden path, not separating at the front door, so that they had to squeeze, laughing, through it together.

Chapter 27

Grand Mal

A week after his final discharge from the forces, John glanced at his family, seated round him on a tube train, on their way to visit the Isle of Dogs. Little Verity sat close beside him, unable to get enough of his company. It had been easy to establish a bond with her. She was seven now, almost the age Erin had been when he went away. It was as though he had left a little girl behind and returned over five years later to find the same little girl waiting.

Opposite him, Daisy had her face turned to the window, her profile, beneath the turban style hat she so favoured, plumper than it had been. He half smiled, remembering the day on his last leave that he had taken her to the pictures. If he had had any fear that his wife might have changed, she dispelled it that day. The film was *Mrs Miniver* starring Greer Garson. The drama unfolding on the screen had roused Daisy to a point when she could no longer contain herself.

The heroine was unwillingly entertaining a German parachutist who had landed in her back garden and forced his way into her house. She was obeying his barked commands and generally suffering his arrogance in silence, when he glowered down at her and brutishly demanded food.

It was too much. Daisy had broken the rapt silence in the auditorium by yelling: 'Hit 'im in the bleedin' eye!' At which point, the heroine did exactly that, causing the house to burst into uproarous laughter and John to shrink back into his seat. She was still the same old Daisy.

Next to her Erin was, as always, reading. John wished he could get close to her but she baffled him. Daisy had been surprised when she had agreed to go with them on this visit to see Danny and Kate. The girl had put a distance between herself and the rest of the family, shutting herself in her room after school, only emerging to say the polite 'goodnight' her mother insisted upon. At first John had thought she resented his homecoming but Daisy assured him the behaviour had started months before.

'She gets a lot of 'omework,' she explained.

'How's she gettin' on at school?'

'She ain't gonna get nowhere. She won't swot. Spends 'er time soddin' about, tearin' 'er clothes She wants to stay on till she's sixteen, but I reckon it's a waste of time.'

Sensing her father's eyes on her, Erin looked up and smiled. John smiled back. She was a good-looking girl. He felt comforted. In a few years she would be getting married.

The train rattled into Mile End station and the family got out to catch a bus to the island. Upstairs on the number 57, they stared out at an alien landscape dotted with familiar landmarks. Daisy sat clutching her shopping bag containing a contribution of tea and sugar, exclaiming at everything she saw. John sat in stunned silence.

On either side they caught glimpses of the old familiar streets. In some places, whole rows had survived. Where houses had been blown away the sawn-off ends of the terraces were supported by wooden buttresses, the naked inner walls displaying remnants of wallpaper or the outline of the stairs that once took the departed family up to bed. Everywhere, on cleared bomb sites, ruins ringed the craters, sprouting now with scrub and ivy.

They got off the bus. It was hard to get their bearings. No one was about. That was the eeriest thing. The emptiness. They found St John's Estate without asking directions. Row after row of neat prefabricated houses. It reminded John of the flat-roofed towns he had seen in the Middle East.

Danny opened the door to John's knock.

'How do you manage to find your way 'ome?' John asked before they fell into each other's embrace.

Erin took hold of Verity's hand and held her back while joyous greetings were exchanged, then Danny saw them and they too were hugged, exclaimed over and welcomed to the house. Kate gathered their coats and disappeared with them into a bedroom.

'Sit down. The tea's all ready,' boomed Danny. 'John, you don't know Florrie, do you?' he asked as a slight woman with greying dark hair backed in from the kitchen, carrying a tea tray. John got to his feet.

'Here. Let me give you a hand with that.'

'It's all right.' She set the tray on a small table, wiped her hands down her apron and held one out for John to shake.

'I'm pleased to meet you, an' I'm glad you got back home all right.' She looked past him. 'Hello Daisy.'

'Hello Florrie,' said Daisy. She made no move to kiss her, but followed her back into the kitchen.

'How are your kids, Kate?' Daisy asked later.

'They're all fine. We got a couple of grandchildren

312

now. They're all settled in Northampton. I didn't really want to come back, but Danny wouldn't hear of leaving the island and I couldn't leave 'im down here on 'is own. Not after he'd been on 'is own for so long. Goin' through all the bombin' and everythin'. Course I know he 'ad Florrie for company for the last part, but I decided to come back. We see the kids every so often. We go up on the coach from Victoria. Makes a nice break.'

The women brought in plates of food until every surface was creditably laden, Kate apologising for having been unable to get winkles.

'You settled in all right, Flo?' John asked awkwardly as he accepted a cup of tea.

'Settled in? Well, yes. I've been 'ere over three years now, but I've got me name down for a place of me own, though it could take years. They've got to re-house families first.'

'She ain't got many points, see?' said Kate. 'She's got a home 'ere with us. She ain't in urgent need.'

'It's lovely here. You should see the kitchen,' said Daisy to John. 'It ain't 'alf lovely. Square, with a big picture window. Just like I've always wanted. You could make a window like that look lovely.'

'What about you Dan,' John asked. 'Are you workin?'

'Yeah. Still in the Millwall Dock. Rivetin'. It ain't like it used to be. The work ain't there. I'm 'opin' it'll see me out till retirement. If not, I got a little disability pension to fall back on.'

'What disability?' demanded Daisy. 'You never used to 'ave no disability.'

'I'm a bit mutton,' said Danny. 'I was standin' too close to the Island Baths when they went up. Blew me right eardrum out. I get a little war pension for that. It

313

ain't much, but it's better than a kick in the teeth.' His gaze fell on Verity.

'You finished your cake?' he asked loudly. 'Wait till you see what I've got for you!' He went to the kitchen and returned with a bunch of grapes. Verity had never seen grapes before. Her eyes grew round with pleasure as she tasted one.

'There's a Greek boat in. I got the stevedore to slip me some. Some things ain't changed.' Danny laughed.

John and Daisy joined in the laughter. Any and everything seemed amusing. It was so good to be together. So good to be back.

Going home on the tube, Erin did not open her book. She faced her mother.

'I didn't even know we had an Aunt Florrie. How is it you've never mentioned her?'

'I don't hardly know 'er meself. She went into service when I was still a toddler.'

'Uncle Dan went away when you were little, but you're always talking about him.'

'He used to come 'ome. Then he lived downstairs. We used to see a lot of 'im.'

'Yes, but you told me all about the brothers and sisters that died, but you never said a word about having a sister Florrie.'

Daisy pursed her lips and turned her head to look through the window in a manner that told Erin it was useless to persist. She sighed in exasperation and leaned heavily back in her seat.

'They lost touch, that's all,' said John. 'Didn't you enjoy yourself?'

'Oh yes, they were very kind, but why are they so loud? Why do they have to shout all the time?'

'Danny 'as to shout because he's deaf,' said Daisy, her own voice rising.

'That's just the way they are,' said John. They might be a bit rough, but they're the salt of the earth.

The curtain came down and rose again on the assembled cast of *A Midsummer Night's Dream*, to Daisy's profound relief. She hadn't understood a word, but she clapped enthusiastically, with the other parents. Erin looked very pretty as Titania, taking her bow in the end-of-term play. This was her last term. She had got a job for the summer in Woolworth's. What she did after that depended on the results of the School Certificate exams.

Daisy gave her a wave, but couldn't be sure that she had been seen. She'd picked a seat in the middle, a few rows back, but her daughter's eyes were fixed at a point somewhere above the heads of the people. John would have liked this bit, but Erin hadn't been able to persuade him to come. He couldn't stomach Shakespeare.

The clapping died away and there was a scraping of chairs as the school orchestra struck the first notes of the National Anthem. Daisy hadn't expected this. In her haste to get out she almost overturned her chair. From her position at the front, centre stage, Erin saw her mother elbow her way to the end of the row. Clenching her jaw and keeping her features rigidly composed, she followed with her eyes, her progress to the doors at the back of the hall. Noisily, Daisy pushed them open and let them close with a crash behind her.

She waited around outside for Erin to change and go home with her on the bus, but after half an hour, she hadn't appeared, so she left, leaving Erin to make her way alone.

John had finished his late shift at Ford's and was sitting at the table when Daisy got in, the remains of the meal she had left for him still in front of him.

'Hello, love. How did it go?'

'Oh it was all right . . . Too many bleedin' thee's and thou's for me. Why can't they just say what they mean? But Erin had a lot to say. I don't know 'ow she remembered it all. Spoke up lovely.'

'Where is she?'

'I waited for her, but I must 'ave missed her. I thought she would 'ave been 'ere by now. She won't be long. She had to wash all that stuff off her face.'

Erin's face was pale and set when she got home just after eleven. John had been growing anxious.

'Where 'ave you been? Your mother's been home more than an hour.'

'I walked.'

'You shouldn't walk 'ome on your own, this time o' night! Why didn't you come 'ome on the bus with 'er?'

Erin cast a bitter look at Daisy.

'Ask her why!'

John turned to Daisy who frowned and looked genuinely puzzled.

'Do you know what she did?' Erin's voice was choked. 'She walked out in the middle of the National Anthem! In front of the whole school!'

'Gawd blimey!' said Daisy in amazement. 'What are you gettin' worked up about? I can walk out if I want to. I don't 'ave to stand up for no King. Bleedin' glorified pauper! He ain't nothin' to do with me.'

'Did you have to slam the door? What about all those people? What must they have thought?'

'I don't give a sod what they thought! And I didn't

316

slam the door. You can't open them doors without makin' a noise. Besides, no bugger tells me what to do. They didn't pay for my bleedin' ticket.'

'And what about me? You don't care about me either, do you? It was my last day at school, and you had to ruin it! Oh, it doesn't matter Mum. Not many people realised you were my mother. They were talking about it when we were getting changed. "Who was that awful woman who walked out?" Only a few of my friends knew and they didn't say anything.'

'That's enough!' John intervened sharply. 'Don't speak to your mother like that. I think you'd better get to bed.'

Erin gave him a despairing look and flounced out, slamming the door.

'You see?' said Daisy when she'd gone. 'You see the way she talks to me?'

'Yes, but you shouldn't 'ave done that, Daisy. You shouldn't 'ave walked out of the kid's school play. You ought to 'ave considered her feelin's.'

'It was only a school play! What did they 'ave to play "God Save The King" for?'

John said nothing. There was no point in arguing. Daisy would never relinquish a point of principle. He felt sorry for Erin, but could not let her know without appearing disloyal to Daisy. He had more than once groped for a way that he might explain to Erin that her mother's passionately held views were part of her strong character, that she was, despite her lack of polish, a woman of integrity, but he had given up, unable to find the words.

He just didn't seem to be able to reach Erin. A couple of weeks later, when he picked up the post and saw that the letter from the Education Authority had arrived, he felt helpless, unsure of how he would handle the situation, whichever way it went.

He laid the letter in front of Erin on the breakfast table. Verity climbed into his lap. Daisy and John watched her read it and put it back in the envelope.

'Well?'

'I failed.'

'Oh, love, I'm sorry.'

His pity was genuine, but mixed with it was relief. He hadn't known how he would tell her that he couldn't possibly support her while she went to medical school. She would have to forget those ambitions now. He held out his arms to her, but she ignored the gesture and pushed back her chair.

'I'm sorry too, Dad. I know you're disappointed. But I knew I wasn't going to pass. It's just . . . you can't stop yourself hoping.'

'Never mind,' said Daisy stoutly, 'You'll still be able to get yourself a decent job. Get yourself a few nice clothes. 'Ave some fun.'

Erin looked hard at her mother and left the room without a word.

'Where's she going?' asked John.

'She'll go upstairs and 'ave a sniffle I expect. Don't worry. She'll get over it. She'll 'ave to. It's 'er own fault. She should 'ave buckled down at school. She'll forget it when she gets a few bob in 'er pay packet.'

It didn't take long for Erin to find a job. She simply picked up the *Evening News*, scanned the long list of situations vacant and chose one in an office in Holborn. Daisy was satisfied. From Erin's two-pounds-ten a week, she took a pound for board and lodging. Ten shillings for tube fare and the rest was hers to do with as she pleased.

Erin didn't say much in response to Daisy's enquiries about her work except to say that she was a filing clerk and that she hated her daily journey on the underground. She once complained of feeling tired, which baffled Daisy. She couldn't understand how pushing bits of paper about could make you tired. Not like loading piles of sacks on to barges.

Daisy gave up dreaming of trips to the shops with her daughter to buy clothes. She was keen to get material to make her a frock to go dancing, but the girl wasn't interested. Daisy couldn't understand it. She would have given her back teeth for the chance. Erin hardly went out, spending most of her evenings reading in her room.

It came as a shock to Erin to learn that her parents were planning to move back to the Isle of Dogs. Daisy could hardly wait to give her the news when she got home one Friday evening.

'Danny's got your father a start in the docks. Well, he's a skilled man with a lot of experience. And I've put our name down for one of them prefabs. I think they're lovely. We should get one no trouble, being displaced islanders. Soon as we get it we'll be goin' back.'

'Well, I won't be coming with you.'

'What do you mean?'

'I'm not going to live in that hole. You must be mad! What about my job?'

'You'll be nearer your job. You'll soon get to like it. The people are genuine. Not like the toffee-nosed lot round 'ere.'

'I don't find them toffee-nosed. And if people on the island are all like Uncle Dan and Aunt Kate, I'd just as

319

soon stay here. Anyway, we can't live in a prefab. They've only got two bedrooms.'

'You and Verity will 'ave to go in together.'

'I won't share a room with Verity!'

'What you gonna do then? Leave 'ome? Where else are you gonna find lodgin's for a pound a week?' Daisy asked the questions as though in posing them she described an utterly impossible situation. It shook her when Erin replied with a glint of determination.

'Yes. That is what I'll do. I'll leave home. And I'll tell you something, Mum. I've been planning to leave for a long time. The only thing that's kept me going for the last five years is the thought of getting out of here as soon as I'm old enough. I don't want to stay under the same roof as you for a minute longer than I have to.'

Daisy felt as if she had been punched hard in the chest.

'Listen. I been a good mother to you. You've always 'ad a good bed and a hot dinner every night of your life. All through the war, you never went without. I seen to that.'

'Oh yes, Mum. I went without a lot of things, but you wouldn't understand. For a start, I could never have any friends. None that I could bring home. I was afraid of what you might say to them. What new ways you would find to humiliate me.'

'Go on, say it! You're ashamed of me. Got too posh to remember where you come from.'

'I'm not ashamed of where I came from. I just don't want to go back, and yes, I am ashamed of you. Not of what you are, but the way you behave. Can't you see Mum? We embarrass each other.'

Seeing Daisy in tears, she went on more gently. 'You think I'm a terrible snob. Well, maybe I am, but so are you. You can't stand to see me trying to better myself. You see it as a betrayal. Ever since I was a little kid I've been determined to climb out of the gutter and you've done everything you can to stop me. Well, I think you've won Mum. Even if you do manage to climb out, the stink of it still clings.'

Daisy's face was contorted with anger. She moved close to Erin and hissed at her. 'You should think your-self lucky to 'ave a mother!'

'Oh yes,' said Erin in bitter mimicry. 'You would have crossed the world to spend half an hour with yours! You might have been luckier than you think, Mum!'

Daisy didn't stop to think. She raised her hand and struck her daughter a blow across the cheek that rocked her on her heels. Erin stood blinking for a moment then, without shedding a tear, walked quietly from the room.

Daisy sat listening to the sounds of her moving about upstairs, knowing she was packing her clothes, unable to bring herself to go to her, to plead with her to stop. The house was quiet, seeming to wait for what would hap-pen next. She looked at her mother's portrait. Charlotte smiled down, having no suggestions to offer. After a while she heard Erin bumping her suitcase down the stairs. Perhaps she might look in to say goodbye or at least to say where she was going, when she would be in touch, but the street door opened then closed. The click of heels on the tiled path came to her then silence closed around her.

The silence rang in her ears. The ringing changed to distant music: 'Ramona'. The lady in the white dress floated towards her, only this time something was different. Daisy had to lean forward farther in the effort to see her face. The swing swooped lower and faster. A low, moaning cry broke from Daisy and she fell to the floor with a crash, white foam coating her lips and her limbs twitching in violent, uncontrollable spasms.

A tea trolley rattled up to the foot of the bed, waking Daisy from a doze. 'Here you are Mrs Fletcher. Soon be time for visitors.'

A teacup and a plate with two sandwiches and a piece of dry Swiss roll were placed on the bedside locker.

'Thanks love.'

It made Daisy feel guilty to be waited on, but it was pleasant to lie propped against a bank of pillows, sipping tea, with a bowl of fruit at her elbow, breathing the scent from the carnations John had brought for her.

She felt quite well now, just terribly tired. No energy for anything. She put down her cup and lay back watching through half-closed eyes, the sunlight dappling the wall on the other side of the ward. The dancing pattern reminding her of another time in another ward and she closed her eyes again, not wishing to think about the day Erin was born.

Footsteps passed her, chairs were dragged up to bedsides and the ward filled with the gentle hum of visiting hour. There would be no visitors for her. John would come in the evening. It didn't matter. She was going home on Saturday. In the meantime, she would just rest. Languor possessed her and she drifted again into a half dreaming state, revelling in the unaccustomed leisure and the comfort of her bed.

'Mum?' Daisy's eyes flicked open. 'I'm sorry. Do you want to go to sleep?'

Erin, clutching more carnations, stood looking uncertainly at her.

'No. I've done nothing but sleep since I got 'ere. How did you know I was in 'ere?'

'Dad met me outside work and told me.'

'He never said nothin' to me.'

'I suppose he wasn't sure that I'd come.'

'And why did yer?'

'Oh, Mum! I couldn't not come! I'll go if you're not pleased to see me. I just wanted to see if you're all right.'

'Course I'm pleased to see yer. I been worried sick. Where 'ave you been?'

Erin drew up a chair.

'My friend at work has got a bedsitter in Wimbledon. I slept on her floor at first. Now I've got my own bedsitter just round the corner from her.'

'What's it like? Is it a decent place?'

Erin laughed.

'Yes, Mum. The landlady is the sister of a woman I know at work. Her husband is nice, too. I've got two little attic rooms, with my own washbasin and a cooker. You can come and see it if you like.'

'And you do cook yourself a dinner every day?'

'Yes. As a matter of fact, I have quite a lot of stews because they're easy to do in one saucepan. Anyway, I want to know how you are. Your face is still bruised.'

'Yeah. I don't know 'ow I done that. I must 'ave hit me 'ead when I fell on the floor. I never 'ad a turn like that before. When I come to, I was all wet, me head was sore and me mouth was bleedin'. Anyway, I picked meself up and I soon got over it. I wouldn't 'ave said nothin' about it, but your father seen the lump on me 'ead and you know what he's like. Made me go round to see the doctor and he sent me up 'ere to the 'ospital. I couldn't believe it when they said I 'ad to stay in.'

'What do the doctors here say?'

'They don't say a lot, really. They done all sorts of tests. A lumbar punch an' all sorts.'

'Lumbar puncture,' corrected Erin.

'It felt like a bleedin' punch afterwards, I can tell you. I never had such an 'eadache. Still, I'm fine now. I'm going 'ome soon. They give me some pills. The doctor said, if I keep takin' 'em regular, I shouldn't 'ave no more fits.'

'Did they tell you what they found out?'

'He said I've got what they call focal epilepsy. Usually brain damage when you're a kid, or when you're born is the cause of it, but they don't know for certain. I reckon it could be one of the clumps I got from Aunt Dolly caused mine. I 'ad enough of 'em. But what difference does it make now? I just got to get on with it.'

Erin picked up her mother's hand and held it.

'I expect it was us having a row that brought on the attack. I'm sorry.'

'Yeah. They told me that upsets can start it off. Still, I shouldn't 'ave hit you like that. I always swore I'd never hit my kids. Will you come back home now?'

'I'll come if you need me to look after you.'

'Oh no!' Daisy raised herself from her pillow. 'I don't need no lookin' after! I'd just like you to come home.'

'Well, I'll come at the weekends, sometimes. Who's looking after Verity?'

'I'm only in 'ere for a week. Your father took 'er to Danny and Kate. She'll just 'ave to miss school for a little while. I'll be all right when I get 'ome. So long as I don't forget to take me tablets.'

'It means you won't see the lady on the swing any more.'

'What does?'

'The tablets. They'll stop you having fits, so you won't see her any more.'

'No.' Daisy shook her head. 'You was right about me 'avin' fits though. You're a clever girl. It's a shame you can't be a doctor.' A thought struck her. 'P'raps you could be a nurse instead. They 'ave to learn all about medical stuff.'

'No, thanks Mum, but I don't want to be a nurse. I thought about it, but it's not what I want. I'm going to join the Wrens.'

'What the bleedin' 'ell for?'

'Because it's got lots of advantages for someone like me and, I can get higher education. I'll be able to sit for my school certificate again. It'll give me another chance.'

Daisy didn't fancy the idea at all. She raised her head to protest but it felt leaden and she sank back again. The ward sister looked up from her desk and rang a little hand bell to signal the end of visiting.

'I'll have to go.' Erin got up. 'Goodbye, Mum. I'll come and see you soon.'

'Wait! I still don't know your address.'

'I gave it to Dad. Don't worry.' She stooped and softly kissed the unbruised portion of her mother's brow. 'Take care of yourself.'

Daisy watched the trim figure retreating down the ward. Shame, she thought. She would have looked nice in a nurse's uniform. Still, a Wren's outfit was very smart. They're lovely, those little shoulder bags they carry. And who knows? She might marry a young naval officer, have a couple of kids and live somewhere like

Clacton, in a nice house with a square kitchen and nice big windows.

She had never given more than a fleeting thought before to the possibility of grandchildren. The generation before hers had marked the advent of grandmotherhood by the purchase of a black straw hat trimmed with a bunch of violets. For the first time in weeks, Daisy grinned. She wasn't quite ready for that yet.

God alone knew what sort of mother Erin would make. She had some queer ideas. Still, she had guts, you had to admit that, and God knows you need plenty. That's something good I've managed to pass on, she thought. She's got my spirit and John's brains. Maybe I wasn't too bad as a mother, considering I didn't have no one to show me the way to go about it.

Her eyes felt heavy. She closed them and turned her cheek into the pillow. For a moment she listened to see if she could hear music, but there was only the ward clatter growing distant and fading away as Daisy sank into contented sleep.